Destined to
Fly

Destined to
Fly

Indigo Bloome

AVON

An Imprint of HarperCollins*Publishers*

DESTINED TO FLY. Copyright © 2013 by Indigo Partners Pty Limited. All rights reserved. Printed in the United States of America. No part of this book may be used or reproduced in any manner whatsoever without written permission except in the case of brief quotations embodied in critical articles and reviews. For information address HarperCollins Publishers, 10 East 53rd Street, New York, NY 10022.

HarperCollins books may be purchased for educational, business, or sales promotional use. For information please write: Special Markets Department, HarperCollins Publishers, 10 East 53rd Street, New York, NY 10022.

First published in Australia in 2013 by HarperCollins*Publishers* Australia Pty Limited.

FIRST U.S. EDITION

Library of Congress Cataloging-in-Publication Data has been applied for.

ISBN 978-0-06-224363-8

13 14 15 16 17 OV/RRD 10 9 8 7 6 5 4 3 2 1

For Roberto

Thank you for being right by my side every step of

this journey and so many others.

For Nix

With much love —

You left us too early!

I have no doubt wherever you are,

you are sure to be flying high …

The limbic system is a complex set of nerves and networks in the brain supporting a variety of functions including emotion, behaviour, motivation, and memory formation. Its purpose continues to unfold, though it appears to be primarily responsible for our emotional life, with feelings such as fear and pleasure. It operates by influencing the endocrine and nervous systems and is highly interconnected with the brain's pleasure centre, which plays a role in sexual arousal.

Preface

Do you ever feel like the hands of the universe have picked you up and hurled you into a sphere that challenges the very core of your being? Somehow, my journey has taken me to a place I never expected to find myself in, let alone knew existed.

It all began with one weekend that awakened my sexuality and ultimately sparked something in the depths of my soul, and I still feel as if I'm tumbling out of control in the midst of a psychological and sexual tornado I have no defence against. I don't know how the kaleidoscopic events of recent times will end and can only hope my loved ones will endure the journey with me.

If I had known then what I know now, I can only wonder whether I would have chosen this path? Perhaps I never had a choice and the path chose me ...

Either way, what has happened in the past has happened, the present is what it is and the future will be what it will be. I can only hope and pray that somehow, I am destined to fly.

Part One

Speak or act with an impure mind,
And trouble will follow you.

Buddha

Lake Bled

Madame Jurilique slaps Josef's cheek in blind
fury.

'How dare you deceive me? After all I
have done for you and your family over the years. This
is how you repay me?'

Josef's arms are secured firmly at his sides by two
hefty security guards, Frederic and Louis, and although
he quickly turns his head to the side, attempting to
deflect her vicious slap, the corner of her ostentatious
diamond ring has slipped to the inside of her finger
and slices his cheek. Her lips curl into an undeniably
satisfied smile at the vision of his blood, forming
droplets on his skin.

'All I wanted from you was her blood. Was that
honestly too much to ask?'

Dr Josef Votrubec remains resolutely silent, refusing
to meet her cold eyes.

'Answer me, Josef!' Her anger is displayed in her fists, bunched into white-knuckled balls, at odds with her otherwise elegant style.

Madeleine considers her options as her previously valued and loyal employee stands defiantly before her. She hadn't wished him any harm until he betrayed her so deceitfully; now she concedes she may be left with no choice but to deal with him once and for all. She cannot allow a single loose cannon on her tightly-run ship.

Madeleine remembered when her close friend, Lauren Bertrand, had called to say that she, Lauren, had been invited to be a member of the elite Global Research Forum. Madeleine and Lauren attended the same Swiss finishing school in their youth before turning a shared passion for chemistry into successful careers. Lauren had since become a leading French chemist who often did consulting work for Xsade. Madeleine had already been keeping a very close watch on the developing Global Forum — the closer she could get to whatever the esteemed Harvard man, Dr Jeremy Quinn, was involved in, the better — and her interest was sparked further when Lauren revealed that Jeremy Quinn was keeping classified research files, including medical records, on the Australian-based psychologist, Dr Alexandra Blake.

Then she learned that Dr Blake's work on visual perception was sponsored by another forum member, Professor Samuel Webster, who was venturing into the field of sexuality and neuroscience. She was hooked. So she organised for her discreet information technologists (strictly off the record, of course) to hack into the two men's computers to find out what exactly what was going on.

Just as a buzzard can sense roadkill, every fibre in her body could sense that Quinn was onto yet another ground-breaking discovery. Her instincts were confirmed sooner than anticipated when her researchers discovered that Quinn's major benefactor, the enigmatic and always-discreet philanthropist, Leroy Edward Orwell, — or Leo, as he was known — was flying into Sydney the same weekend as Quinn was meeting up with Dr Blake. As Xsade was on the verge of finalising a patent on their 'purple pill', developed to combat female sexual arousal disorder, she knew she would hit the jackpot if she could continue to access information on what Quinn and Leo were up to.

Madeleine and Lauren were on a one day conference together when Lauren informed her that the forum's planned experimentation might not go ahead after all. Madeleine was left with no choice but to anonymously blackmail Quinn into continuing what he had been planning so meticulously for months. Much to her relief it seemed to work, as the testing went ahead as scheduled and the results she obtained from both Quinn's and Webster's computer systems were far beyond anything she had ever imagined.

Lauren's casual phone call to Madeleine from Singapore, mentioning she had just bumped into Alexandra Blake, before she boarded a plane to London was the icing on the cake. Having been thwarted by strengthened security on Quinn's and Webster's computer systems, Madeleine felt as if the universe was delivering Dr Blake to her doorstep and compelling her to act; accordingly, she arranged for the Blake woman to be forcibly escorted to a chateau in Slovenia and then to Xsade's off-the-grid facility under Lake Bled.

Madeleine was sure she was on the cusp of discovering the source of the anomalies in Alexandra's blood, unlocking potentially limitless profits for Xsade and earning herself the level of personal and professional power she had dreamed of for years. The best part would be finally outwitting the great Dr Quinn. There was no aphrodisiac more meaningful to her than social status and positional power. Quinn had, in fact, achieved her own ideal version of a networking nirvana in the pharmaceutical and medical worlds. In her mind, he rather arbitrarily and haphazardly stumbled upon the miracle cures that the world adored him for. It bewildered her that, apparently, money was never the driving factor for Quinn. He certainly never sold his formulas for the highest offer, because if he had Xsade would control the entire market. Well, this time, she wouldn't let Xsade be ignored because of some misguided moral stance of Dr Quinn's. She would discover his secrets before they went to the marketplace. This time it would be she who gained both the notoriety and the superprofits of the next great drug to save the human race, leaving Quinn to fade into insignificance. If she didn't achieve this and at the same time regain access to the enigma of Dr Blake's blood, she could at least take comfort in the fact that she had personally destroyed their credibility in the eyes of the world.

Everything was going according to plan until Josef let her down at the last minute. As if mere pinpricks of Alexa's blood were ever going to be enough for the detailed analysis she had in mind. All he had to do was extract a large sample of her blood while she slept after having ingested the purple pill. So simple, so easy and no one had to get hurt. She had no doubt that results from tests on Alexandra's blood would have been remarkable and she is furious that she didn't just do the blood extraction herself which, in hindsight, would have been far more effective, if slightly messy.

A smile that looks more like a snarl curls Madeleine's lips as she allows her mind to wander indulgently further afield. If Alexa's children's blood is anything like hers, the possibilities are endless. Even if she cannot gain direct access to them, perhaps once the world sees the scandalous pictures of their mother Madeleine has up her sleeve, they might be taken into care. Then she could even offer to foster the children and have their bodies continually available to her for experimentation.

Despondently, she admits to herself that this is merely a daydream and snaps back to the matter at hand.

As she stands in front of Xsade's version of Judas — and not in front of the one person in the world she wants under her control, Dr Alexandra Blake — rage twists in her belly. This man, a trusted employee for the past five years, managed to ensure Blake's escape from their facility and personally delivered her into the hands of her lover, Dr Jeremy Quinn, in Dubrovnik. Had she not treated him fairly? Paid him handsomely for his work as Xsade's lead physician and Head of Research and Development? She can't understand what drove this madness in him as he stands defiantly before her, secured by her henchmen.

Josef is valiantly maintaining his silence in the face of his boss's venomous wrath. He knows only too well from previous experience that nothing he says will be tolerated until her fury subsides. Madeleine Jurilique is determined, powerful, manipulative, cunning, dangerous and, in general, should never be crossed — even more so when she is in this ferocious frame of mind. He has overheard muttered conversations in the staff canteens as colleagues likened her to the White Witch of Narnia or a barrel of aggravated, poisonous snakes and Josef can now understand why.

As the European Managing Director of Xsade, Jurilique is one of the most powerful executives in the global pharmaceutical marketplace. She seems to have an uncanny ability to deliver the next 'big drug' to consumers, as well as huge profits to the Board of Directors and Xsade's shareholders, so much so they have gradually allowed her to run the company more or less as she wishes. Jurilique's unstoppable ambition has made her more callous and reckless with each passing year, enabling her to make increasingly dangerous decisions and take unprecedented risks on behalf of the company. But as long as the money keeps rolling in, it seems the executives are happy for her to have free rein.

Josef himself has ignored his conscience and turned a blind eye, but her treatment of Alexandra Blake proved to be the final straw for him. At first he believed that Alexa, like so many others, was willing to sell her body for money or for the sake of research. It wasn't until he found some of his boss's files that he understood she had been specifically brought in for reasons other than what she had signed up to in her contract.

Under such extreme circumstances, she handled herself with a dignity he didn't often find in people and he could sense the goodness within her. Jurilique's demand, her order that he drain over a litre of blood from Alexa while she slept, had violated his personal and ethical values beyond any degree of conscience; no amount of money could make up for what she was asking of him, or the risks she was willing to take in relation to Dr Blake's life. He could take no more.

As their standoff continues, Josef refuses to meet her eyes though he can feel the breath pass her porcelain-capped teeth before it hits the bloodied skin on his face. She slides her hardened, glossy nail under his chin, silently forcing him to meet her lethal gaze.

'Be under no illusions, good doctor. You will be going nowhere until I have what I need, and you will be assisting in the process.' She slides her nail along the line of the wound on his cheek as she watches him flinch before her. 'So you can kiss goodbye to the thought of seeing your sweet little wife again any time soon, just as you can kiss your professional future goodbye when all of this is over.'

An involuntary shudder ricochets down his spine at her words.

She steps back and issues her command to her ever-faithful henchmen. 'Lock him up. He is boring me and the sight of him is making me ill.'

With a flick of her wrist she goes to dismiss them. She notices Josef is finally struggling against the firm grasp of her men.

'To ensure he is secured I'll organise for Dr Jade, our new head physician' — she glares at Josef viciously with hate in her eyes — 'to administer the same drugs that paralysed our dear friend and escapee, Alexandra, when we were moving her from the chateau to this facility.'

Panic and dread settle into Josef's bones. He understands that this woman is beyond simply ruthless as he had presumed — she is a sadist. Her extreme lack of conscience now fosters a dangerous love of violence. He realises that his hope that her fury would dissipate and he could reason with her was futile. For the first time since he was taken, he suddenly fears for his life. There will be no escaping if he is completely immobilised by those drugs.

Madeleine finally sees in Josef's eyes the fear that she has been longing to provoke. It inspires her further.

Josef continues in his attempts to struggle free, his efforts creating a sheen on his face. 'Madeleine, please, you can't do this, please, my wife —'

She raises her eyebrow at Louis who instantly bends Joseph's wrist back onto his arm causing him to shriek with pain, effectively silencing his words.

'Take him to the lab and I'll page Dr Jade to meet you there. Under no circumstances let him out of your grasp, boys. You know what I pay you to do.' She turns and a smile plays on her lips when she hears the distinct sounds of suffering in Josef's screams as he is dragged out the doors backwards. She silently congratulates herself: at least she can always count on Louis and Frederic to obey her every command.

Alexa

I lean against the doorframe to gauge the intense conversation between the two powerful men in front of me. Jeremy Quinn — who is, and if I'm completely honest always has been, the love of my life — and Martin Smythe, an ex-US marine who now looks after security for the mysterious and elusive Leo, one of Jeremy's closest friends and major benefactor.

I can't help but consider that the difference between males and females becomes even more pronounced in times of danger or unease, in that men require action and females need reflection and supportive discussion. Or perhaps that is just me.

Their focussed debate has been going on since I received a horrifying blackmail letter — from the same woman who abducted me less than a month ago when I had arrived at Heathrow to meet up with Jeremy and the other members of the Global Research Forum.

My stomach is still tumultuous from throwing up moments ago in the kitchen sink, which occurred seconds after I'd finished reading the letter's contents. Emotions swirl in my nervous system, spinning between pain, anger, regret and surprisingly, a hint of ultimate acceptance. Acceptance that this is my fate until this nightmare is resolved, comes to an end. At least I hope it does. Surely that can happen in life, not just in stories? I have more than a sneaking suspicion that it won't come to an end until we understand exactly how and why my blood is what it is: an enigma which seems to vary its state depending on the hormones released in my body at any given time. Apparently, the more extreme the scenario, or my situation, the more intriguing the results, or at least that's what Jeremy and his technicians tell me. Why? Why me? I have absolutely no idea. There is still so much I don't fully understand.

My fragile stomach and pounding head force me to turn away from their action-orientated strategising about my future, and I make my way into the en suite of the master bedroom. Attempting to distract myself from the reality of the threats hanging over my head, I splash my face with cold running water before collapsing on to our king-size bed and gaze out at the orchestrated picture-perfect scenery from our Disney Resort Hotel suite in Orlando, Florida. I am situated in what is marketed as 'the happiest place on earth' and ten minutes ago I would have argued vehemently with anyone who told me that wasn't true.

I had been blissfully happy. More happy than I almost believed any person deserved to be in a lifetime … but in one puff of smoke or, more accurately, one A4-sized envelope later, my happiness turned to dread and fear, thanks to Madame Madeleine Jurilique, the Managing Director of Xsade's European Division. Also known as Madame Goldy or the Wicked Witch of Kidnap and Abduction. My body shudders in response to my memories of being abducted from Heathrow airport in London, drugged, taped to a wheelchair and concealed under a burka, and finally being transported through Europe in a suitcase to Xsade's facilities in Slovenia. I retch again but there is nothing left to bring up except a lingering acidic taste of bile. What the hell am I going to do?

Dr Josef Votrubec, who worked for Xsade, risked everything to ensure my escape from the facility beneath Lake Bled, before they could more or less drain me of a significant portion of my blood. Thank god he contacted Jeremy directly who, via the seemingly endless global resources of his friend and mentor Leo, managed to ensure my ultimate safety. Appallingly, the same thing can't be said for Josef, who was captured at gunpoint by Xsade mercenaries just after handing me over near Dubrovnik. Jeremy, Martin and I managed our getaway in a sleek speedboat to rendezvous with a luxury cruiser. Although I had only known Josef for a short time, he risked his entire career to ensure my safety and for that I will be forever grateful. He is a kind man with a good heart. On the drive to meet with

Jeremy, he told me of his love for his wife and how, so far, they had been unable to have children, a thought that always causes me pain knowing how forceful my own urges were to procreate when the time came.

I can only hope and pray that he has been safely reunited with his wife, though as much as I want that to be true, I know deep down that the two men on the pier with the guns aimed toward Josef would in all likelihood have been Louis and Fred. They were the men who had guarded me in the castle embedded in the hills north of Ljubljana. Madame Goldy's right-hand men.

Josef's betrayal of both Xsade and his boss, Madame Jurilique, would surely precipitate a reaction no human being would choose to experience. I have never met a more dangerous and narcissistic woman. Since my escape, Martin has provided us with regular updates and background on her, which makes her even more sinister. She operates in society as an elite, well-educated leader of industry and moves in circles of influence most people only dream of ... well, people other than Jeremy and Leo, I suppose. Yet she has about as much heart as a ravenous anaconda carefully manipulating and devouring her prey. Shivers ripple through my body as my concern for Josef's wellbeing reaches fever pitch. And now she wants me back within her vile corporate web for further experimentation, explicitly involving my blood.

I have no doubt that Madame Jurilique will follow through on the threats contained in her letter. I still hold the letter apprehensively in my trembling hands, and I read it again as though I'm somehow willing its contents to have changed.

Dear Doctor Blake,

    I do hope you have had a wonderful time recuperating in the Mediterranean with your lover and have enjoyed the delights of Disney World with your sweet children, Elizabeth and Jordan.

    It is so unfortunate that you were not able to properly conclude the entire 72 hours at our facility. After having provided us with such useful information, there is but one element we now require.

    Should you not be forthcoming in relation to our requirements we shall once again be forced to take circumstances into our own hands. The enclosed news headlines are but a sample of the strategies we will employ to ensure that we acquire what we need from you, so please let me be clear.

    We need your blood.

    If, for some reason, you decide not to cooperate with our request within the next ten days, we shall be forced to proceed with our global 'Do you really know Dr Alexandra Blake?' campaign. Needless to say, I shouldn't have to remind you that we have some wonderfully explicit photographs and video clips to authenticate our headlines.

While I have your attention, I should also
mention that should this not procure your
participation, we would look to acquire the next
best thing — the blood of your children.
I shall look forward to working with you
again in the very near future.
Sincere regards,
Madame Madeleine de Jurilique

If she can't have access to me, she will ensure no one else does either, in any way, shape or form. I also have no doubt that keeping Jeremy and me apart would give her an added sense of psychotic joy, knowing that she is controlling me and he cannot do anything about it. The thought makes me nauseous all over again.

Salina, who works for Martin as part of Leo's security team, is still in Europe attempting to locate both Josef and Jurilique. During her investigations she discovered that Lauren Bertrand, the French member of Jeremy's Global Research Forum, was bitterly disappointed that Jeremy was given the role of Project Leader rather than herself. An email exchange between Lauren and Madeleine promised that Jeremy would get what he deserves both professionally and personally. They just needed a little more time and patience.

If anything happened to Jeremy or my children I don't think I could live with myself. No, I know I couldn't live with myself. The sheer evil of her suggestion is mind-blowing ... if I don't meet her demands, she will endeavour to procure the blood of my children! How dare she? She is one sick woman whose desire for power, money and ultimate market control means she will stop at absolutely nothing. How dare she threaten my children! They are my world, they mean everything to me. I will protect them with my life. And my blood.

Once again, I return to the room Elizabeth and Jordan are sharing. My profound need to see their small bodies resting soundly is overwhelming. It's difficult for me to believe that they are already nine and seven years old. Time has flown by so fast. My emotions are as raw as my love is strong. As I gently smooth the hair away from their angelic faces and kiss their foreheads, I lay my palms against their hearts so they can each sense my love for them drifting through their innocent sleep.

'Sweet dreams, my cherubs. My love for you is as deep as the core of the earth and as high as the stars in the sky.' My voice is low and heavy within my chest, and I breathe their presence deeply into my lungs before gently closing the door behind me.

I return to the kitchen where Martin and Jeremy are still huddled over their notepads, brainstorming strategies and the next steps in my life. As soon as Jeremy senses me in the room he rushes to embrace me in his strong arms. Arms I so desperately long to be cradled in forever, but I know this will be impossible in the short term.

'Don't worry, sweetheart, we will get through this.' He searches my face and cups my cheeks gently between his palms, tilting my head upwards to meet his gaze. I can't help but notice that his beautiful features are riddled with anxicty; his green eyes are even smokier than ever given the depth of his emotion for me. 'I won't let her touch you or the children, Alexa. We will protect you at all costs. I promise you.'

I swallow the lump in my throat that threatens to break me, knowing that Jeremy's word is his bond and this is never more true than when his promises involve me. I have never in my life needed to be stronger with him than now.

'Please sit down, Jeremy.' I guide him back to his seat at the table, knowing I need the advantage of my standing position. I pause until I have their undivided attention.

'I have made my decision.'

He immediately jumps back up. So much for that strategy.

'What do you mean, you have made your decision? We haven't discussed anything yet, besides Martin and I have been working through options —'

'Jeremy, please,' I interrupt, 'there is nothing to discuss. If my children are at risk there is only one solution.' I steady my hands against the table and take a deep breath, preparing the words I need to release before they falter. 'The bitch can have my blood. It's only blood. I want this nightmare to end. If she gets what she wants, maybe my life will be left intact rather than in the pieces in which she seems determined to shred it.'

19

I'm always shocked to hear myself unexpectedly swear, but it seems Madame Goldy brings out the very worst in me.

'Over my dead body, Alexa. It is not going to happen.'

A heaviness descends on his mood and the seriousness of his voice confirms that my decision is far from agreed from his perspective. This could be a very long night. He indicates to Martin by a nod of his head to pack up the notes on the table, then takes a firm grip of my elbow and steers me into the lounge room. I hear the front door quietly open and close. Here we go. I brace myself for the inevitable conflict and decide to make the first move.

'I will *not* put my children in any danger, Jeremy, ever.'

His arms wrap around me and he doesn't let me go. He holds my head against his chest, pressing my ear to the beat of his heart, his lips touching the top of my head. I try to stay strong. I try to push him away before I am forced to tear myself away, away from the man I have finally been reunited with after all these years, the man I have loved since I first understood what love could be.

'Let it go, sweetheart. You don't need to do this alone. I am here for you. Please, let me be strong for you, for all of you.' His words penetrate through my implacable facade and my body crumples within his firm grasp. Tears spill from my eyes as his body remains the rock his words promised. Although I still know what path I must take, I have to concede that Jeremy knows exactly what I need right now. He secures me in his embrace until my tears subside, understanding my emotional exhaustion before effortlessly scooping me up and carrying me into the master suite, placing my weary body and mind carefully on the bed as if I'm made of eggshells — a good reflection of how I feel, actually.

'Do you need something to help you sleep?' he asks gently.

'You know what I'm like, Jeremy. Even the weakest drug seems to hit me hard. I'll see how I go. Right now I have so many uncontrollable thoughts running through my head. I feel like I've been punched in the gut. I don't know what to do.'

'Can I help in trying to subdue them for a while?'

'How?' Wondering where his mind is going.

'I could run a bath.'

'Ah ...' I relax a little. 'What a perfect suggestion.'

'Lavender?'

The tiniest of smiles appears on my face, accompanying the worry that creases my brow. 'Of course.'

A few minutes later, slightly calmer, in the serenity of the surrounding warmth of scented water, I snuggle close into Jeremy's chest as I lie nestled between his legs.

'Just when everything was going so well, she pulls the rug from beneath our feet — again. Why can't we find her, J? Why hasn't she been brought to face any form of justice?'

'Her time will come, sweetheart, I promise you. Someone like Jurilique will come unstuck eventually, even if it is by her own doing.'

'Eventually isn't soon enough. I need her to come unstuck in the next ten days before my life implodes into the unknown yet again.'

His legs immediately tense around my body. 'You will not be going anywhere near that woman, Alexa.'

I know this isn't going to be an easy argument to win with him, but he must know that I don't have a choice given the circumstances, surely?

'You've gone quiet. Why?' he murmurs into my hair.

He has always been able to ask me the unanswerable. I am quiet. I'm quiet because I don't want to have this argument, one we should never be forced to have, an argument that will cause us both no end of pain because of who we are and what we know is imperative to our lives. Me to him and my children to me.

I release a deep sigh filled with both frustration and resignation. 'I honestly don't know what to say. I feel numb.'

'I can understand you feeling numb. Just as I feel furious with her heinous demands. But I know you too well, AB, to think that you don't have thousands of thoughts running through that beautiful head on your shoulders. Please, share them with me. Now more than ever we need to communicate openly with each other. Don't let her get between us by sending a piece of paper.'

An anxious chuckle escapes me at his oversimplification of my dilemma. 'Is that how you would describe those headlines if they were about you, Dr Quinn? A mere piece of paper.'

The image of those headlines has been burned indelibly into my brain:

Slut mother shuns kids for kinky sex experiment.
Dr Blake bares all — check out her best angles here.
Psychologist turns Psycho — would you leave your
    kids with this mother?
Adultery — sadomasochism — is this what you teach
    your kids?

'I'm not saying it's great, obviously. But it's nothing we can't deal with. We are stronger than that.'

'The photos, J, you should see the photos she has of me. As if the headlines aren't bad enough but she has the graphic evidence that, shown in the wrong context, supports them. If they were just between you and me, I've no doubt we'd find them privately provocative. But to share them with the world ... I'm a mother, a professional. This exposure will ruin me, ruin us. The way Jurilique presents them means they can only be seen as seriously f'ed up from society's perspective. I don't want to be in a world where they exist publicly. And imagine if the kids ever saw ...' I choke on my tears, which prevents me from continuing.

'They won't, Alexa.'

Frustration at his dismissal of my fears tumbles out in my words. 'Don't tell me they won't when they will. You don't know what she's like. I'll end up as a recluse if I don't give her what she wants in ten days. Unable to work any more, unable to face the world, or even my own family if the truth be known. I swear to God and to you, I will never allow her to touch my children. She can have my blood and I'll keep my life. It's the only way to deal with this.'

I feel Jeremy's chest rise and fall with each breath, and I sense his attempt to control his anger and anxiety for my sake. His palm is absentmindedly stroking my shoulder and now I wish I could hear his thoughts. I'm as concerned about his silence as he was with mine. We both know this argument is not going to be resolved tonight, so I change tack. 'Can you promise me one thing?'

'Depends.' His mood remains dark; he is still far away from me, absorbed in his thoughts.

'We only have a few more days left at Disney World with the kids until we meet up with Robert. I don't want them to know anything about this. I want to enjoy this time with them in case—'

His hand immediately covers my mouth, stopping me from saying any more.

'Don't ever speak like that, Alexa. I literally won't let you.' He maintains this position to give more credence to his statement and grips me tight against his hard body, as if buying time to get his own thoughts in order. His legs anchor around mine and twist around my ankles, spreading me as wide as the bath will allow. I'm fully restrained against him. 'But I think it's a good idea,' he continues. 'We should maintain the status quo while we're here, for the sake of the children.'

I immediately relax as he accepts my suggestion and my body melts into the warmth of his.

'Now that we have at least agreed on one thing, I have some additional business to attend to.' I try to speak, but his hand still covers my mouth. I think he is enjoying controlling the silence, possibly the only thing he can control about me at the moment, so I remain still against him. He can sense my question. 'Well, sweetheart, if you're not going to accept any drugs to help you sleep tonight, then the least I can do is provide your mind and body some relief and distraction from your endless thought processes.'

His free arm slides beneath my body and arrives conveniently between my legs, tantalisingly close to my sex. His hand around my mouth now stifles my groans, rather than my words, and he doesn't hesitate to slip his finger in to torment my tongue. He has deftly pre-empted any potential protest as his magic fingers work between my legs to send my body into a frenzy. Almost instantly my 'endless' thoughts vaporise into the steaming water surrounding us.

I would have sworn that it would have been impossible for me to orgasm in my current state of angst. I was wrong. Twice, as a matter of fact. What is it about us and baths?

Needless to say, my emotional exhaustion, and the ultimate escapism he provided enabled me to achieve just what the doctor ordered ... a dreamless night's sleep.

* * *

Wishing time would stand still rather than marching determinedly forward, we spend the next few days wholeheartedly engaged with Elizabeth and Jordan at Disney World. We water slide, fall from terrifying heights, get splashed on boat rides, experience 4D movies, see ghosts, meet Mickey and Minnie and Donald's entire family, Lightning McQueen, Tinkerbell and Ariel, and they all still managed to touch the kids' hearts, as did their rides. Martin is never more than a few feet away from us and it was obvious he and Jeremy have reinforcements, who, even though they attempt to blend into the crowds, are continually loitering in the background. I don't want anything to distract me from the kids' joy so I don't discuss it with Jeremy, knowing it would be a yet another redundant argument. I can't help but notice the tentative looks that continually pass between him and Martin whenever we are out in public. Each time I catch them, Jeremy immediately masks his concern with a smile and enthusiastically captures the kids' attention to distract me, and them, from my impending doom.

Our initial plan is to check out of the hotel tomorrow night and fly to Los Angeles to meet up with Robert, before heading back to Tasmania. I'm not sure if I want Robert involved in any of this chaos. I just want it to be over as soon as possible. Jeremy has asked me to think about whether or not I would have Elizabeth and Jordan's blood tested; perhaps I'm being naive, but I want them to enjoy the holiday without needles and my mess impinging on their happiness. So many irresolvable thoughts, questions and logistics cascade through my head.

We haven't had further discussions. We are both desperately trying to live in denial as long as we can stretch it out. A few times during the night, when we are meant to be sleeping, I notice Jeremy out in the lounge room with only the lamp on. One time I catch him pacing the floor and speaking in hushed, anxious tones on the phone. As soon as he sees me in the doorway he quickly hangs up and wraps me in his arms, ushering us both back to bed. The look in his eyes clearly informs me that any questions I have will not be answered right now, but I try anyway.

'Jeremy, we need to talk. There is so much to work out and I'm starting to freak—'

He silences me with an index finger across my lips, looks something up on his phone and slips it into the docking station before whipping into the bathroom and returning with the ylang ylang massage oil. No doubt he senses my restlessness, but he hasn't uttered a word since ending his phone call. When he returns the acoustic sounds of classic Australian songs filter through the room.

He slides off my pyjama top (I thought it was best to leave the negligees for when we're on our own, for the kids' sake) and guides me onto my stomach. Straddling my buttocks, he positions my arms either side of my body and rubs his hands together in the slippery oil. His large hands slide along my back and shoulders, loosening the tension that has been building since the arrival of the Wicked Witch's letter. This feels *so* good.

He continues along my arms and hands, ensuring no part of my upper body is left ignored. I release a sigh as some more of my tension eases. After his thorough absorption with my back, he guides me to my front, now straddling my hips and thighs. He re-anoints his palms with the oil and begins the same process over my belly, chest and breasts. I feel my muscles melting under his firm rhythmic touch.

I stare into his eyes, which seem to be searching my soul in our silence. As if sensing my thoughts he lifts my wrist to his lips and kisses my bracelet.

'Anam Cara,' I whisper, knowing we are soul companions, knowing this bracelet symbolises our union and connection to each other. From a practical perspective, it also ensures he can never lose track of me given its GPS chip, something that was weird for me at first but which I'm forever grateful for since my abduction. And they've modified the bracelet again to ensure I can be tracked absolutely anywhere ... underground, underwater or whatever. Knowing that it can't be removed protects me and links me to

Jeremy always. It binds us together even when we are forced apart.

My heart strains as I acknowledge how hard it will be for him to let me go, or for me to be taken away from him again, but I also know I don't have a choice. I must do this for my children and for our future together. Surely he realises there is no other way. A tear slides down my face and his kiss is now tender against my cheek instead of against the precious jewellery encircling my wrist. More than anything, right this second and forever more I want Jeremy's body and soul with me, just as he is now, with focus, dedication and an intimacy and knowledge that has only strengthened between us over the years.

He has been swelling in anticipation since rendering me topless and it is only a few seconds before both our pyjama bottoms are tossed to the floor. He holds himself above me, allowing me to feel his heat and hungrily caress his body.

I am more than ready for him, but suddenly he is in no rush; he kisses me in four places and lingers on sucking and nibbling of each one of my erogenous zones until I'm as wet with perspiration as I am below with desire. His lips reach my lips, his teeth nibbling, his tongue playing until I'm rapturous with desire and he slowly slides his full length into me. I wrap my legs around his taut butt as he anchors my hands to the bed with his. He adjusts slightly to find the perfect pressure point deep inside me, matching the same pressure with his tongue, almost suffocating my mouth with the same fullness as below.

We build together, we move together and we erupt together in perfect synchronicity and with a whispering scream we cry out each other's name in the height of our shared ecstasy. At this moment there is a part deep within me that fully comprehends that having finally found me again, he will never let me go.

Alexa

It would have been sad to leave this magical
artificial world under normal circumstances, let
alone the cloud of threat we are under. The kids
want one more ride around the park on the monorail
to say goodbye before we depart and I can't say no.
Who knows if we will ever be back here?

Jeremy seems more than agitated when I agree to
their request as he moves around the apartment making
sure we have packed everything. 'There is just so much
stuff.'

I can't help but laugh. 'Welcome to the world of
kids, J. There is always stuff, everywhere, every day.'
I grab hold of his waist as he flies past me in a flurry.
'What is it? You don't seem yourself today.'

I wasn't sure whether I'd done something to
specifically bother him or whether he was finally starting
to crack under the stress of our undiscussed situation.

'I'd just rather you not go on another ride. Haven't you all had enough?' Something is definitely bothering him. His anxiety has been rising as our departure grows imminent.

'How about I go with the kids and you stay here and have a moment on your own to get everything together? There's really only your work things and we're all set.'

The kids are playing rock, paper, scissors next to us so I have my 'everything is perfectly under control' face and voice on. I'm getting better at it and he seems in no mood to be confronted by my concerns.

'No, Alexa, I'm not letting you out of my sight.'

It is this statement that triggers the realisation in my mind that I actually haven't been alone with Elizabeth and Jordan since the first night we arrived. Jeremy has been with us constantly. They immediately look toward Jeremy sensing the change in the tone of his voice.

I embrace him, pulling his head toward me so I can whisper: 'Please, one circuit on the monorail. It will be good for us and it will give me an opportunity to be with them alone.'

'No, what if —'

I quickly cut him off with a promise. 'I will take Martin and one of those other minders. We will get on, complete one circuit and get off at the same station. I promise you. Please,' I plead with him. 'We'll be fine, honestly.'

Exasperation shifts to acceptance as he extracts me from his arms and strides out to arrange it personally with Martin. I sigh into the room as I acknowledge how even the simplest of things in my life have become increasingly complicated since meeting with Jeremy all those months ago.

He kisses me out the door, holding my chin between his fingers and making direct eye contact, as if to ensure he has my undivided attention. 'One circuit — no getting off.'

I stand on my tiptoes and peck his lips. 'I love you too, J.'

We leave serious Jeremy behind and the kids are thrilled we have the green light to go. Thankfully, they don't understand the particulars of why this needs to be such a big deal, and are now so used to being trailed by our keepers, they don't ask any questions. And so, we say farewell to a place they have loved visiting, one last time.

Jeremy appears to be calmer and in a much better mood when we return and even has a skinny flat white and a firm embrace waiting for me. He visibly relaxes the second we walk in.

'See, safe and sound.'

'Just as well, sweetheart, or I would have had Martin's head.'

I look warily toward Martin, not necessarily doubting the sincerity of Jeremy's words. He nods his thanks to Martin; they have already been through more than enough drama together because of me. It will end soon, I reassure myself. As soon as I give Jurilique what she wants. I hope. I stop my brain from considering the possibility of any other outcome.

I quickly drink my coffee as the minders take our bags to the stretch limousine waiting downstairs — more fun for the kids.

'Alrighty, let's go.' We gather our things together as the kids pick up their newly-acquired stuffed animals and we assemble ourselves into the lift and out into the limo. I lean into the car to ensure the kids are settled in their seats and as I back out to collect my other bag, Jeremy shoves me straight back inside and closes the door. Good grief, what now?

The doors immediately lock and the kids stare at me with wide eyes and surprised faces. No doubt the look on my face isn't helping. I gaze out the tinted windows to see Martin has apprehended a woman with a white envelope in her hand. She looks shocked and immediately drops it on the ground and tries to pull away from his grip. Hotel security arrives, though I can't hear what they are saying with the windows up.

It appears to get sorted out rather quickly. Jeremy nods to Martin and he bends down to pick up the envelope and place it inside his jacket pocket. Jeremy then slides into the back of the limo with us as if nothing out of the ordinary has happened. The kids remain silent, which is unusual at the best of times, awaiting my response.

I decide now is not an appropriate time to question Jeremy and suggest a game of I-spy for distraction as the car slides smoothly out of the Disney fantasy and into the real world. Jeremy looks relieved at having avoided my inquisition yet again.

The return trip to the airport seems to be taking much longer than I remembered on arrival, but the kids are chatty and happy so I fully engage with them and enjoy their giggles and recollections of our past week together. That is until I see high-rise buildings glittering in the distance against a clear blue sky and Martin is driving the limo on the freeway directly toward them.

Shocked, I turn to Jeremy.

'Do you have anything you need to share with me?' I utter the words under my breath, thankful the kids are now happily absorbed in their technology and not me. His grip around my hand tightens as he shakes his head. More silence from him. 'Well, I think you do and I'd like you to share it now.'

I shuffle around in my seat so I can make better eye contact with him. He shakes his head again. Damn him, he knows I'm not going to make a scene in front of the kids.

'Please tell me where we are going, J, because if I'm not mistaken, it appears we are heading toward Miami and nowhere near Orlando International,' I say sternly and as quietly as possible. I try to release my hand from his grip, but he tightens it further instead. 'You're not going to tell me what's going on are you?'

'Not here, no.' He indicates toward the children.

Jeremy never eases his grip on my hand. I can sense his nerves and anxiety, which just go to heighten mine. Our eyes eventually connect. His are cloudy, blanketed with intense emotions, and he mouths the words 'I love you' as I notice a tear well up in his eye. Oh, dear god, this must be killing him just as much as it is me. I close the distance between us and snuggle underneath his shoulder. He releases my hand, only to quickly clasp it again with his other hand, so he can wrap his arm around me. We remain this way in silence while we watch the rest of the world go by, on our way to our yet-to-be-disclosed destination.

Part Two

Sex is the great unifier. In its big slower vibration, it is the warmth of the heart which makes people happy and together, in togetherness.

David Herbert Lawrence

Jeremy

I embrace Alexa as close as I acceptably can in the presence of the children. Martin is driving the limo fast, but within legal limits, to Adam's penthouse in South Beach, Miami.

Adam is Leo's brother. He inherited the same wealth as Leo and he is, potentially, Robert's new boyfriend, based on their recent successful rendezvous in London. I contacted Robert, Alexa's husband, after we received the letter, informing him that she was at great risk again. He agreed without hesitation to meet us on the East Coast and Adam offered his place as the meeting point given its convenient location and additional security. It also had a helipad if we happened to get hold of Leo in time. So our plans seamlessly fell into place.

I thought it would kill me not to discuss and work out a response to Jurilique's letter, as per Alexa's request, but in the end it worked out for the best. We've been able to ensure the kids weren't affected and still enjoyed their holiday, and I've been able to make arrangements during the evening when Alexa has been asleep. If she thinks for one second I would let that bitch lay another finger on her, she can't know me as well as I thought.

After pulling a few medical strings, I've been able to access Elizabeth's medical records from when she was in hospital with appendicitis two years ago. It appears that she has type A blood rather than type AB like Alexa, so it is impossible for her to have the same unique allele, or alternative gene, that we discovered Alexa has during the experimentation process, which is something of a relief. But that's assuming that this type of anomaly is genetic, rather than, say, being triggered by some specific medical condition or reaction ... that would be highly irregular, though everything about Alexa's blood is unusual to say the least. From the tests we have done to date, her particular anomaly only appears to relate to XX chromosomes, not XY, thereby specifically impacting females. If this finding proves to be true, there is then no need to test Jordan's blood, and we could confirm that the children are of absolutely no value to Xsade, or anyone else for that matter. I haven't wanted to bring it up with Alexa until we know for sure. Given that she wasn't keen on the idea of testing the kids in the first place, I decided to let sleeping dogs lie, not wanting to upset her further given everything she is going through.

This may be good news for the kids, but from my perspective, this knowledge puts Alexa at significantly greater risk because she appears to be one of a kind, at this stage anyway. I also know that, once a company such as Xsade discovers what we know of the composition of Alexa's blood, they would keep her in their facilities as a human laboratory rat until they extract every last detail about her to fulfil their research requirements. Who knows if she'd ever see the light of day again?

I know I'm a dominant presence in Alexa's life, but I also know I'll need more than a strong hand and weighted odds to be able to convince her of our plan. She must be made to understand that under no circumstances will I ever submit her to personal risk and danger. Thankfully, I will have a few people on my side before we embark on such a discussion.

Finally, we arrive at South Beach. I open the car window hoping that the crystal-clear sky and the smell of the ocean spray will lighten her mood, but it is clear to me that this change of plans has heightened her anxiety, maybe even sparking anger. Nothing I haven't handled before, just the circumstances are now more extreme.

We stall at a boom gate before security allows us entry and we descend into the darkness of the garage. A security team surrounds us as we pull in to park and Martin turns off the engine with a relieved look on his face that I register through the rear-view mirror. A bystander would have to conclude that our arrival, surrounded by such heavy security, indicates fame, politics or the filthy rich! Alexa takes a deep breath before allowing me to escort her out of the car. She indicates for the children to stay behind in the car and promptly shuts the door on them.

'Jeremy, tell me what the hell is going on here?'

She is seething, not a good start.

'We can talk about it in the apartment, AB. Not here.' I shift her aside and quickly open the car door. 'Come on, kids, you can hop out now. I have a surprise for you upstairs.'

I help them shuffle out of the limo, more to avoid her death stare than anything else and we make our way to the lift. If we weren't in Miami, I would swear I'd been frostbitten by the icy atmosphere.

Martin enters a convoluted code and the lift finally begins to ascend. When the elevator doors open, even I'm taken aback at where we find ourselves. It's a penthouse suite that looks out toward the aquamarine waters of Biscayne Bay and the depths of the Atlantic Ocean.

I'm temporarily distracted by the view as the kids rush past calling out, 'Daddy, Daddy', and then I notice that both Adam and Robert are standing by the mirrored bar in the centre of the room. While they are in the midst of hugs and introductions, I turn to Alexa, whose face has gone from furious red to deathly pale and for a moment I don't know quite what to think. She appears to have gone into shock so I gently guide her to the lounge, sit her down and fetch her a glass of mineral water in between greeting the men.

It has been a while since I've seen Adam but I've known him for almost as long as I've known Leo, and that's well over a decade. He isn't as tall as his older brother and has a stockier build, but he has the same light brown hair and blue eyes and seems as friendly and outgoing as ever.

Robert looks simultaneously relaxed and nervous, which I suppose would be the case when your children first meet your 'new man'. It's weird to think that they need to go through what we've just been through with the kids. Everyone has appeared pretty adaptable to date so hopefully that will continue.

It has taken the children all of two minutes to notice the swimming pool just beyond the sliding glass doors so now they are hassling Alexa for a swim. 'Please, Mummy, please. Can we? We've got our swimmers in our luggage. Can we?'

I'm not sure whether she is going to faint or be furious, which is strange because she is usually so easy for me to read, but then again, I'm still adapting to the 'mother' version of Alexa.

'Why don't you ask your father? He seems to have more of an idea about what is going on than me,' she responds quietly and I swallow my discomfort at her words, knowing that our change in plans has hit her hard.

The kids take her words in their stride and merely bounce back to Robert. 'Go on, dad, please, can we?'

He looks toward Adam, who shrugs. 'Sounds like a great idea to me.' He picks up the intercom and asks

43

for the luggage to be brought up. Robert walks over to Alexa and affectionately squeezes her shoulder; she doesn't respond.

'How about we leave you two alone for a bit?' He glances cautiously at me. 'I'll get the kids organised. We can talk later.' He gives me a very blokey 'good luck, mate, she's all yours' look before bunching Elizabeth and Jordan up in each arm. 'This way, kids. Let's take a look around.'

Martin remains stationed at the lift doors looking nonchalant.

I walk over to AB and kneel down before her so we are at eye level. She is sitting still though shivering and deathly white. 'Please, have a drink of water. You need some colour back.'

She eventually swallows a little as I bring the glass to her lips. The last time I knelt before her like this was at the InterContinental when I asked her if she would spend the weekend with me. God, what am I asking her to do now? Is it any better? Shit. She might hate me forever.

'Alexandra ...'

'Don't you dare "Alexandra" me, Jeremy.' Her voice is low and lethal. 'What the hell have you done?'

'We are meeting here to work out the next step.'

'Next step! My next step is perfectly clear and has been since I received the letter. I am giving the Witch what she wants so she will leave us alone. That is my next step, J.'

'Well, unfortunately, I beg to differ.'

'You can beg to differ all you want but that's what I'm doing.' She gets up off the lounge and strides over to the lift where Martin is standing and attempts to press the button. I'm not sure whether she truly expects that she can leave, or is just proving a point to herself. Martin blocks her, knowing that she is not to leave the apartment without my express consent. 'Martin, please?'

He shakes his head but remains resolute. 'Sorry.'

'There are other options, sweetheart. Honestly, we can get through this without her blackmailing you.'

My words and Martin's actions seem to break something within her as she spins around and lashes out toward me, her small fists pounding against my chest. 'Don't you understand, there are *no* other options.'

I hold her against me as her bravery dissolves and she bursts into tears, knowing she is fighting an invisible fight, shadow boxing. A fight that we know we can't both win. I'd do anything for her not to be going through this anguish, not to experience the pain she is being forced to experience. It's hurting both of us and I vow that Jurilique will pay for putting her through this nightmare. I lower her body back onto the lounge, still holding her tight.

'You must understand that you are not alone in this,' I say with the same level of intensity, and add with conviction, 'I will not allow you to hand yourself over to that evil woman, Alexa, under any circumstances. As I said before, it will be over my dead body.'

'God, Jeremy, please … you can't … The kids … the risk … you have to let me go, you must. I survived once, I'll survive again.'

Oh god, this is almost killing me, just as it is breaking her. She is so distraught, so fragile.

'I don't think you understand me, sweetheart. I've lost you to her once. I will never allow that to occur again. I'm sorry it has to be like this, but it is the only way.'

Her sobbing reaches new heights causing the pain in my chest to intensify as if I'm being stabbed. Her face looks as if she is experiencing the exact same sensation. This is the first time she has reacted this way since receiving the letter, almost as if she is finally giving herself permission to express the distress she must be feeling, knowing the kids now have their father around. She has experienced a watershed, something has broken in her.

I hadn't realised she was keeping herself together to that degree for them, but of course she would. That's what a mother would do, wouldn't she? Anything to protect her children, and there is no doubt Alexa is a formidable lioness. I'm not a parent but I imagine I'd be exactly the same.

'I must … I have to …' Her words are muffled as she sobs hard into my chest and all I can do is hold her for as long as it takes. Forever, hopefully. She is the love of my life and I know she won't be leaving this building until we have worked out a way forward that doesn't involve her returning to Xsade and walking back into the hands of that psychopath. Even if she hates me for it.

I'm not sure how long we've been entwined in each other's arms on the lounge by the time Adam deposits two cups of green tea on the coffee table. The kids are squealing in delight in the pool with Robert, and poor Alexa looks like she has been put through an emotional wringer.

'Hi, I'm Adam.' He stretches out his hand to Alexa as a way of introduction. I feel a little guilty that this hasn't already happened; it is his place, though these are unusual circumstances and I'm sure he'll understand.

She quickly wipes her eyes, her natural politeness kicking in. 'Hi, I'm Alexa. I'm so sorry about this mess.'

'Not at all. Thanks for sharing your man with me,' he responds with a cheeky wink. God, could this be any more awkward? Much to my surprise, his acknowledgement makes Alexa smile for the first time in ages.

'My pleasure, Adam. I hope you are enjoying each other.' She too, gives him a wink with her puffy, tear-stained eyes. This may not be too bad after all, what a relief.

'Would you like me to show you to your room? I thought you might like to freshen up.'

'That bad, hey? Jeez, what a first impression.' She smiles weakly at him. What is it about gay men and their ability to connect with women? At least she is smiling, that's more than I could achieve. I keep my arm around her as he shows us to our room.

'How long are you expecting us to be here, Adam?' Even in the state she is in, she doesn't miss the opportunity to ask him, not me, in the hope of eliciting some answers.

'That is entirely up to you, my friend.' Good answer. He shows us to our suite and indicates the fresh towels. '*Mi casa, su casa*. Don't rush, I'll be out bonding with the kids.' With those words he closes the door behind him and leaves us with our green tea, our luggage and each other.

She looks exhausted, overcome. 'Please tell me, what are we doing here, Jeremy?'

'I'm sorry you're not happy about this, sweetheart, honestly I am.' I smooth a few strands of hair away from her accusing eyes. She no longer has the resolve to keep me at a distance. 'We need to make some informed decisions about what is best for you and your children and we can't do that without Robert's input.'

'And Adam?'

'It looks like he's as much a part of his life as I am yours, my love.'

'Great. Anyone else you think should be involved? Do you have my parents' number?' she adds sarcastically.

'You know I wouldn't do that without your knowledge, but there is someone else ...' I trail off, not knowing whether now is the best time to mention it.

'Oh god, who?'

'It looks like Moira has located Leo —'

'Leo is coming here?'

'Sometime in the next 24 hours.'

'I don't believe this!'

'We are here to help, and we will get through this together.' I go over to place my hands on her shoulders and this time she does have the energy to brush me off. This is not good.

'I need some time alone, J, to thinks things through.'

'We are all here to support you, Alex.'

She glares at me. 'Support me in every way except in what I have decided. Yes, believe me, your support is loud and clear — everything on your terms.'

'You're not going to do anything rash, are you?' I suddenly can't keep the concern for her welfare from my voice.

'Can I get out of this apartment without your assistance, or approval?' she asks acerbically.

'Well, no. Not unless you decided to abseil from the balcony.'

'Exactly, just as I thought. Another ambush and I'm trapped. Again. Well then, no, I won't do anything rash just yet. I need to think. I'm going to have a shower in an attempt to clear my head.'

I feel terrible. She has been hurled into the unknown one too many times since she met up with me. I'm not even sure how much more she can take. She's strong, but the circumstances she has found herself in since our weekend together would be sure to break a weaker person.

'Okay. Good.' I try to remain calm but I'm not sure the panic I'm feeling on the inside is completely masked. If she were to do anything that involved self-harm ... I can't think like that! It must be old ghosts haunting me and bringing out past fears from being unable to save my own brother. But I know extreme circumstances can create irrational behaviour ... No, she's not like that, it's not in her psyche. 'Can I get you anything before I leave you alone?' I ask gently, concern catching my voice.

'Nothing just yet.'

Thank god, she finally softens and holds my hand, kissing the back of my hand to let me know there is still hope for us, even though there is pain.

'Don't take too long though. You know I start to twitch convulsively when I can't lay my eyes on you.'

A tired laugh escapes her. I return a kiss on her hand and leave her in peace, at least for a little while.

I join the others poolside where Adam is entertaining the kids with some form of water volleyball. I kick off my loafers and join Robert, dangling my legs in the water.

'How is she?' he asks.

'Pretty pissed off at me bringing her here, but I know she never holds a grudge for too long.'

'Yes, thank god for that.' We both laugh empty laughs, recognising our shared knowledge of Alexa's personality.

'How serious is it, Jeremy? How much danger is she in?'

'I'm not going to lie to you, Robert, it's very serious and she is in real danger. They seem to know our every move. We received another threat this morning before we came here.'

'Shit, really? She's not considering going, is she?'

'She believes it's the only way the kids will be safe. She's not willing to risk anything when it comes to them.'

'I can understand that. But they need their mother. I'm not willing for her to risk anything for that arsehole company.'

'I know, that's why I need your help to convince her that it's not an option you're willing to sanction on the kids' behalf. Based on what we already know, the children are of no value to Xsade, only Alexa.'

'Can't she just send some of her blood to them and be done with it?'

'I wish it were that simple. Unfortunately, having conducted their own experiments on her and having hacked into our systems they're aware that, given certain scenarios, very specific hormones are released into her blood. So they need both her body and her blood to discover what we know.' I decide not to mention any of the healing characteristics; the fewer people who know that the better.

'Well, we just have to come up with another way. We need to keep her safe. Even though I'm not married to her any more, Jeremy, she still means the world to me and our kids. I couldn't bear for anything to happen to her.'

'I'm pleased to hear it. We just need to convince her of the same thing.'

'You do know how stubborn she can be?'

'Why do you think I've called for reinforcements? I'd never be able to do this alone.' We share knowing yet concerned smiles.

'Well, we'll do whatever we can to keep her and the kids safe.'

'Thanks, Robert, I really appreciate your help. By the way, I've been meaning to ask, how was London?'

'Let's just say it was like a homecoming in every possible way,' he says with a smile that reveals his joy in the decisions he has recently made in his life.

'That's great, I'm really pleased for you.'

Pleased for his happiness though still unsure of my own, I lift myself up to go and check on Alexa, when he says, 'Now we just need to get this mess sorted and everything will be perfect.'

I look down at him hoping his words are true. 'Absolutely, that's the plan.'

On my way back to our room, I remember I haven't checked in with Martin regarding the envelope that woman was trying to hand to Alex and backtrack to the lift.

'Hey, Martin, have you opened it yet?'

He nods. 'It states that sending her blood alone is an unacceptable proposition and outlines exactly when and where she should be in seven days time before their "campaign" begins.' He hands me the note.

'Fuck.' I automatically rub my hands through my hair after having scanned the words.

'I know. It's not good.'

'What's not good? Why are you swearing, J?' Alexa's voice startles me.

'Oh, sweetheart, there you are. I was just coming in to check on you.' Her wet hair is slicked back and she is wearing a white cotton robe tied around her waist. Could her timing have been any worse?

'What's happened?' She immediately notices the note between my fingers. I anxiously look at Martin, not wanting to hand it over.

'Jeremy, please, don't insult me.'

'I would never insult you, just promise me you will never go to Jurilique, ever, and it's yours.' I can only hope.

'You know I will never do that. Give me the damn note.' Her voice indicates that she is not to be messed with. There is absolutely no playfulness left, so I reluctantly hand it over.

She reads it and abruptly collapses to the floor in a crumpled heap as if her legs can no longer bear the terrible weight she carries. She rips the note to shreds as if it is poison in her hands and her entire body starts trembling. 'What am I going to do? She'll never leave me alone. Unless we find her, she will find me. We know that's the truth. She probably knows exactly where I am right now, even after your surprise detour. I can't take any more of this, I just can't. I'm captive here and I'll be captive there. There's no way out, no end in sight.'

There is nothing I despise more in myself than being at a complete loss for words or unable to take action.

Unfortunately, that is exactly how I feel at this precise moment ... utterly redundant. Moments pass as we wonder what will happen next. I don't know what to say or how to console her.

Fortunately, Robert walks back inside leaving the kids outside drying themselves with their towels. Alexa looks up at his face and suddenly kicks into gear in a way that shocks us all.

'Right, if you want to know how to support me in the short-term, this is how. Robert, you're on kid duty as the responsible parent for the next twenty-four hours. Jeremy, I need a drink and make it strong. I need to feel numb for a while.'

Robert and I both try to speak at the same time before her words and strengthened voice override ours. 'I don't ask for much and this is what I'm asking.' She then adds in the same clear, firm voice. 'I'm deadly serious. I need a drink. Now.'

Okay, clearly we have reached breaking point. Robert and I look at each other and nod, knowing full well that if we were in her shoes, we would have demanded exactly the same thing days ago.

Adam appears, suggesting that we make our way up the spiral stairs to the sun deck and he'll bring up some drinks. I nod in agreement and attempt to dislodge Alexa from her seated position on the floor surrounded by the scraps of scattered white paper. She appears to have gone back into shock.

Eventually, realising she is incapable of moving herself, I pick her up in my arms and carry her upstairs away from the children and deposit her on a comfortable sun lounge with a view as far-reaching as the eye can see. She has her swimmers on under her robe. She must have been going out to join the kids.

I'd go down and fetch a hat but I don't want to leave her in this state so high up, given the nothingness in her face. This whole situation has finally taken its toll, become too much. I think back to being at my hotel, One Aldwych in London, just after she had been abducted. All I wanted was a drink to numb the pain. How can I condemn her for wanting the same thing? Her body is immobile so I gently push her head back and stretch out her legs so she is fully relaxed on the lounge, as I wait anxiously in the silent breeze for Adam.

Finally, he arrives with two Long Island Iced Teas. I raise my eyebrows, questioning his choice.

'Well, she did say strong. Here's the intercom if you need anything else.'

I thank him for the drinks and wave one in front of AB's face to get her attention.

'Your drink, m'lady,' I try to say as light-heartedly as possible. She finally comes out of her trance and takes hold of the long glass, rips the straw out along with the umbrella Adam has decorated it with, and gulps it down. This could get very messy, very fast. She draws breath only to repeat her action, downing three-quarters of the drink in record time. I have to physically prevent myself from stopping her by removing my added extras and taking a sip as well. Finally, she makes eye contact.

'This is good.' And polishes off the rest. 'I'd like another.' She looks directly at mine and I deliberately take a huge mouthful before handing it over. Bloody hell, it's strong even for me.

'Promise me, you'll at least try to sip it?' I add hopefully but to no avail.

After about ten minutes of silence between us, with me anxiously awaiting her next move, she finally speaks. 'Ah, that feels so much better.' She picks up the intercom. 'Hi, Adam, that was perfect. Would you mind making another just like it? Excellent, thanks.' I can tell by the look on her face that she is enjoying my reaction to her shenanigans. 'What a great guy Adam is, don't you think?'

'Yeah, he is. Looks like you two will get along just fine.'

'Don't look so disheartened, Jeremy, I'm meant to be the one feeling that and for the next few hours I just want to forget about everything. Otherwise my brain and heart may implode. Can you do that for me?'

She discards her robe and I'm left with the breathtaking vision of her curvaceous body in a retro, red halter-neck bikini, soaking up the sun. For someone under so much stress, she looks stunningly gorgeous. If anything, having kids has given her body more shape and her breasts look sensational. I can't believe my dick instantly springs to life. I feel like a teenager with the impact she has on me.

'Yes, I will always do anything for you, sweetheart.'

She scoffs. 'Only if it is aligned with what you want.'

'And you know that what I want is always what is best for you.' I kiss the top of her forehead. 'I'm just going to get your hat, sunglasses and your next round of beverages. Stay put.'

'Where else could I go?'

* * *

When I return with a tray holding the drinks, some Lebanese bread, tzatziki dip and sunscreen, Alexa is nowhere to be seen. Her robe is still on the sun lounge, but she has vanished. I slam down the tray on the side table and quickly scan the area. Shit, please no. Not again. My stomach goes into free fall. I have been gone less than five minutes. I race around the structure where the stairs come up from the apartment, then to the other side, my heart pounding in fear.

Nothing. No one. I run to the edge of the balustrade and look below, hoping, knowing she would never jump. It's not in her nature. I scan the sky with the fleeting thought that maybe a helicopter has scooped her away, not that I heard any noise. Oh, god, no. Please, this can't be happening again.

Then suddenly I feel her fingers pinch my butt and I turn around in a frenzy to grab hold of her with all my life, sheer relief mixed with angst and anger at her antics. She tries to run, but I capture her around her waist and haul her over my shoulder.

'Never — do — that — to — me — again!' I slap her butt on each word, and she is screaming and laughing as I unceremoniously dump her beautiful body back on the sun lounge. 'I swear to god, Alexa. You just about gave me a heart attack.'

She's laughing uncontrollably now; once she starts, she always finds it hard to stop. Still beside myself with fear, adrenaline surging through my veins, I quickly pick up the tie from around her robe and deftly wrap it around her wrists, tying each of her hands to the side of the lounge.

'What ... what are you doing? You ... can't ...' She staggers between her hysterics, laughing so much she has no hope of preventing my actions. I ensure they won't loosen.

'This way, at least I know you will stay put.' Much better, I think to myself. She looks so sexy restrained to the sun lounge in her bikini. Now that I know she is safe, I'm pleased that she has had a good belly laugh.

'Jeremy, please untie me.' She's still laughing at my reaction. 'Anyone could come up.'

'After having you vanish on me like that, I don't care what they think. You know I'll go to any extreme to keep you safe. After that behaviour, how can I trust you not to disappear again? Besides, everyone just left for an early dinner, so I'm afraid there is no reason whatsoever to untie you.'

Finally, she is able to get her breathing under control. She tests her restraints. 'Honestly, you know this is not necessary. Release me.'

'Never. You just about scared me to death.'

'But I can barely move.' She struggles again.

'Exactly, sweetheart, that's my intention and it gives me great peace of mind. More than I've had for days, actually.' I allow a smile onto my face.

My innuendo is impossible for her to ignore. I place her sunglasses over her eyes and the hat on her head. I can't resist kissing her lips while I'm in the vicinity, knowing there's physically not much she can do to resist me.

'Well, could I at least have my drink please?'

'Are you going to apologise?' I hold the drink up toward her face.

'For pinching your butt, never!' Her cheekiness is contagious.

'Alexa,' I admonish, and move the glass away.

'Okay, I'm sorry, but it was pretty funny.' Her giggles begin again.

'You know as well as I do that the word "but" negates everything that comes before it.'

'Alright, I'm sorry, I didn't mean to alarm you, really. I was just having some fun. Can I now have a drink? Please. I shouldn't have to beg.'

'It's so good when you do, though …' I raise the potent drink to her lips and she takes two quick mouthfuls.

'It's nice to see you laugh, AB. It's been a while.'

'Yeah, great, I laugh and end up tied to a chair.'

'But this way, I get to look after you.' I feed her some bread and dip before taking off my shirt and straddling her trapped body. Her sharp intake of breath confirms she likes what she sees. 'And do what I want with you.'

I nuzzle my face in between her bountiful breasts before nipping her pert nipples through the fabric of her bikini, which is met with both struggles and squeals of delight. I trail my kisses along her belly before pausing at the top of her bikini bottoms to look up at her face. Her eyes are fused with lust and excitement.

'God, I love you like this, but to go any further would be indecent.' Confusion crosses her eyes. 'We are here to drink. After all, that is what you requested.'

She unconsciously attempts to move her arms toward me, momentarily forgetting they are trapped. 'Jeremy!'

I shift away from her to pick up the drink and have a sip, and then pass it to her for another few mouthfuls. Her body relaxes back into the lounge, absorbing the feeling of the alcohol.

'You're right,' I say. 'These are good, aren't they? You know, our life would be so much easier if you just accepted what I asked of you, knowing it is always in your best interests. Perhaps the easiest option is to just keep you captive myself until all of this passes over.'

She looks at me, assessing my seriousness. If only she knew.

'No, Jeremy, don't even joke about it.'

'Perhaps that is the solution. I've been trying to reach a compromise, hoping you would come to your senses and give yourself to me rather than the Witch.' I take another sip and offer it again to Alexa. 'So much food for thought. Choice or no choice.'

'Choice, choice is always better,' she replies with haste. 'But she has given me no choice. I can't protect anyone unless I do this. You must understand. I need you to understand, J.'

'But you need to understand that I must protect you, and it seems that *you* have given *me* no other choice.'

The last thing I want to do is embark on another futile debate with her when she has finally given herself permission to let go and be comfortably numb for a while. So after a quick scan of the environment I confirm that we are atop one of the tallest buildings in SoBe, Miami, hopefully guaranteeing our privacy. It would be such a shame to waste this decadent opportunity.

'It's the lack of choice that —'

I ignore her words as I eagerly embark on my sexual mission. Knowing distraction is by far the best strategy at this stage, and with my target being trapped on the lounge, well, let's just say it's my best-case scenario under difficult circumstances.

Her cries of protest about choice quickly turn into cries of pleasure as I focus solely on liberating her body and mind and doing what we do best. I can't deny the sheer joy I receive from having unhindered access to her body. So much joy, that I spread her legs wider to gain greater access to the playground my lips and tongue love to explore. My palms can't get enough of massaging her sensational breasts now sitting squished together above her bikini top. As my tongue escalates the tension on her sweet spot and I roll her nipples firmly between my finger and thumb, she arches her back and calls out my name. I want her as much as

I've ever wanted her. I know we'll never be able to get enough of each other. Her pleasure is my world. She is my world and I'll never give her up. Ever.

The sexual tension between us is electrifying as I tease her clitoris with my tongue and feel her body tighten against mine, struggling to free her bound wrists. I can feel her conflicted fight for both control and surrender and I cherish that in this moment, I can control it for her. I can give her the release she needs, take away her fears, her apprehension, her hurt, even if it is only for a few moments. I feel her build and I want her to explode with the passion that is so much a part of who she is, who she has allowed herself to become. But not yet.

I establish a smoother rhythm. I want her to ride with me, forcing her to come with me on my terms, terms I know she loves. She is panting, her heart thundering in her chest. I realise how much tension I've been holding onto while facing the risk of losing her. I want this control, need it at this juncture of our lives where we seem to have control over little else, so I play with her body as if it is the last time I'll have access to it. I want her to feel every bit of extreme pleasure pounding through her.

Without pausing I want her to build again, from a higher starting point, until her orgasms cascade over each other so she becomes mindless for as long as possible, so she becomes mine for as long as possible, unresisting and fully surrendering to the needs of her body. I continue my relentless kissing and sucking and playing, and feel her swell. I'm needing to be closer to her than ever before.

Her voice is hoarse. 'Please, now Jeremy, release me.' Finally her words concur with her body's desires.

'I thought you'd never ask, sweetheart.' And she gives herself over to her body and to me, exploding in ecstasy as I ignite her clitoris with forceful suction that coincides with my twisting and releasing of her nipples and she screams uncontrollably. I suck up her juices as quickly as they are expelled in the spasms contracting every muscle within her sex.

She is riding uncontrollable waves, they are picking her up and taking her away from the pain and heartache of the real world and I want to give her more, more of this freedom: knowing she can't deny me access, knowing she won't say no, knowing she won't run from me and knowing that we need this more than anything, this physical closeness, this union, our togetherness. I need her to feel raw and pleasured, need her to release herself to me so she understands this is how we are meant to be … never apart, never separated.

I drop my jocks and take her. She is wet and contracting around me. I fasten my mouth over hers so she can taste her own pleasure and consume her from above and below, catching her cries and spilling my own tears on her face. I blanket her body with mine as she spasms with a joy she has no control over, no say in, no choice but to lay beneath me and accept. Passion trembles through her muscles rendering her mind utterly numb, just as she wanted. She is overcome, incapable of words; the only thing left is her shuddering from the aftershocks of her multiple orgasms — for the short term at least.

The passion between us has only intensified over the years, as if our absence from each other served to escalate our sexual urges and lovemaking. Now more than ever, I cannot get enough of the woman I love. If only she granted me the same access to her mind, we could work through this together rather than be at loggerheads with one another.

I pull up my pants then reluctantly draw hers up as well. I release her wrists and snuggle her limp body into mine on the lounge, enjoying the silence and closeness I sense I'll be granted for a while longer. I can't help but ponder in the back of my mind how she is going to respond to Leo's plan. How she reacts remains to be seen and, knowing Alexa as I do, may well be completely beyond the power of any of us to control, even given our best intentions.

Alexa

I curl into Jeremy's warmth, unable to think or move as he wraps his arms around me. His body feels wonderful against my skin, as does the sun shining down on us from above. How does he do this to me? He sends me to a place I never knew existed before him, or maybe it's a place that only exists between us, though I doubt that. It's as if we're at one with the gods, with the universe, where there is no beginning or end, no pain, no guilt, just complete freedom. Our lovemaking is intense; it overwhelms me and lingers with me long after the actual event. Our bodies combine in the sheer joy and pleasure of each other. It's as if I'm a magnet unable to prevent myself from being drawn into his sphere. He becomes my world, both physically and metaphorically and overtakes my being. Just when I think I can't take any more, he takes me further and higher. I know that any energy I have to fight the man I love, to go against his wishes and his will, is fading fast, particularly as I want what he wants for me. I know he can't bear to lose me just as I couldn't bear to lose him, which is what makes this so difficult. Our love is literally tearing us in different directions.

I know that his actions, even more than his words, are screaming at me to listen to him, to acknowledge his love and commitment to me. It's becoming impossible to fight and it's a fight I don't want to have in the first place. I don't want to return to Xsade, not one part of me wants to engage with that woman ever again. Though my heart knows I must because it has a direct connection to my children.

It's unfair to expect Jeremy to understand that; it's impossible until you become a parent. I've never known a love like it. But his love for me is so strong I feel like I'm bound to him in invisible chains. Chains I couldn't bear for him to unlock, chains that are wrapped so tightly around me I don't think my heart would continue to beat without them.

And now this. Ensuring I stay open to him, taking me on his wave of desire and not letting me off until I'm at one with the serenity he has created. It's this peace, this silent pulsing energy that completes me, heals me from within. I've never been able to achieve that state unless he leads me there. It's only when I truly surrender to him, his desire, his love, that I can reach such unity and perfection. I'm floating, I'm drained, I'm desperately in love and dreadfully scared of the consequences for my loved ones if I accept his hand and embark on a different path.

I let my mind remember simpler days, easier times when he wasn't part of my life. Like the family's favourite place in the Huon Valley, watching platypus frolic in the stream after the kayaks had been laid to rest, and the kids riding Rusty the pig and milking Honey the cow, the milk to be turned into scrumptious soft Brie over time. Sitting by the campfire with fresh, steaming hot damper, singing and dancing to folk songs from the past as the sun sank behind the lush green hills of the valley's fertile lands. Or skinny dipping in the perfect water rolling into Wineglass Bay at Freycinet Peninsula, its saltiness tantalising our skin and its freshness awakening our senses long after the hiking tourists have disappeared. The shining sun lengthening summer days and squeezing the darkness of night into its shortest hours of the year. Such abundant, natural beauty surrounding me, wrapping around my body and restoring my vital essence, but even then, in the midst of all of that, I still knew deep down something was missing, that there was a hole in my soul that yearned to be filled.

It dawns on me how much I long for the peace and solitude nature provides me, how much I have missed this sense of tranquillity. The recent events of my life have been hurling me into the unknown, epitomised by my time at Xsade's laboratory, so artificial, so contrived. I feel as though I've lost touch with the core of my human nature. Fear trembles through my body at the thought of re-entering that soulless environment in the next week.

'Alexa, are you back? Are you okay?' I feel his soft lips whisper against my ear and my groin responds instantly, as if his voice is invisibly connected to my inner sex. You'd think it had been neglected for years instead of minutes.

'No. Not quite, still far away.' I feel him snuggle my body tighter into our spooned position on the sun lounge.

'Don't leave me, J. I need you as much as life itself.'

'As I need you, sweetheart.'

It would be so much easier if I could just promise him the same thing in return. The truth is his words fill me with both comfort and fear.

Whether it's the alcohol, our lovemaking on the rooftop, or not being responsible for children for a few hours — perhaps all three — it feels really nice knowing my emotions are comfortably numb for the first time in a long time.

Robert, Adam and the kids eventually come home and I'm finally in a better state to interact with them normally, rather than as a crumpled heap on the floor. We still haven't worked out any details regarding our short-term plans and none of us want to discuss anything until the kids are in bed. They appear to have adjusted incredibly well to having the four of us around and shriek with delight and responses of 'awesome' and 'that's so cool' when Robert informs them everyone will be staying a night or two, and it's no wonder —

they have discovered they will be sleeping in Adam's dedicated games and movie room where they've been given permission to play until they fall asleep. Oh well, I did give Robert responsibility for the next twenty-fours hours so I'm not really in a position to disagree. I hug each of them, pleased to see their smiley faces before they excitedly disappear into their room.

They bought pizzas home for us and Adam opens a crisp Viognier from the Napa Valley. Our chatter flickers easily around the mosaic-mirrored dining table as they share stories with us from their time together in London, ensuring the conversation doesn't focus on anything to do with my recent experience and I can't help feeling both engaged with the banter but also dissociated from its flow. My husband, my lover and my husband's lover sitting around the table catching up like old friends. It seems so ill-conceived yet feels so right.

Adam amps up the volume of some pumping tunes and I feel the overwhelming need to dance. It's as if this place is designed specifically for parties. I finish yet another glass of wine and throw my arms around Jeremy.

'Dance with me?'

He smiles his cheeky smile and cups my face in his palms. 'How could I not? It's so great to see you relax.'

He teases a kiss across my lips and I feel weak at the knees, just as I did years ago at university, and I'm thankful he's holding me tight. My body melts and gravitates toward this man as though he is directly descended from Eros. God, he is smouldering and I regret asking for a dance instead of a quick trip to our bedroom or the rooftop again ... Would that be weird, I wonder, in front of Robert? Perhaps not.

'I just need to return a phone call and I'll be right with you,' Jeremy says.

Adam immediately swoops over and takes my hand, distracting me from my delicious thoughts about how I could play with Jeremy's body.

'I'll dance with you, gorgeous girl. Let's go poolside, the speakers are on out there.'

I glance questioningly at Jeremy. He used to call me GG, or Gorgeous Girl, in our younger years, so how did Adam know to use that moniker? His hands fly up in mock protest. 'What? I've said nothing, just a lucky guess I assume, but it's the truth after all.' Jeremy winks and slaps my butt. 'Go dance with Adam, I'll be out in a sec.' My eyes follow his triangular torso as he walks away from me while Adam drags me in the opposite direction.

The night is warm and clear, a half moon sharing the sky with a few stars, as we boogie. And we boogie hard. It feels great to dance, to release my pent-up energy and stress. The music pounds in my ears and the world whooshes around me as Adam, who is proving to be an exceptionally skilled dancer, flips and turns and spins me in multiple directions. Luckily I've had quite a few drinks by now so I confidently assume I must look equally proficient given his strong lead. It's exhilarating.

He leaves for a moment to refresh our drinks and I keep dancing, the music enabling me to fly away from the dramas, to remove myself from reality. My hands are in the air like I just don't care, dancing and pounding, my feet bare, grooving and moving like there is no tomorrow — until I turn around and notice four male figures watching me intently from inside the glass doors. This distracts my excellent rhythm to such an extent that I stumble over my feet, lose my sense of balance and fall inelegantly, splashing into the pool. How absolutely embarrassing!

Grateful I still have my bikini on underneath my now see-through short summer dress, the men appear poolside, with Jeremy and Robert offering me their outstretched arms to haul me from the water, trying to restrain their chuckles.

'Not a word,' I lightly threaten them, as they attempt to hide their smirks. Adam hands me a towel. 'Thanks.'

Standing slightly back from the others is the fourth man who I don't recognise but who I intuitively know is the reason I lost my balance. He steps forward.

'Well, hello, you must be Alexandra. I'm Leo.' He holds out his hand toward me. I cannot believe I am meeting Leo for the first time like this.

'Oh, Leo, great. Hi. I'm sorry, um … I'm wet.' I quickly wipe my hand against the towel so I can shake his hand and see the twinkle of amusement in his azure eyes.

'I see that. You are also quite a dancer.' Oh, dear lord, how long had they been watching? Visions of me

71

thinking I looked like a disco goddess quickly vanish and are quickly replaced by the reality of a tipsy mother in her mid-thirties, with two left feet, falling into the damn pool. Okay, now would be a good time for the ground to swallow me up or for me to jump back in the water and stay under with my eyes closed until the men disappear. Typical! Of all the times I could have met Leo looking sleek, confident and relaxed, instead I'm sodden, see-through and in a bikini, my wet hair slathered against my face and body and completely flustered.

'Just … please … I just need a moment to, you know … sorry. I'll be back …' I quickly excuse myself and run into the bedroom to catch my breath and pull myself together.

Leo is here, right now, after all these years. Jeremy's hero, his mentor. The person who helped him out of the emotional hole he went into when his brother Michael committed suicide and when none of his family and friends could reach him, me included. I'm in awe of this unknown man, even possibly a little jealous of him for being able to achieve what I could not, though grateful nonetheless. But we were so young, I was so young.

I can't imagine how Jeremy — so strong, so alpha male — will behave with someone he admires so much, when he is the one who is used to being in control. Suddenly this piques my interest, my first and maybe only opportunity to see these two men interact with each other, two men who have had such a profound effect on each other's lives. Fascination begins to compete with my mortification at my poolside performance. Of all the times …

'Sweetheart, are you lost in there?' Jeremy lightly taps on the door before entering the room.

'That couldn't have been more embarrassing, J. You could have warned me he was about to arrive.' I can still sense the amusement beneath the mask he is trying to maintain for my benefit.

'You were in the moment, AB, letting yourself go, just as you did when you sang and played guitar on our last rooftop together.' His arms snake around my middle. 'There must be something about you and rooftops, something seductive and delicious.' His lips nip my neck. 'I need to remember that … I'd never interrupt you when you're in that space. It's when you are at your most beautiful.'

'Nice words to hear, but not helpful right at this moment. Leo! After many years of hearing about him and this is how I meet him.' I indicate my state so he doesn't miss my point.

'He doesn't care, you care. Come on, let me help. I want you back out there sooner rather than later.'

I slide my arms around his torso and kiss his chest. 'If you help me get dressed, I may never get back out there.'

He guides my meandering hands away from the zip of his cargo pants.

'You're incorrigible and still a little tipsy, I see, even after your dunking.' He pulls the wet dress over my head and begins to dry my body with the towel. A few seconds later, a dry dress is whipped over my head.

'Jeez, you are moving so fast it's making me dizzy,' I complain.

He towel-dries my hair before looking for a brush. 'You need to meet him properly. He has come back specifically for us.'

Suddenly I feel dread in the pit of my stomach. For us? 'What do you mean, for us?'

I sit on the edge of the bed as he gently but quickly brushes my hair, something I'd usually enjoy under different circumstances.

'So we can consider all the options.'

Clearly my time of being free from reality has come to an abrupt end.

'Okay, you look fine.' He grabs my hand and pulls me off the bed.

'Jeremy, what are you planning?' I sense he is up to something.

'We're just talking, Alexa. Now that everyone is here we can work this through.' He looks directly into my eyes, his hands cupping my face, ensuring I meet his gaze. 'You know how important Leo is to me, Alexa. Please don't let me down.'

Talk about playing his trump card! What do I say to that? He plants his arm firmly around my waist and steers my reluctant body out the door. There is only one feeling you have when you are in a position such as this.

Foreboding.

I'm being led into a room full of testosterone — Leo, Adam, Robert and Jeremy. Men who have presumably come together for the sole purpose of talking me into doing something I know I can't do.

Ladies, where are you when I need you? I'd give anything to be having a movie night with my girlfriends back at home, sipping tea, eating chocolate and having a laugh or a cry. Instead, I'm literally being dragged into probably the most significant discussion I've ever had in my life, knowing the odds are well and truly stacked against me. I will attempt to keep an open mind, as I drag a heart full of apprehension down the hallway.

Part Three

Cooperate with your destiny, don't go against it,
don't thwart it. Allow it to fulfil itself.

Nisargadatta Maharaj

Alexa

I re-enter the living room with Jeremy; everyone seated around the dining room table is apparently awaiting our arrival. Four sets of ominous eyes immediately gaze toward me. How could I have possibly forgotten Martin, who adds significant weight to the alpha dominance in the room. If Jeremy wasn't holding on to me with a firm grip, I swear my legs would give way beneath me. I glance around, looking for any excuse to flee for a moment. I need an opportunity to clear my head before facing them and their potentially pointless arguments about what is best for me. Then genius strikes.

'Ah, I'll just go and check on the kids. I'll be right back.' I attempt to turn away from Jeremy but he has me anchored between his arms and steadily guides me toward one of the spare seats at the table.

'They're good, Alexa, sound asleep. I checked them less than ten minutes ago.' Robert's words effectively cut me off from any potential means of escape, even though they seem genuinely laced with sympathy. He pulls out a chair for Jeremy to place me in. Trapped, I start to fidget. Jeremy holds my hands together on my lap beneath his palm, possibly showing his support or ensuring I don't run. In my twitchy state I can't decipher which.

My heartbeat quickens as silence descends on the round table and everyone's eyes focus on Leo, except mine, which are fixed on the table in front of me. His strong presence looms and it's difficult to deny the respect he has from each of the men around the table.

'Let me just say, it is so wonderful to finally meet you in person, Alexandra. I've been hearing about you for many years from Jaq and now here we are, brought together by such an uncanny sequence of events.'

It surprises me that Leo calls Jeremy Jaq, using the initials of his full name, Jeremy Alexander Quinn, just like his parents. I haven't heard him called that for many years.

Unable to put it off any longer, I finally look up to meet his gaze and acknowledge his introduction, and I suddenly have an overwhelming sense of déjà vu. I've seen him, met him somewhere before. I become lost in his glistening blue eyes as if they are a window to his soul, potentially even my own soul. It is a feeling I haven't experienced before, like some weird kind of sixth sense. A wave of kindness and protection veils me like a warm cloak as if time suddenly stands still; it momentarily disarms me, taking my breath away.

Forcing myself to disconnect from his eyes, I realise everyone is waiting for me to respond, and my natural politeness kicks in.

'Likewise, it's lovely to meet you, too.' I shake my head in an attempt to focus on the here and now as if I had just experienced some sort of time warp. 'Though I have the strangest sense that I have met you somewhere before.' My voice is soft, unsure.

'Interesting ... in another time, another place perhaps. Many paths are crossed during our lifetimes.' His calm, philosophical response poses more questions that it answers. I think to ask a few of them, but instead I keep them to myself, shifting my bottom in the seat from the recent memory of my so-called 'punishment' at a time when questions were forbidden. Jeremy doesn't miss my adjustment and tries to hide his grin, squeezing my hands within his palm.

'Now, let's progress to the discussion we have been waiting to have. Martin, I believe you have an update.'

It's as though he is chairing a formal meeting — a mandatory one, clearly. All eyes turn to Martin.

'Thanks, Leo. Salina sent through an update two hours ago. She now has confirmation that Jurilique is underground, situated at the Xsade laboratory in Slovenia where Alexandra was taken. She believes Votrubec is also being held there.'

Straight to business.

'So he is alive?' I can't help but interrupt.

'He made recent contact with his wife but she has not seen him since your escape. He told her he was working

81

on a project requiring his presence around the clock and it may be a few weeks until he completes it.' My heart sinks. The Witch is definitely holding him captive there, but at least he is alive which is a huge relief.

'It is our understanding that she requires his expertise to conduct the testing, and experimentation on Alexandra's blood. His potential release is dependent on her return and involvement.' God, this just keeps getting worse. I lower my head as if both he and I are doomed for execution.

'And did you meet with my contact at Interpol?'

'Yes. On standby awaiting further instruction.'

'Good, I'm pleased to hear it. Anything else, Martin?' Leo asks.

'Only that we received additional correspondence from Jurilique this morning, via a guest of the hotel who was asked to pass the message on, detailing Alexandra's instructions for the meeting point.'

How has my life come to this?

'And I assume you have passed that on?'

A pause. 'Well, no, not exactly.'

'Oh?'

'It was ripped to shreds, but we have collected the pieces.'

I immediately flush scarlet — everyone around the table knows that I was the shredder. I may as well sound a siren it's so obvious.

'I see.' As if he couldn't see. I silently thank Leo for not making issue of it. 'Thanks, Martin. Any questions before we move on?' Heads shake no.

'Okay. I think it is clear from the conversations I have had with each of you around this table where you stand in relation to responding to Jurilique's attempted blackmail. Everyone except Alexandra.'

All eyes swivel to the bright beacon of my face. Leo continues to address me by my full name, which, along with his demeanour, provides me with an unexpected and surprising reassurance.

Jeremy hasn't uttered a word since this meeting began and I half expect him to speak on my behalf given our recent disagreements. He remains silent and they wait patiently for me to respond. I release my hands from beneath Jeremy's palm, take a sip of wine from my glass as my mouth has gone dry, pray for some Dutch courage and prepare to speak. Here goes nothing.

I explain what I have been trying to convey to Jeremy since the arrival of the letter. My fear for the children. My desperate need for this to be over to resume our normal lives, our careers. My desire to exist in society rather than become an outcast, a recluse. I talk for a long time and they sit and listen, not one interruption or question, just patience and understanding from around the table, which frankly, I find astonishing — not what I expected. I talk until I have almost no words left and finally sum up.

'That is why there's no other option than for me to give her what she wants, for the sake of all our lives.' I take another sip of wine and only look up to meet their eyes when I replace the glass on the table.

Jeremy and Robert's faces are brimming with emotions I can't bear to register. Adam looks toward his brother and as they lock eyes, their heads tilt ever so slightly, acknowledging some silent agreement between them.

Leo speaks first. 'You know that everyone around this table cares for you deeply, Alexandra, that we wouldn't be here if we didn't?'

'Yes, of course. And I want to thank you for all you have done to protect me. I don't know how I can ever repay you.'

'Life isn't about repayments. It's about experiencing and learning, exploring the unknown. Something you have enabled quite a bit of recently.'

'Don't I know it,' I say under my breath. Thankfully, Leo's lips curl in a half smile rather than annoyance. He certainly is incredibly handsome and has aged magnificently for a man nearing fifty. He is fit and tanned, no doubt from his recent time in the heat of the jungle, with playful, reflective azure eyes that are bordered by thick black lashes and a classic, perfect American smile. I can see why people, at first glance, may consider that he and Jeremy could be related. They are of a similar build and stature, both exceptionally good-looking in the sense that the majority of straight woman and gay men could easily be caught staring idly at their bodies for far longer than would be deemed appropriate in public. Both share the same suave presence and intellectual confidence, the key difference being Leo's relaxed and charming personality, compared to Jeremy's more professional, urbane and commanding demeanour.

'Yet, you see the only option available to you is the one provided by Madame Jurilique?'

I nod in silent agreement to Leo's question.

'Thank you for sharing your fears with us. Jeremy, would you like to share your perspective?'

He nods and states his side of the argument we have been having for days as though he is a barrister delivering his concluding argument to the judge and jury. If I didn't fundamentally disagree with his case, I'd be bursting with pride at his succinct yet heartfelt delivery. In this particular instance, it doesn't help me one bit. Nor does his reference to his concern that if one pharmaceutical company is interested in 'acquiring' my blood's unique capability, that it would only be a matter of time before others cotton on and want access to the same thing, by any means, just like Xsade.

'And Robert, anything to add?' Leo certainly can't be deemed anything but egalitarian. Robert quickly aligns himself with Jeremy, stating that giving in to Jurilique's demands will not serve to keep either me or the children safe in the longer term and, like Jeremy, will not support my returning to Xsade under any circumstances, regardless of the impact of her smear campaign against me.

I'm a little aghast at both his knowledge of the issues we face and the depth of his convictions. Robert and Jeremy share solemn looks between them before looking back to Leo. God, what hope do I have? I look pleadingly toward them, feeling my energy to fight them draining from my limbs as well as from my words. 'Please, both of you … how can you say that? You know I have no choice …'

'Alexandra, I have an alternative option for you to consider this evening. One that, in all likelihood, hasn't crossed your mind and one that I'd like us to explore, if I may. Would you care to hear it?' Leo's eloquent phrasing takes me by surprise every time he opens his mouth. I had always assumed he would be as direct as Jeremy can be, but it's not the case.

How could I not be open to options? Particularly in circumstances such as these. What else is there to do? Resigned to the fact that I'm in his brother's house, surrounded by men who admittedly care for me deeply, yet want me to do anything but what I need to do, I reluctantly nod.

'Yes, Leo, of course.'

I hear Jeremy physically exhale at my agreement. His previous silence had been distracting me from thinking about the stress he must be feeling. We make eye contact and he kisses my palm, relief and tension still weaving through the muscles of his body.

Leo explains his proposal, describing the potential risks and dangers, and painting a detailed vision of a potential nirvana, the best-case scenario if everything goes according to plan. His monologue is compelling and allows me to wallow in a vision of the future that I have been incapable of considering given the immediate nature of Jurilique's threat. What he is suggesting is beyond anything I could ever have conceived and goes so much further than merely the next few days. His passion makes the impossible seem possible, helping me to start believing in the idea that these horrible events have happened for a reason. That they have a purpose we are yet to discover and offer a path for us to take that would otherwise have been unavailable to us.

His language is engaging, enthusiastic and it opens pathways, as if he is reaching out to me and tempting me to escape with him, to take a risk, a journey not taken before, an undefined path. And I want to believe in him, more than I've ever wanted anything before. We are all mesmerised by his words, as if we are in a trance; he has captured the imagination of every mind around the table. I should have known that for a man like Jeremy to revere Leo like he does, he would need to be exceptional. He is.

As his speech ends, Leo meets my eyes and it's as though I'm hypnotised by his, until my mind abruptly flashes with a shock of recognition. Leo is my owl, the owl in the dream I had on the plane to London. The one who is looking out for me, the one I acknowledged with a bow of my head when I had transformed into an eagle.

How much do I trust in my dreams? Should I give them credence? Questions scatter through my brain in less than a second before they are silenced. In this moment, I recognise that it is my destiny to fly with this man, in uncharted skies. I know I need to trust him with my life, as scary as that may be, but knowing too that my life depends on it. The perceived kindness and sense of calm I experienced just a short time ago gives weight to this notion. Perhaps Leo is the wise owl guiding us toward our undiscovered future. He certainly ensured Jeremy's redirection many years ago and has stood by him ever since.

This male ambush was nothing like what I had expected; perhaps had been programmed to expect. They have surprised me with their sincere response to my situation, while remaining calm, kind and rational.

I'm forced to question why I wouldn't allow myself to consider any other options, would barely engage in the discussion. My only conclusion is that my ego got the better of me. The threat of the world seeing me in a different light to the public persona I have so carefully constructed and managed throughout my life, allowed me to be held to ransom.

I am beginning to understand that my true learning has only just begun, although Jeremy began the process by awakening me to the potential integration of my distinct parts, shining light on what was previously dark. I feel like the universe has thrown me a huge curve ball and I must choose whether to duck or bat. I decide to play.

'I have two conditions for all of you to consider before I accept this proposition.' Jeremy looks anxious, Leo allows a small smile on the edge of his lips as though he has expected as much.

'Yes, Alexandra?' Leo asks.

I glance toward Robert. 'Elizabeth and Jordan come with us.'

No one responds but looks are exchanged around the table, laden with unspoken words.

'And the other?' Leo enquires with an aura of calm the others don't have.

'That Salina gets Josef away from the Witch,' I state firmly and with a vehemence that shocks even me.

Leo's body language gains a regal stature as he senses imminent alignment and he makes eye contact with each of the men around the table, as if reading their minds. One by one, their heads nod in agreement with my conditions. My palms moisten at the thought of what I'm about to sign up for.

'Your conditions are reasonable. Robert and I discussed the children earlier as we suspected that this would be a major factor in your consideration of our proposal. Robert has reorganised his work commitments and will come with us, ensuring they will have at least one parent with them at any given time. A tutor has also been organised to continue their schooling whilst we are away. All other logistics have or will be taken care of by Moira, upon your agreement.' Of course, Moira would have everything under control, Leo's be-all-and-end-all assistant. She clears the logistical path of his life so he can do what he does best — whatever he wants.

I can't believe my life has become such a bartering tool. I think on what I've done in the past weeks: promising Jeremy 48 hours, no sight, no questions.

Negotiating and signing a contract with Xsade; post-abduction; and now this. I am about to hand myself over to Leo and embark on a journey that defies logic, until the stars align, whatever that means. Yet everyone around the table appears to be in full support of a plan that is more bizarre than any dream I've ever had. Even Jeremy, who is always so rational, analytical and scientific, is clearly willing me to accept.

'So, essentially, you are asking me to go with the flow, let be what will be. In your words, "let the past reconcile with the present and let the future unfold". Is that right?' I ask.

'That's correct.'

'I'm putting my life in your hands, Leo ...'

'In *our* hands, Alexandra. Please trust that we will never let you fall; we each have our distinct roles to play in this journey.'

Sometimes the path of least resistance may be the most difficult decision to reach, but the simplest road to follow. As I finally relinquish my previously resolute plans to return to Xsade, and agree to accept the path now laid before me, there is a collective sigh of relief around the table. A palpable release from anxiety and tension. I too exhale, exhausted from forcing myself to swim upstream against the tide. It is as frightening as it is invigorating, an intoxicating relief to defy the path of fear and replace it with one of hope.

Jeremy embraces me as if his life depended on it. Tears spill from our eyes. Leo joins our embrace, as do Robert and Adam, completing our union and solidarity in what lies ahead. Martin is already on the phone making arrangements for goodness knows what. I have no idea what will unfold from this point forward although I do know I need to be as fearless as I've ever been. Walking into the unknown, knowing I'm risking my life as I know it for a better future for me and my loved ones. And having to trust in others to ensure the outcome.

Jeremy

Thank Christ, is all I can think. Leo has been able to achieve what has been impossible for me. Alexa has consented to our plan rather than handing herself over to Xsade, which was never going to happen anyway, but now life is far simpler without us arguing every five minutes about which direction her life should take, or being in a state of limbo where we disagree but don't talk about it.

Admittedly, when Leo first discussed his alternative proposition I was a little sceptical. Well, very sceptical. It goes against my nature in every way and if anyone other than Leo had suggested it, I would have immediately written it off as insanity. But Leo did suggest it and frankly, if it saves Alexa from a death trap, then the least I can do is keep an open mind for my friend who seems intent on risking everything for us.

Besides, if he discovers what he is hoping to — and knowing Leo, who am I to say he won't — then the results could save Alexa from being the target of every pharmaceutical company around the globe.

Leo's recent trip to the Amazon to live with the Wai-Wai people brought him in contact with one of the most powerful shamans he has had the privilege to meet — his words. The shaman was willing for Leo to journey on a 'soul flight' with him, where they apparently perceived some form of enlightened state together.

I can't deny this sounded like mumbo jumbo to me, but Leo has been studying this stuff for years and genuinely believes it could provide the missing link to understanding the enigma of Alexa's blood, though I'm not sure how exactly. The link that our studies, even with round-the-clock work by our analysts and technicians, has yet been unable to provide.

My areas of study have always been considered 'outside the medical box' so to speak, but this will take our research way beyond the realm of traditional scientific methodologies and that's how Leo finally convinced me to take this journey with him: he'll coordinate the mumbo jumbo — that is, whatever preparation is involved for Alexa to participate in soul flight — and I, other than being there to support Alexa, will gather the research data and provide medical assistance, which hopefully won't be required. So in essence, Leo will coordinate the spiritual and I'll be responsible for the scientific. We're both hoping that the answers to Alexa's blood fall somewhere in between.

I've organised for my protégée at Harvard to be on standby in Boston so she can start analysing any data we send through without delay. Leo, Alexa and myself will begin our jungle trek from the Avalon base in the Amazon, in northern Brazil, to the shaman near Mapuera village in the state of Pará.

I have no idea what we are letting ourselves in for but I trust Leo with our lives and he seems to be adamant that this is the path forward. He is so sure of himself, in fact, that any argument I put forward bounces back as if he is protected by some intellectual force field that I can't penetrate. It's a weird feeling and not one that I'm used to. His hypnotic speech to those of us around the table was another example of this; as much as you might try to rationalise his words, they seem to engage some level of the subconscious so that you find that you are willing yourself to believe in him. It's a strange sensation.

I've witnessed him do it before to people, but was never sure whether it would work on a defensive Alexa. Either way, I'm not arguing. In my mind he has already achieved the unachievable and she has agreed to remove herself from the outside world for as long as it takes.

And everything is still in motion behind the scenes, for this blackmailing to come to an end. Leo's connections with Interpol will try to fast-track any red tape to indict Jurilique and get her behind bars sooner rather than later. Hopefully, the authorities have been able to track Xsade's systems and are better positioned to protect Alexa. Even in the worst-case scenario, if Salina and her team are unable to penetrate Xsade to bring down Jurilique and rescue Josef before her vile campaign against our reputations begins, at least we will be so far removed from media and western society that we can protect Alexa and the kids from any ramifications. But we still have five days, so anything is possible.

The more Leo discussed it with us, the more it seemed like our only viable option. It was also abundantly clear that he was never going to take no for an answer. And I certainly know what that feels like. Her eventual consent was like breathing life back into a situation which was previously doomed, allowing me to relax my tense muscles for the first time in what feels like forever.

Part Four

One must learn to love, and go through a good deal of suffering to get it, and the journey is always towards the others soul.

David Herbert Lawrence.

Lake Bled

S alina can't believe her luck. Finally, after a long time of hunting, she has managed to locate one of the secret entrances into the facility. She just needs to confirm it.

Since Alexa, Jeremy and Martin returned to the States, she has been investigating Jurilique and Lauren Bertrand and attempting to locate their whereabouts in the hope of finding Josef Votrubcc. Though she has been sending progress updates regularly to Martin, she still hadn't managed to access the entrance to Xsade's facility. She was starting to think it might be impossible, but now, she thinks she has succeeded. Martin will be pleased and that makes it even more worthwhile.

Salina had had a sneaking suspicion there was something dubious about the hospital morgue where she had seen Alexa's apparently dead body. Alexa was there one minute and gone the next — as if by magic.

Then they had been sent on a wild goose chase by a doctor who seemed to vanish into thin air, and Salina had been unable to find the man again. In her mind, that had to be the place that held the key, even though the thought of it gave her the creeps.

The main obstacles were the entrance and the emergency room, which she moved through smoothly. Once again she was thankful that Lake Bled hospital was a quiet community facility and staff seemed to be few and far between. She noticed some spare lab coats in one of the rooms and grabbed one to cover her black clothing; with her black hair slicked back from her face, she instantly looked like a medical professional. She continued down the stairs and paused briefly before slipping into the room she remembered as the morgue, and after she making sure she was alone she quietly locked the door behind her.

One at a time, she opened the heavy doors to the refrigerated holdings, exhaling in relief not to encounter any bodies.

'This has to the way in,' she muttered to herself as her eyes scanned the room for any other openings. She took a deep breath before lifting and sliding her body on to the metal stretchers and commando-crawling to the far end, pushing against the wall to assess whether anything would give. She was not sure whether to be relieved or disappointed that it was totally solid. She wriggled out and tried the next one. Again, nothing. By the third she had started to question what she was thinking with this theory. As if anyone would be allowed to access a facility via these cold chambers. As she half-heartedly tested the last one, she sensed some give, which hadn't been the case with the others.

Using her flashlight, she scanned the wall. There was a tiny silver button located on the bottom corner. She pushed it. Instantly, the back of the chamber slid open. She quickly turned off her torch and allowed for the forty or so seconds it would take her eyesight to adjust to darkness before sliding down into what is presumably the outskirts of the Xsade's facility.

She was in.

* * *

Salina now notices some form of rail track, like an old-style roller coaster, and is immediately reminded of the salt mines she recently took her nephews to in Salzburg. It's a similar set-up and looks as if you could get up quite a bit of speed twisting and turning deeper underground. She can't risk such an entrance, so she removes her white coat and stuffs it into her backpack; it may come in handy later.

Her black clothes blend in with her dark surroundings and she follows the path of the tunnel on foot. Only once does a trolley come whizzing past and she crouches down into a small ball. Only when it passes does she venture a glance and sees that there was nobody on it — this must be how they transport goods. Relieved, she continues her journey into what seems like the bowels of the earth.

Alexa

The last twenty-four hours have passed in a blur since I abandoned plans to volunteer my body and blood to Xsade. Since then it's as if the world around me has been on fast forward and has suddenly come to an abrupt halt now that we are comfortably cocooned in one of Leo's private jets.

Our arrival at the private airfield could have easily equated to a secret service operation. The kids, Robert, and Adam arrived by limousine and Jeremy, Leo and myself departed in stealth from the apartment just after dark from the rooftop via helicopter — just in case we were being followed. We are now flying to another one of Leo's secret Avalon properties in South America.

Leo still doesn't want the exact location to be known to me, as apparently it is more important that I feel the energy of the environment than have any predetermined opinions of its location. Whatever ... go with the flow, I keep telling myself. This mantra helps when I consider the alternative; I involuntarily shudder at the prospect.

I made phone calls to my family, explaining that we were staying in America for a few months due to work commitments, which was met initially with shock, then understanding, bless them. My emotions were shaky when I heard the concern in their voices, just as they probably sensed my worry, but I strengthened my resolve that being with my immediate family was the best option for us, even if I was disrupting so many lives. Robert organised for the kids' absence from school, and for one of our friends to house-sit for a month or three, without a hitch. Moira had coordinated everything for my work, so I didn't even need to call or email the university, which feels weird.

Going against the force of Leo and Jeremy's plan was impossible, regardless, every option sealed, as if they were intent on creating a protective bubble for me to exist in outside the real world. I attempt to push aside my recurring dread about how my family, friends and colleagues might react should Jurilique follow through with her smear campaign; it makes hiding in the void of denial that much easier for now.

Everything was arranged so smoothly there was no need for me to communicate with anyone other than my family. There was no doubt in my mind that these plans had already been orchestrated prior to my consent. I'm sure they would have worn me down eventually, and it's obvious that there was no way

Jeremy was going to let me return to Xsade. He has barely let me out of his sight since we were reunited in Europe. I couldn't even leave the apartment of my own free will. A nervous laugh escapes me as I acknowledge that I've been held captive by love in Miami instead by fear in Slovenia. I sigh at the thought that this is what my life has become; it's emotionally exhausting to fight and I suppose ultimately it makes no difference.

After making the necessary calls, everyone's phones are confiscated by Leo. Jeremy stifles his amusement at my bemused expression, no doubt remembering how angry I became when he 'stole' my phone at the commencement of our weekend together in Sydney. Gosh, it seems like forever since we embarked on this wild ride, so much has happened since then. I don't say too much this time when he has to hand his mobile over as well, but I relish the moment and poke him in the ribs as Leo explains that there will be no reception where we are going, only via satellite phone. It would also be best to leave them behind, he told us, in case any were being traced, which admittedly makes sense. Jeremy then has the opportunity to poke me back when Leo also asks for my watch.

'My watch? Why?'

'We've discovered that Xsade bugged it, that's why they have known your exact location at any given time.'

'Oh, really?' I dejectedly hand it over to Martin, who never moves too far from the lift doors, as if he thinks I may flee the second he's not paying attention.

'We'd already debugged your phone, but it wasn't until a few hours ago we discovered a signal was still being emitted from another source. Other than the one in your bracelet, of course.'

'Of course.' I remember everything was taken from me at the facility except the bracelet, which they were unable to remove.

'Don't look so sad, Alexandra. There'll be no need for watches or keeping time where we're headed. This way we can leave your watch here and they'll think that's where you are.'

There was no use fighting it. Everything that needed to happen to disconnect us from the real world on the last day, has happened. Now, it's just our little group on the plane who know anything about our journey at all. Obviously, we can't risk any knowledge of my whereabouts falling into Xsade's hands. It's quite a weird feeling having your family and friends not actually knowing where you are or what you are doing. I desperately hope I'm not being selfish in wanting my children with me; I'd die if anything happened to them because of all this. Them being here gives me a greater sense of security and comfort than I've had in months, so I'm immensely grateful to these men in my life who allowed it to happen.

Leo has asked Martin to return to Europe to liaise directly with Interpol and assist Salina in rescuing Josef, hopefully ensuring Jurilique's threats remain just that. I also have a sneaking suspicion they fear Martin's presence makes me focus more on what we are risking, distracting me from the whole purpose of our journey. If so, they are right. Every time I look at Martin, I am reminded of the danger that lurks out in the real world for my family. My stomach continues to churn with dread for Josef's safety, and for Salina's as well, even though she's a professional like Martin. So I'm pleased Leo is taking serious precautions and I know he has every faith in Martin's ability, as do I. Even though I was less than pleased when he wouldn't let me out of Adam's apartment under any circumstances, it reinforced to me how seriously he takes his job and he is exceptional at it.

We've swallowed or been jabbed with everything under the sun today — yellow fever, hepatitis, typhoid, cholera, the list goes on. My upper arm still throbs from the tetanus injection, and I'm pleased the kids are finally asleep so they won't be feeling any pain. Their little systems are no doubt awash with many miniature versions of disease. Jeremy was as gentle as possible with them, but it's always difficult to see your children endure needles. They were very brave, and just so excited to be embarking on yet another adventure. God, I hope I've made the right decision having them come with us.

I smile a weary smile toward Robert who has Jordan nestled on his lap just as Elizabeth is on mine. The others are chatting at the front of the plane.

'How are you, Robert? Are you sure you're okay with all of this?' I'm suddenly aware that we haven't really had any time to chat privately since arriving at the apartment.

'You ask me now?' he says with a laugh. 'I'm okay, Alex, all good. It's weird though, isn't it?' He raises his eyes to our surroundings. 'I could never have imagined this turn of events.'

'I'm still coming to terms with how my quiet life has been turned completely on its head.' I'm aware my voice sounds a little wistful which Robert notices.

'This has been pretty hard on you, hasn't it?'

I reluctantly nod, scanning our previously intact family unit and trying to keep my emotions contained on the inside as my eyes well up. 'Yeah, it has, but I'm hoping it will work out in the end.'

'Any regrets?'

I smile at his recognition of one of my life's values. 'No, I don't think so, but it doesn't make this any less weird. I'm just so sorry that you have to be involved … and the kids … I never wanted …'

'It's alright, Alex, I have no regrets either, honestly, about any of this, or us.' His voice is sincere as he acknowledges both of our new and old relationships. 'Besides, from everything I witnessed with the kids today, they are very excited about being jungle explorers.' He deliberately lightens the mood and I laugh at the memory of them stalking around the apartment earlier as the various wild animals they may encounter.

'Do you think I made the right choice?' I ask earnestly.

'The only one you could have. Really, you will get through this, we all will. And look at us now, a functional extended family, still talking to each other, still supporting each other and our kids sleeping soundly on our laps. It's not all bad.' He regards me with both sympathy and strength.

'Thank you. You are an incredible dad. I never want them to lose that. You've been so great through this when I've been so, well, overwhelmed, I suppose.' I hope he understands that the children we made together are what binds us together and I'd never undo that bond.

'And you're a great mum. We both know we made beautiful children together,' he says with a wink, confirming his understanding.

I glance toward Jeremy, who has been sporadically keeping an eye on me during his conversation with Leo, Adam and Martin, and smile. I have nothing but platonic feelings for Robert, which has been the case for years, but I still love and respect him, now even more so than when were officially together. I feel secure in my relationship with him knowing that our love for our children will override any personal issues we may face.

Jeremy catches my gaze and returns my smile both with his lips and his eyes, and my heart floods with warmth, spreading a tingling sensation from my head to the tips of my toes. I blush from the strength of these physical and emotional feelings. It's as if we are bound together with invisible ties and he too, gives me a knowing wink, never one to miss the slightest change in my physiology.

How blessed I am to have these two men in my life, both of whom I love, but in completely different ways. The turmoil I have been thrown into as a result of saying 'yes' to Jeremy, always saying yes to Jeremy, is nothing short of unbelievable. But he has brought more love, and play, and feeling into my life than I ever believed possible, resuscitating my heart and rescuing me from the brink of endless inertia that was surely eroding me with each passing hour of my life. The drama, pain and angst of the lows, perhaps contribute to me feeling so alive during the euphoric highs. This is certainly one hell of a wild ride, and no doubt will continue to be, but finally I am now brave enough to embrace the journey surrounded by love and supported by the most special people in my life right by my side.

I quietly reach for a blanket to put over Elizabeth and place her head on a pillow, carefully extracting myself from beneath her body. As I stand, I give Robert a kiss on the forehead as a symbol of just how much he means to me, to us. Then I walk over to stand by Jeremy, needing to be near his strength and the muscled warmth of his body. His arms immediately wrap around me like a cloak and I snuggle into his chest, knowing that whatever happens from this point forward, I am where I should be.

After however many hours, we arrive. Once we land, we are escorted through some militarised security checkpoint, board two helicopters for an hour or so and then travel by jeep on forest tracks taking us deeper into the jungle.

The warmth and humidity hits us instantly, as soon as we are exposed to this new environment, creating an instant sheen on our skin, turning into perspiration and eventually making me feel like I desperately need a shower. Finally, we turn a corner and reach a clearing. Before our eyes, is the wondrous Amazonian version of Avalon.

Lake Bled

Martin finally arrives back in Ljubljana, slightly weary after more than 48 hours in transit around the globe. The weather makes a pleasant change from the humidity of the jungle; he has never really understood why people like to spend their holidays sweating and baking under the sun — give him skiing and trekking any day.

He grabs a sugarless, double shot macchiato before jumping into the hire car to make his way to Lake Bled and Salina. Pleased he is finally back in communication with the world, he connects his phone in the car and makes the calls that will bring him up to speed.

It's a relief to hear that Interpol is finally taking Dr Blake's abduction allegations seriously. Until Leo organised for his contact in the FBI to get involved, they had been refusing to consider that one of Europe's most respected executives could have gone so spectacularly rogue. Finally, the evidence they packaged together has fallen into the right hands and he will have the official support he needs to bring this woman down.

Martin's first stop is a meeting he has organised with the Slovenian Ministry of the Interior. The ministry has appointed a local liaison officer to coordinate between the various authorities, and given the US Federal Bureau of Investigation has an international partnership with them, it should reduce any red tape considerably, smoothing the path for Martin's team. He has also been informed that they have the on-ground support of a National Police Force special task squad should he require additional resources.

Leo gave him the green light to use every means at his disposal to ensure Blake and Quinn's reputations remain intact, and that is exactly what he plans to do. Salina has made great progress and he knows Leo will be pleased now that he has the Ministry's commitment and the ground support of the police. Given they had no knowledge of Xsade's secret facility, they have also alerted other departments to start investigating tax fraud and evasion in their country.

Things are certainly not stacking up very well for Jurilique. Her previously immaculate corporate reputation is beginning to collapse like a house of cards and Martin knows they are very close to her demise. It's the first time he has allowed a smile on his face for a very long time as he updates Moira with the latest details, as is procedure.

Martin has been trying Salina's number since his

arrival and is a little concerned she isn't answering. She is one of their best European operatives and has been instrumental in getting this case to where it is now. During their time together trying to locate Alexandra, he became very fond of her and, if Quinn hadn't been with them, Martin suspects something may have happened between them. In this job, neither of them have much chance to form liaisons with others, but if they had the time and opportunity who knows ... Martin, his focus always on the job at hand, knows that Salina, like him, wants to see this bitch fall and fall hard for what she has put them through, justice or no justice.

He finally makes contact with Luke, the junior operative working with Salina, who confirms she had managed to find access into Xsade two days ago and re-entered the underground facility early this morning. Before re-entering she contacted Luke and said that she had discovered they were having an orientation training session for their new inductee scientists and planned on joining the group, disguised as one of them. It was the only way she could get into the facility, as her explorations had come to a dead end without higher security access.

'When did she leave?'

'She left at 6.00 a.m. so she's been gone almost nine hours now. I'm assuming she's in, but I'm not sure whether she has merely been unable to contact me or if she's been taken.'

'But she always keeps her phone on, yes?'

'That's right. We've had no luck trying to gain access — it's like an impenetrable fortress. And as it's underground there's no guarantee our phones will get a signal. But as last reported, we have confirmation that both Votrubec and Jurilique are currently inside.'

'Blake says she believed she must have accessed the facility via the hospital, because she wasn't taken anywhere else and only escaped via the boathouse with Josef's security pass.'

'Correct. Salina was scouting both areas in an attempt to gain entry. We were able to acquire a security key from an employee who refuses to undergo any more testing on behalf of the company. He's feigning sickness to avoid going in.'

'I'm assuming Salina is armed?'

'Of course.'

Martin shakes his head. 'I don't have a good feeling about this. She would have been in contact with us by now if everything was okay.' He pauses for a moment to assess his options while Luke waits on the line. 'I'll organise for police backup to be on standby in Bled, just in case. Meet me at the hospital and we'll agree next steps from there.'

Alexa

An environment as rich, thick, colourful and bountiful as this is difficult to describe. It's as if we have arrived in the midst of the heart and lungs of the earth. It's overwhelming. Everywhere I look is teeming with life; foliage is the greenest of greens; the flowers and multicoloured birds are brighter than anywhere I have seen. It's as if I'm seeing everything for the first time through a special fluorescent lens. I have the sense of suddenly feeling like an insect in a land so vast and massive that it's almost impossible to gain any perspective. The sounds of the jungle almost drown out our voices, as if we are rudely interrupting nature's conversations when we speak. I breathe in the intoxicating freshness of the air. My lungs have never experienced anything so pure; it immediately energises my body, which is hungry for more of this invisible feast.

Leo has built a small village of elaborate and luxurious huts scattered around a main building which resembles the other Avalon I visited at the end of my weekend with Jeremy. There is no ocean here, we are embedded in the fertility of the dense jungle which is littered with streams and tributaries that no doubt lead into the massive river system that feeds the mighty Amazon river. The sound of water trickling is never far away, like tiny bells tinkering in the wind. I feel like I've landed in the jungle version of the Faraway Tree and half expect to stumble upon Moon-Face or the Saucepan Man. This place is pure magic, its energy flows right through my body, enhancing my mood and enlightening my spirit.

Surprisingly, we settle in very quickly to this new world. We go for walks on tracks that need to be remade and hacked out with machetes after each wet season and we are situated near the most gorgeous water hole to swim in, already a favourite pastime for the kids. It has a waterfall and a natural water-slide and is surrounded by water lilies and the vibrant sounds of nature. The water is cool and fresh and provides great relief from the humidity and heat of the day.

It's difficult for me to consider the imminent threats I faced in my old world as I eagerly immerse myself in this one, happily distancing myself from any potential danger my children and I face. Every time the headlines in Madame Jurilique's letter pop into my mind I resolutely push the thought aside. There's nothing I can do about it now. I've put my trust in Leo and all

I can do is see it through. Who knows, it may have already begun and I'd be none the wiser, so I continue to embrace this 'unreality' while it lasts.

Our diet consists mainly of fish, vegetables and fruit sourced from the jungle, with plentiful treats such as sweet berries fetched from the trees … and we've even adjusted to the bitterness of the chocolate made from cocoa beans. Our food looks like a festival dancing on our plate with so many rich, diverse colours competing for attention. The kids love the taste of maracujá ice cream and tapioca and are having a ball climbing to reach the purple grape-sized berries from the açai palm trees. They haven't asked for any fast food yet so hopefully the abundant supply of *papas fritas*, otherwise known as chips, is keeping them sated in the short term.

* * *

We've been practising meditation and yoga exercises each morning and evening as though we are on an extended family health retreat and we feel happy, vital and alive. Our delight in this no-technology, simplistic, healthy style of living surprises us, except for Leo of course, and even the kids have taken naturally to having a siesta. We eat when we are hungry, sleep when we are tired and play when we are in the mood. I have no complaints about going with the flow, as I don't remember ever feeling this content in my life. The days meld into nights and the nights into days, and just as Leo requested I have no real sense of time or how long we have been here. Living this lifestyle, it becomes absolutely irrelevant. I've never experienced such a sense of timelessness in my life and I feel myself soaking up the experience of being where there is no such thing as a deadline.

As I'm swinging in the hammock from the balcony of the main house, I notice Leo and Jeremy walking outside fully armed.

'My goodness, where are you guys off to with all that?'

'We're having guests for dinner tomorrow, so we're killing a pig.'

'Good grief, have you ever done that before?'

Leo smiles. 'I have. Jeremy assures me he's good with a scalpel.'

'Are the others going to help?'

'Adam? No way, not quite his style. He'll eat it, he won't kill it.' Like so many of us in the world, I think.

'Robert's at the water hole with the kids. We weren't sure whether you'd want them around,' Jeremy adds.

'Oh, right ...'

'Don't look so shocked, AB, you know this is where food comes from.'

'I know, but ...' I can't help thinking of a documentary I saw a few years back where some mother pigs were confined in their pens, unable to move freely, as their piglets suckled on them constantly. I have only eaten free-range pork since. I shake my head to remove the disturbing image. 'Oh well, at least I know they are — were — happy pigs. So who's coming, anyway?'

'A few senior members of the tribe, maybe a couple of others. They'll be taking us to the shaman. It's our first meeting before our journey commences, a celebration of sorts.'

Well, this is certainly news to me. 'Does it involve me?' I ask, naively. They both chuckle in response.

'Sweetheart, it's all about you, that's why we are here,' Jeremy says with a smile and a sense of the unknown in his eyes.

'Should I be worried?' I yell out as they walk away toward the animal pen.

'Not in the least, but you must be there,' Leo calls back.

Right, well, that clarifies things ... or not. I lower myself back into the hammock as they wander off to hunt and slaughter in the pig pen. As much as I try, I can no longer concentrate on the book I was enjoying moments ago and the butterflies that have been lying dormant in my stomach recommence their flight.

The next night is full of festivities after a day of preparation on all our parts. Our guests have arrived, five in all from the Wai-Wai tribe. Two elders and one young man, one teenage boy, and Yaku, an apprentice medicine man, who appears to be somewhere in the middle of the bunch age-wise and can speak a little English. Their dress is partly casual western, partly native. They are all wearing camouflage-patterned, or khaki, cargo trousers, some with black singlet tops, some without, but their upper bodies are painted traditionally and they are adorned with headdresses of varying leaves and feathers.

Their small-statured bodies are muscle-toned and they look extremely serious until their giant white-toothed smiles illuminate their faces against their darkened skin. The shaman, referred to as Yaskomo in their native language, rarely travels from the village. The elders, who are said to share some of his magic, are to take us to him when the time comes.

The concept of timeframes tends not to exist in the same way here as it does for us in the western world, with everything happening when it feels right rather than at any pre-arranged time. I imagine the notion of meeting a deadline is just not understood in these parts, which in itself makes life so much less stressful.

The pig is sizzling on the spit over the fire and there are plenty of vegetables roasting underneath. After we have eaten, we relax and enjoy their local music. The beat of a tribal drum, a wooden flute and a guitar keep us entertained as we celebrate the coming together of our unlikely gathering.

Leo has been studying their language for the past few years and assists in translating between our groups. Elizabeth and Jordan are quite taken with the teenage boy who has travelled here with the men. He is teaching them some of his tribal dances, they are teaching him the macarena. They are having lots of fun and it's wonderful to see them communicate so effectively without the use of a common language. Global lessons for adults in the art of the unspoken word!

They are happily sharing their *água de coco* with each other while the adults, or should I say, the men and myself, are drinking beer, or *cerveja*, or aged *cachaça*, a local alcoholic drink made from distilled sugar cane. We haven't had any alcohol since we left Florida so it's going straight to my head. The locals suggest adding sugar and lime juice, essentially transforming it into a *caipirinha*, which makes it easier to swallow and a rather refreshing cocktail, particularly in this humidity. Mind you, I only dare sip it and slowly at that. The party is in full swing around our campfire and we are singing, laughing and learning a new fused style of dancing.

Eventually the festivities die down, the live music fades into the background allowing nature to reign in this rich part of the world. The kids are bundled on top of some straw matting with their new friend, having fallen asleep. I notice Leo is in deep conversation with two of the tribal elders; there is no question he is intrigued with their world. Robert and Adam are next to one another, enjoying the fire and the last of their local cocktails. They have their hands on each other's knees — the first public display of affection I have been witness to. Their togetherness makes me smile, as does mine with Jeremy. We are swaying together, arms wrapped around each other, as the remaining locals play soft music, or perhaps I am swaying and Jeremy is keeping me balanced. Either way, it feels fantastic being able to be with him like this.

All the troubles and dramas of recent weeks have faded into a dark spot in my mind and I feel like I'm almost home as I nestle comfortably against his firm, warm chest. Jeremy raises my chin toward his face with his index finger.

'You look more relaxed and happy than I've seen you in a long while.'

'Very observant, Dr Quinn, and that's because I am.' He bends down to kiss me ever so gently on the lips. I feel like I could literally float away with the sensations this one gesture provokes.

'I love seeing you like this. There is nothing that makes me happier.'

'Well, let's just stay like this. Forever, if we can.'

Even in the dim flickering light of the fire I can't help but notice the small frown creasing his brow at the hope in my words. It's as if he wants to give me the world but knows he can't right now.

'What is it, J?'

'You know this can't last forever, sweetheart, don't you?' He searches my face before continuing. 'The elders' presence here indicates the next step in the journey that Leo has been talking about.'

'Yes, I know,' I say reluctantly. 'I'm just putting it out of my mind until it happens, and thankfully, right at this second, my mind is fully occupied with other thoughts.' I slip my hands beneath his trousers and cup his butt.

'Oh, really, Dr Blake? And what might they be?'

'I'm sure you could hazard a guess.'

I stand on my tiptoes and engage him in a longer, almost indecent extension of his earlier seductive kiss. Being under the stars, by the fire, with the music, dancing and drinking has sent my carnal desires for this man into overdrive. I can feel him swell against my belly. If we were alone right now and I had my way, we'd be writhing around naked paying sexual homage to the gods. Unfortunately, for so many reasons, we are not in that position.

'Christ, Alexa, I'm going to have you drag you inside this second if you keep that up.' Jeremy's eyes scan the rest of the group. He seems relieved to find no one is paying us any attention.

'You won't be hearing any complaints from me,' I say, both cheekily and seriously.

He shakes his head with a smile on his face, takes firm hold of my hand and drags me off to say goodnight to everyone. Adam and Robert are equally as wrapped up in their own world as we are in ours. I give them both a quick kiss on the cheek and a wink and then I'm guided over to Leo and the elders.

'Perfect timing,' Leo announces. 'Would you care to join us for a moment? We have just been making the final arrangements.'

The sexual energy pulsing in my groin takes an instant dive straight down my legs and escapes out my toes before I can even blink. I try to pull Jeremy subtly toward the house, silently relaying my preference to retreat quickly to our bedroom, to no avail.

'Sure. Of course.'

They shuffle around so we can join their gathering by the fire. I look anxiously toward Leo, whose eyes, once again, give me a sense of calm and take the edge off my nerves. I honestly have no idea how he is capable of that but regardless, it works, and I make myself comfortable in a chair.

It is at this point I understand that Jeremy's commitment to Leo, in relation to my embarking on this journey, is absolute. He will not say no to Leo, just as I cannot say no to him. It's an intriguing dynamic that unfortunately I'm not given a chance to explore right now.

The tribal elder says something to Leo in his native tongue, which Leo translates. 'Alexandra, would you mind standing for a moment? The elder would like to feel your forest energy.'

At this unusual request I look at Jeremy and Leo, who both nod, encouraging me to do so. I stand and the elder steps toward me. He is slightly smaller and stockier than me, and places his palms on the bare skin of my shoulders with his head lowered toward the ground.

We remain like this for some time until I feel his pulsing warmth connect with my body. As this occurs, he looks up until our eyes connect and we remain standing silent and unblinking. I suddenly feel as though the ground is shifting beneath me and I'm off balance. It's as though I could stumble and fall, but his gaze provides me with an equilibrium that keeps me firmly anchored. As quickly as this feeling comes upon me, it immediately disappears and he removes his hands from my skin. My mouth opens in shock, but I don't speak, unable to break the momentum of whatever just happened. He takes my hands in his, turning them this way and that, as if he is sensing me rather than studying me or looking for anything in particular.

As he releases me, I feel paradoxically energised and tired and I ease my body back down into the chair. Jeremy reassuringly holds my hand, yet has a quizzical look on his face, while we wait for the elders and Yaku and Leo to consult with each other. After a few minutes Leo turns to us.

'As you both know I have been visiting the Wai-Wai people on and off for the past three years. They have been generous in allowing me to live with their tribe and understand their way of life, including their ancient traditions and connections to their spiritual world, for which I am eternally indebted to them. During my last trip, I had the privilege of taking a five-day journey with their head shaman, who guided my first experience of soul flight.'

Conscious that the elders understand very little English, Leo takes a moment to acknowledge the tribe's generosity toward him, in their native language, before continuing. 'It became clear to me during this experience, and after having read your thesis, Alexandra, that the events which have transpired over recent months are in no way coincidental.'

'My thesis?' I squeak, my voice coming out rather high-pitched.

This comment certainly has my attention. My original thesis, which I completed almost fifteen years ago, was on masochism and the ego in relation to the female form and specifically explored the work of Sabina Spielrein. It was also the reason Jeremy organised the specific style of my submission for his experiment, after I admitted to him in a moment of youth-infused weakness that it had been an unfulfilled fantasy of mine, something I had never been brave enough to explore personally, only via research. Something he remembered when I thought it had been long forgotten. I should have known better.

'What on earth has that got to do with any of this?' I continue, my eyes flickering nervously between Jeremy, Leo and the elders. Not in a complete panic but not far from it.

'Surprisingly, quite a bit. That is what we hope to discover and in doing so, we aim to unravel the apparent mystery of the healing element in your blood.'

I feel like I have gone into a state of semi-shock as my brain processes the links between my thesis, the experiment and everything that has happened since.

'Would you like some water, AB?' I nod confirmation to Jeremy who seems forever attuned to my needs.

Once we are again settled and silent, Leo continues. 'Tonight I want to provide you with some insight on soul flight and the necessary preparations you must undertake before you embark on this unique and privileged experience. The Wai-Wai people are chosen for this journey only when the shaman deems they are spiritually ready. Ever since the tribe was discovered in the twentieth century, white people have asked to be able to participate. Those who are obsessed with power, wealth and material possessions, are greedy or destructive or experience ongoing stress in their lives, are told they will never be ready for such a journey and leave disappointed that no amount of money can sway the shaman, as that is not what he values. Those who embody humility, kindness, forgiveness and generosity, who engage in exploration of the imagination, the unknown or unfamiliar are more likely to be given the gift of soul flight. It is a gift in the sense that not everyone who attempts it is capable of achieving it. It requires an instinctive intelligence and a strong sense of spirit, which we believe you have.' He gestures toward our small fireside gathering, and they nod in agreement. 'This, combined with a willingness to explore the heart and soul of your nature, will, we hope, guide us to the source of what science has not been able to discover … the enigma of your blood.'

I can't help but inhale deeply at the enormity of his statements and the huge expectations they create. Leo notices at once. 'Don't get me wrong. I appreciate a sceptic's viewpoint, and scientific verification of presumed "miracles", as much as the next person, which is why I dearly value my esteemed colleague and wonderful friend.' He acknowledges Jeremy and this time it is my turn to squeeze his hand. 'And that is one of the roles he will play on this journey. Our best scenario is that he will provide us with the scientific verification we aspire to, but I am under no delusions, however. Without Jeremy I would never have been able to convince you to take this journey with us, for which I will be forever grateful to him. I'll say again that all of us being here together is beyond coincidence. I believe we are on the brink of a connection to the untapped universal web of nature, sexuality and spirituality, which is yet to be understood by science and western medicine. It is my opinion that a combination of these will provide us with the opportunity to seek the truth and will take us to a new level of understanding; a level that east and west have been skirting around, but as yet have not successfully integrated. Alexandra, I believe your blood is potentially one of the critical elements that can help unlock the key to this integration. This is why the paths of our lives have crossed at this point, at this time.'

My mind slowly absorbs Leo's words and the peaceful, yet abundantly alive, forest surroundings. The elders look as if they have tapped into an inner silence unknown to us and are seated in an almost trance-like state. The rhythm and intonation of Leo's words can make you feel as if you're floating, he is an amazing orator. Jeremy has subconsciously moved closer to my body, forever fulfilling his role as lover and protector.

'Any questions so far before I move on to the specific preparations?' Leo glances around our small group; we are still mesmerised by him. 'No? Okay. It will take us a few days of jungle travel to reach the shaman. During this time, Alexandra, your immersion in the nature that surrounds you is fundamental. The elders will let us know when the time comes that we are no longer to speak to you.'

'What?' I screech out before I can stop myself. Not more conditions?

'Engaging with your inner silence is imperative and we will all support you in this process.'

'But what if I need to say something, to ask something?'

'You may ask, but your voice is the only one you will hear on our travels. Silence is preferred, no artificial input should intrude on your journey and human voices will be kept to a minimum. This will allow nature to be your key source of communication.'

'So I can ask, but you won't respond?'

'Not in a verbal sense, no.' Great, I think semi-sarcastically. He continues. 'When you eat, you will eat only lightly and naturally. We will be living off the jungle, eating food we gather, preparing lotions to protect our skin and drinking special herbal teas that may cause sensations of an altered state of consciousness. They will not be harmful and will only affect you in the short term. Having experienced this myself, I would recommend that you embrace these changed states wholeheartedly, for this is where true learning and understanding occurs.'

Leo had alluded to this before we left Miami so it doesn't come as too much of a shock. I'm actually quite keen to experience what happens, or if anything really does. I wonder if more natural, herbal medicines could possibly have the same impact that western chemicals have on my body — an interesting experiment from a scientific perspective, though I can't say what my beliefs are on the spiritual side. I suppose I'll find out soon enough. I nod in agreement and a quick thought crosses my mind.

'Can I write?'

'You mean on our journey?'

'Yes, can I write about my experiences, thoughts, feelings as we go?'

Leo has another brief discussion with Yaku before answering me. 'Should you be that way inclined, it's an excellent idea, Alexandra. I was anticipating that Jeremy would be doing the analytical side but to do it from yours would be brilliant. I have a journal you can use and you can decide if and when you are happy to share it with us.'

'Great, thanks.'

I sense that something has shifted in Leo and the elders but I don't know what. This thought scatters through my mind and disappears. I love keeping a journal and haven't written for months with everything else that has been going on. This somewhat lessens the concerns I have about the 'no talking to Alexa' rule. God, imagine telling the girls back home that? I can talk, but you can't talk back! For someone like me that could be likened to torture. Although you never know, it could be good for me. Maybe.

I think about the times I wished for a bit of peace and quiet when the kids were little and just wouldn't shut up, particularly when I was on the phone. I can't help but smile as I think of the saying: 'be careful what you wish for' ... And here I am.

'What are you smiling about, AB?' Jeremy enquires, as always homing in on my facial expressions.

'Oh, nothing really ...' I return my attention to Leo. 'Can I ask another question?' I shift in my seat. I suspect I'll hesitate about asking questions for the rest of my life, thanks to Jeremy!

'Of course you may.'

'What was the elder doing when he touched me?'

'He was checking to see if you are ready to embark on this journey.'

Oh, that's news. 'And am I?'

'Yes, you are ready,' he says, with a hint of pride and approval in his voice, which is a strange sensation. 'We will be leaving tomorrow.'

Ah, so that is what had shifted between them moments ago.

'Tomorrow. So soon?' I can't keep the tremble out of my voice.

'Yes. And there is one more thing. There will be no sexual relations allowed with you on this journey.'

'What? You have to be kidding me!' Jeremy snaps out of his reverie, leaps from his chair and shouts into the night air. Well, this is obviously a shock to him, just as much as it is to me. If I wasn't so amused by his reaction, I'm sure I'd be just as aggrieved as him, too, but I find it impossible to keep the smirk off my face. This is hilarious! There is nothing I love to see more than the oh-so-calm, cool and collected Dr Jeremy

Alexander Quinn completely out of his comfort zone. Leo maintains a more mature approach than I do in relation to Jeremy's outburst.

'No, I'm not kidding, Jaq. It is imperative for what we are *all* hoping to achieve.'

Jeremy looks exasperated, almost physically pained at his words. 'How long will this journey take anyway?'

'As long as it takes, my friend, as long as it takes.'

'Fine.' He is clearly not fine, he is clearly very disgruntled, I could even surmise he may be pouting. 'But we have tonight, don't we?' he asks defiantly.

'Yes, you have tonight.'

Still trying to stifle my laughter at Jeremy's reaction to Leo's words, I find myself suddenly swept up from my chair and slung over Jeremy's shoulder, caveman-style. I'll never understand how quickly he can do that to me. How embarrassing, in front of the elders! I attempt to swat his backside in reproach.

Leo shakes his head and chuckles. 'I gather we won't be leaving at first light.'

'You've got that right, my friend,' Jeremy responds as he makes a beeline to our cabin. The door shuts behind us and he throws me gently onto the bed.

'What's up, J? Finally a condition you find difficult to accept?' I know I shouldn't tease him but I just can't help myself, his reaction is priceless. 'How is this any different from the conditions I had to accept during our weekend together? You can't possibly think —'

He has stripped naked and has me ambushed on the bed before I can even finish my words. 'Don't push your luck, AB. The last thing you'll want for your journey tomorrow is a sore, red arse and the mood I'm in now, I can't deny it's a possibility.'

'And how, pray tell, would you explain my inability to sit down to your dear friend, Leo?' I ask cheekily.

'I can assure you, sweetheart, it would be nothing he hasn't seen before.'

'Really? I wouldn't have thought he was that way inclined.' I'm a little surprised at this admission from Jeremy and notice that something in his demeanour alters ever so slightly.

'He isn't.'

Hmm, sounds like he is trying to shut me down, which just serves to pique my interest.

'Well, what do you mean then?'

My clothes meet the same fate as his, landing scattered on the floor. No doubt a direct attempt to dissuade me from questioning him further, so I sit up to look at him eye to eye, which he avoids. Intriguing.

'Jeremy, seriously, I know there is something you're not telling me. Haven't we been through enough recently without keeping more things from each other?' Possibilities flicker through my brain in an attempt to connect his words, a sore arse and Leo. And then it hits me like a brick. Something that should have dawned on me way before now.

'He was there, wasn't he?'

J shuffles around the bed uncomfortably as I pin the words on him just as I straddle him physically while he weighs up his answer.

133

'Please don't pretend to not know what I'm talking about. I learnt my lesson about doing that to you the hard way. It would be insulting if you tried it in reverse.' My tone is deadly serious. 'He saw me, during the experiment? My pleasure, my pain, my arousal. He saw it all, didn't he?'

I don't even need Jeremy to answer me as I can hear the truth in his silence, see it in his body language. Nevertheless, I need him to acknowledge this to me now, personally.

'Yes, Alexa, he was there,' he admits solemnly.

'Why didn't you tell me?'

'I wasn't sure how you'd respond. I assumed if you had wanted to know who was there you would have asked by now. But I can't deny that I didn't want you to be uncomfortable around him when you met him for the first time knowing what he had observed.'

'And it was after ... when he, well, saw me, experienced me like that, he asked for my thesis?' I ask perplexed, this new version of events tumbling around in my mind.

'Yes.'

'Why?'

'To be honest, since all of this began he seems to have been on some sort of quest. It's as if everything that happened during our weekend in Sydney sparked something in him. That's why he offered me Avalon for your recovery and went to every extreme to ensure you were protected. After he received your thesis in the States he came straight down here to spend time in the jungle to experience soul flight, as you're aware. When Moira eventually got the message through to him that you had been abducted, he was beside himself, apparently, stopping at nothing to help me help you, any way he could. Since then he seems to believe we have the key to the missing link he has been looking for his whole life, that us being here is much more than coincidence, as he said by the fire. But he can't explain any more than that to me at the moment. It's as if he's depending on your own experience of soul flight to shed light on everything that seems to be in darkness at the moment.' He allows me to remain straddling his body, gently stroking the curves of my waist, as I absorb his words.

'Now you know everything and I am truly sorry if you are upset that he was there.'

He lowers his eyes as if giving me time and space to consider my response.

Am I upset that he was there? I may have been if I had known before, but now that I know him, have seen the look in his eyes, how he provides me with a serenity I've never experienced before, I know I'm not upset. Something seems exactly right about him being there. It's as though my dream about the owl with Leo's eyes, and my flying as the eagle — trying to protect my eggs in the nest lest they should fall — is making some strange kind of subconscious sense. Everything seems to have unfolded in a perfectly timed sequence of events for me not to be upset or angry, just accepting of this reality. Maybe the unusual connection I feel to

Leo is founded on something after all, just something I don't have the knowledge to understand yet.

Jeremy is patiently waiting for me to process this information before seeking my response.

'Would you have told me if I had asked?' I say.

'Asked if he was there?' I nod. 'Of course. I can't lie to you, AB.'

'And you'll tell him that I know?'

'Only if you are comfortable with that.'

For some reason, I feel that Leo knowing that I'm aware that he was there, is a critical piece of this mystic puzzle but I have no idea why.

'Yeah, I am actually.' Jeremy's face collapses in relief that we have managed to work through this potential danger zone between us.

'Is there anything else you want to ask before I claim what's mine for the foreseeable future? Or at least for tonight.' His mood changes and his eyes glaze with lust. I can see the heightening of his erection and shake my head, indicating the matter is closed for the moment, which may be likened to waving a red flag to a bull.

Jeremy has clearly taken Leo's sexual ultimatum as a challenge to possess every orifice of my body. We fly to heaven and back too many times to count, my voice becoming too hoarse to achieve any further coherent sound, which should no doubt benefit my future silence. Our sexual intercourse is akin to the jungle animals surrounding us. It is as if he has been told he could never touch me again in his life, such is his desire for me tonight. The man is insatiable. For the first time in my life, I finally decide to swallow his seed, which leaves him utterly dumbfounded and, seemingly, in absolute awe of me. The euphoria I feel at succumbing to this final act of surrender with him is an astoundingly and surprisingly beautiful moment between us, one neither of us will forget, so firmly emblazoned is it in our memories.

* * *

Many, many hours later, I'm finally allowed to fall asleep in sheer physical and sexual exhaustion. Not that I'm complaining, it is a blissful, sated sleep for me. I can't say the same for him.

When I awake, Jeremy has a bath running and my tired limbs appreciate soaking in the warmth for the last time in however long.

'Oh no, you've got to be kidding.' I shake my head in response to the erection striding toward me. 'You can't possibly have anything left in you.' His face says it all. Apparently he does.

Eventually, we make it to the main house of our jungle village for breakfast, though I'm sure we've well and truly passed that time of day. I'm absolutely starving and thankfully Jeremy, who seems to have more energy after our activities rather than less, is happy to whip up a storm in the kitchen, which I enthusiastically devour. The kids are racing around gathering things together.

'Jordan, what's going on, what's the rush?' I manage to catch him as he passes in a frenzy of activity.

'We're going to the village to live with Marcu and his friends for a few days.' I remember that Marcu is the teenager who now knows the macarena.

Elizabeth joins him, equally excited. 'They've invited us to go and we're leaving in the next hour. It's going to be a real jungle adventure.'

They continue past as I stare after them, astonished. When was all this decided? My motherly instinct automatically kicks into gear. I'm not used to plans about my kids being made without my direct involvement. Thoughts of anacondas, tarantulas, panthers, piranhas and giant sloths falling from trees, bombard my brain, as I fear for their safety.

Robert appears conveniently from around the corner with a backpack ready and notices the concerned look on my face. 'It's okay, Alex. Adam and I are going too so there is no need to worry. It'll be a great experience for them. They'll love it, just like they loved the wilderness in Tassie. Besides, how many kids get to have an experience like this in the Brazilian rainforest?' I remain unswayed. 'Anyway, Leo tells me you have an adventure of your own starting today.'

At this reminder, butterflies take off in full flight in my belly and I'm at a loss for words.

'Thanks for worrying about us though,' Robert continues, 'but we'll be fine. The kids have been waiting for hours to say goodbye to you. We were told to leave you both alone,' he says with a cheeky grin.

'I … oh … yes, well …' I blush as I glance at Jeremy who is standing innocently at the sink, pretending to focus on doing the washing up.

'And now they can. Elizabeth, Jordan,' he yells, 'as soon as you say goodbye to Mum, we'll be ready to go.'

Their excited faces bounce toward me as they wrap their arms around me in little bear hug goodbyes. There's no time for any emotion given their enthusiastic swarm of activity before they vanish.

I turn toward Jeremy just as Leo appears from the room next door to join us and I just shake my head at the perfection of their planning. There's nothing quite like having every detail of your life coordinated to the extent where it is absolutely impossible to go against the flow of the tsunami. Men!

They both smile knowingly, their conspiracy a success. They knew full well that saying goodbye to the kids would be the most difficult thing for me to do, but it only took a few seconds and they magically disappeared. Deep down, I know it is foolish to underestimate the intelligence of the men standing before me, so why am I so surprised it has happened this way? Maybe I'd always secretly hoped that I could outsmart them. Even more idiotic on my part. I don't bother saying anything, it would be futile anyway so I just accept what is.

Jeremy reassures me with a kiss on the lips that all will be okay and hands me a jungle-strength coffee. Leo, still with the grin on his face, places his hand on my shoulders. A warm electric current immediately shivers through my entire body. I really need to get to the bottom of why he has such an effect on me.

'Good to see you're making the most of kisses and coffee before you go. We'll leave as soon as you're ready.'

Jeremy growls at him and turns to me. 'That's us being told, sweetheart. The time has come.'

I realise most of what I may need has already been thoughtfully packed on my behalf, so I'm concentrating on toiletries in the bathroom, though how much I'll need for a jungle trek I'm not too sure. It's not like it will be five-star, or even one-star for that matter, though I suppose it will definitely be millions of stars if I consider a different perspective. I'm fossicking through the cupboard when Jeremy appears at the door.

'Nearly ready? I need to do your medical before we leave.'

'Medical? Honestly?' He stares at me with a 'What else would you expect from me' look. I should have known that Jeremy would take his 'scientific' responsibilities as seriously as he does his career. 'Great, so the research begins …' His smile is both kind and non-negotiable. 'I'm just looking for a new contraceptive patch. I've just realised I haven't changed it since we've been here, I'm sure I must be well overdue.'

'I'm afraid you won't find it in there, sweetheart. It wasn't packed.' My searching pauses, but I don't absorb his words.

'Would it bother you, going *au naturel* for this trip?' He slides his arms around my waist.

'Oh, well, I'm not sure, I haven't thought about it. I suppose not, but I've had a patch since Jordan was born ...'

'We were hoping you wouldn't mind your hormone levels returning to their natural state in your body for this trip. I meant to speak to you about it on the plane, but it slipped my mind and I haven't thought about it since we've been here.'

'Well, it would have been nice to be consulted, I must admit. But what about —'

He pre-empts me, 'No sex rule, remember? That should keep you safe.' He turns me around so I'm facing him, and I see genuine regret in his eyes.

I just shake my head, flabbergasted, yet knowing there is no use arguing about it. 'Whatever ... go with the flow ...'

'Thanks, AB, and I'm sorry, I did honestly mean to discuss it with you.' He looks relieved that I'm not making an issue of it. I throw my toothbrush, toothpaste, deodorant and some moisturiser into my toiletries bag and at the last minute, a packet of tampons. Just what I need in the jungle, a humongous period. I hope they realise what they're in for with the mood swings that will accompany *'au naturel'*!

Dr Quinn goes into full professional mode conducting his medical on my body, recording every response with great finesse. There is no deterring him from his task, although he concedes a few smiles at my cheeky passes at him. Blood tests, body measurements, pap test, reflexes, blood pressure ... the list goes on.

Eventually, we are ready to go. The good news is, I don't have to carry a single thing except my water bottle, which is fantastic for me. My main aim apparently is to absorb myself in walking to the rhythm of the jungle. Can't be too hard, surely. Oh, and make the most of conversation while others still have the right to engage with me. I have no idea what I'm walking into and I know that backing out now is not an option. Everything that has happened up until now has been preparing me for what lies ahead.

I feel a little anxious, but with a touch of excitement, which surprises me though I'm not sure whether that puts me in the category of brave or stupid. No doubt I'll find out soon enough.

Jeremy rubs his hands along either side of my arms as though he can actually feel the nervous tension building in my system. 'I will be with you every step of the way, sweetheart. Always by your side.'

'And you trust that this will work out, J?' I can't help but question his commitment, one final time.

'I trust Leo wholeheartedly. He's never let me down in all the years I have known him, so yes, I trust that we should embrace this process and see where it leads us. Any other path is even more fraught with danger.'

I swallow my fear at his words, knowing them to be true and pull his head toward me to make my last contact with his lips. Jeremy packs up his medical kit, which will no doubt be accompanying us and I put my Jungle Jane clothes back on — sadly, they are not quite as attractive as the movies depict — and we join the others who have been patiently waiting.

I sense that now is the beginning of the end of my journey. One that I have committed to take, which is why we are here. There is no looking back. I need my companions' bravery as much as I need my own as we take our first steps into this unknown adventure together.

Lake Bled

S alina feels as though she has struck gold when her plan falls into place. She reaches the end of the track and appears in a lobby where the group of people are preparing to enter the facility. They have white lab coats on and not a hair our of place, so she quickly assembles her hospital outfit and grabs a pair of thick-framed glasses out of her backpack, ensuring her small Smith & Wesson Bodyguard handgun is tucked discreetly in her coat pocket.

Leaving her backpack in the shadows, she casually meanders over to join the main group and blends with Xsade's new inductee scientists. Shiny silver doors ping open to reveal a large elevator. They cram in before descending further beneath the lake.

The facility is more impressive and high tech than she expected and she stares at the silver-suited volunteers her group passes in the corridors, trying to imagine

Dr Blake in similar attire. Salina has memorised every detail of the case and feels like she knows both doctors, Blake and Votrubec, intimately.

She continues along with the inductees and is pleased they are encouraged to ask questions, helping her to establish the basic layout of the lab. She wonders where they could be keeping Josef. For all she knows, they could have a whole series of lower levels. No wonder Alexa's bracelet didn't register; it's as though they are in the depths of the earth. Her phone is definitely useless down here and she hopes Luke isn't too concerned about how long she's been gone just yet.

One of the young, eager scientists asks their tour leader if Madame Jurilique still intends to address the group at the end of the information session. Indeed she does. Nothing quite like having internal verification that the target is in the building.

Part Five

The day science begins to study non-physical phenomena, it will make more progress in one decade than in all the previous centuries of existence.

Nikola Tesla

Alexa

O ur little group consists of the two tribal elders, Yaku, Leo, Jeremy and myself. The jeeps picked us up from Avalon and delivered us to the spot from which we will commence our trek. I didn't think it seemed possible to be more deeply in the jungle than we were at Avalon, but once again I tell myself to always expect the unexpected, the new mantra for my life as my preconceived constructs continue to be eroded.

Now that our actual journey is underway, I do feel a sense of calm ... it is virtually impossible for any Xsade spies to have a clue where we are. These thoughts, among others, meander through my mind as we continue our climb upward through the mountain jungle. The heat and humidity is at breaking point and I'm looking forward to the daily afternoon downpour that leaves you soaked to the core but also refreshed and revived. I'm continually drinking my water, which is tinged with citrus and mint, replenishing what I'm losing in perspiration. Conversation has been sporadic as we settle into the rhythm of our steps, each finding the pace that suits us best. Nothing can be rushed in this heat; it would leave you with no air to breathe. I begin to find it quite meditative, slowing my breathing, easing my pace but knowing I'm slowly moving forward, step by step to somewhere, even if it is unknown to me.

The jungle is brimming with insect and bird life and is almost dreamlike in its vibrant beauty. Leo was right, you don't need much conversation when you immerse yourself in a natural wonderland such as this.

Our little group pauses at a small clearing to take in the magnificent forest below as the rainclouds come tumbling in. I smile at Jeremy and inhale the scent of the rain deeply into my lungs before it actually arrives. It is one of my favourite smells — the earth's perfume as she awaits the liquid that will quench her thirst and give her the gift of abundant life.

There is no need for umbrellas or coats as the rain cascades toward us. I stand with my arms outstretched, welcoming its temporary cool wetness against my skin.

'You still love the afternoon downpour, AB?' Jeremy knows I've embraced the heavy rainfall that arrives religiously every day.

'I love everything about it, the smell, the feel, the taste, the sight of it. It's as if Mother Nature is tantalising us with her brilliance. Just when the heat becomes too oppressive, almost unbearable, she provides us with this. Overloading our senses but continuing to hide her secrets.'

'I feel the same way. It is indeed a gift to be able to experience nature like this,' adds Leo, as we stand in awe of the beauty surrounding us. I'm suddenly a little overwhelmed with gratitude for what Leo has done for us. I turn to him beside me.

'Thank you, Leo. For everything. I would never have believed this journey was possible, let alone that I'd have the opportunity to experience anything like this with both of you, my family and tribal elders guiding our path. There is magic in its unexpectedness.'

His eyes reflect the deeper meaning of my words and even though he remains silent, I know he understands.

I hug Leo and feel the same familiar electricity, emitting kindness and a sense of calm over my psyche that occurs every time our bodies connect, even now when we are completely saturated. I don't know why it's like that between us but since I met him in Miami, his presence seems to give me the courage to accept my fate, knowing he will be by my side. Even stranger is when I have spoken to Jeremy about this he shows no jealousy or concern, just acceptance that this is the way things should be. Perhaps he is more Zen than I ever give him credit for.

After our brief respite, the rains pass and our journey continues up and over the side of the mountain.

We eventually arrive at our evening destination, our first bivouac truly under the stars and I'm infused with excitement. I gaze around and am immediately drawn to a magnificent tree looming high above us, its branches outstretched like arms ready to either embrace or to capture our small gathering. This contrast intrigues me.

'Leo, what tree is that?' He has a brief discussion with the elders who seemingly nod their heads in discussion and approval at my question.

'That is the grand lupuna tree, which contains a spirit that is regarded as the guardian of the rainforest. Its trunk is said to resemble a human abdomen and must be treated with the respect its majesty deserves.'

'Are we able to walk up to touch it?' I can't explain it, I've always had an intense desire to touch giant trees and this one in particular is pulling me irresistibly toward it. Again, he confers with the elders.

'Yes, you may. Follow Yaku, he will take you. The local legend is if you insult the tree it is known to take revenge with its magic. If you respect its presence, it will protect you from the dangers of the rainforest,' he says with a wink and a smile.

'Nothing but respect, Leo, I can assure you.'

'I'd never doubt that, Alexandra.' His words make it sound as though he's known me for years rather than weeks. 'We'll stay here and set things up for tonight. Enjoy.'

I go to give Jeremy a quick kiss and his arms hold me back. 'Sorry, sweetheart, I promised.'

'Really?' I ask, shocked. 'Not even a kiss?'

'I'm afraid not.'

'Jeez, I would have made more of an effort to have a decent farewell.'

'I don't think we did too badly, AB,' he adds with the cheeky smile I love. As soon he mentions it, I feel the lingering tenderness in my groin.

'Hear, hear,' confirms Leo with a laugh. 'We had to wait for hours for you two.'

I blush. 'Okay. I'm sorry. So my celibacy begins,' I say as I take one last swig of water.

I look toward Leo anticipating a joke or some additional sarcastic comment. None arrives. I'm getting to know that Leo doesn't joke about things he firmly believes in.

I reluctantly shake my head in acceptance as I stride off to commune with the tree.

What a wonder. The tree is huge, well over fifty metres tall with a trunk almost ten metres wide. Its roots are seriously anchored within the forest floor and its leaves stretch way beyond the canopy in search of the sun. As I touch its massive belly, the energy surrounding the tree encompasses me, giving me a sense of its strength and serenity. I can understand why this spiritual tree demands respect.

I stand with my palms pressed against the trunk for a few minutes before finding a position on a rock where I can observe the tree's massive form and sense its energy more fully. As I watch from a distance, Yaku pays homage to the giant lupuna by chanting and meditating on his knees at its roots. After a while he carefully pierces the trunk and extracts some sap from underneath its bark to put carefully in his pouch.

As he does so, it dawns on me that I'm in a giant natural pharmacy, where people knew, and some still know, how to heal using what the plants have within them. I suddenly have a deep understanding that nature is offering us so much more than we realise if we just open our eyes to the opportunities of nature and medicine combined.

Just as these profound thoughts flood my mind, I hear a loud sharp screech high above our heads. Yaku appears to give thanks to both the tree and the eagle we see soaring high above us.

'Harpy eagle. It is sign, we are ready,' he says in his broken English.

I glance up at the huge eagle swirling high above us, around and around the lupuna tree. It appears nature is well and truly talking to Yaku and I know that very soon, nature will be the only thing talking to me. I, too, pay my respects, copying his actions and we return silently to the group.

Our camp beds are laid out in the clearing around a fire that should protect us from wild animals during the night. Yaku is eager to explain exactly what happened at the lupuna to Leo before he leaves to consult with the two other elders. They start preparing some potion with leaves and the extract from the tree. I try to remain as calm as I was in the presence of the tree before the eagle's screech, but I can feel the adrenaline creeping into my nervous system as I sense my spiritual journey is about to begin. I tell myself over and over that it will be fine. I can do this.

As we gather around the fire, my stomach is rumbling from not having eaten for many hours. I take a sip from my water bottle, but it's now empty so I go to fill it when I notice everyone is seated around the fire.

'Alexandra, please. Come join us,' Leo calls.

The time has come. Oh, jeez, why am I so nervous? He places his hand in mine and guides me to the seat next to him and beside Jeremy. Immediately his touch allows me to inhale and exhale more slowly and provides me with a sense of calm. I don't withdraw my palm when I'm seated; it gives me the security I feel I need. I glance at Jeremy and hold his hand as well, with a half-hearted, nervous smile.

'All will be well, Alexa. We will be here with you physically every step of the way.'

Even though it's not the physical component I'm worried about, I still appreciate his words, making the most of what may be the last of his voice. But I have to wonder where in god's name will I be? I'll be fine, I reassure my mind; plenty of people have done this before. People have been doing it for years to achieve an enlightened state ...

I glance around realising that everyone is waiting for me to be present with them, as if they can hear my internal chatter themselves. That would be embarrassing. I breathe deeply again, relax, just relax.

Leo, naturally, leads the description of what happens next.

'Yaku tells us that the harpy eagle, the most powerful raptor in the Americas, has signalled that the spirits are ready to accept and guide your entry into their world. Usually the soul flight of a westerner would only occur with the shaman, but apparently the spirit of the lupuna, the most powerful protector in the jungle, will ensure your safe return to this place and the elders have been granted permission for you to commence your journey a little earlier than planned.'

I can't really speak, not that I have too much to say. I feel like I'm going into some form of surgery that all the doctors are completely comfortable with because they've done it so many times before, neglecting the fact that it may be the patient's first time under the knife and they are utterly petrified. Apprehension is whooshing through my body so profoundly I'm surprised they can't hear it.

'In experiencing soul flight, we are able to tap into nature in its purest form, our original human design. We have the opportunity to ask ourselves whether we are living the life that is our destiny, the reason we were born. It inspires us to re-align and adjust our lives in the present and awaken the innocence in our hearts. It isn't about exploring uncharted territory so much as simply coming full circle, returning home to our purest self, our simplest essence and deciding whether we accept this into the here and now. On occasions, soul flight may show us glimpses of our ancestral past; this can serve to provide greater understanding of our future, though it may not be clear at the time. Once your journey commences, Alexandra, you will only commune with nature, without human interference, until your journey concludes. It will begin with your first sip of this drink, prepared by the elders. Its ingredients have been determined via messages from the spirit world.'

I decide to ask while I know someone will still answer: 'How long will I be gone for?' I raise my fingers to highlight the word 'gone'.

'No one knows the answer to that question; it depends on your own journey. Just like in dreams, sometimes what seems like a long time occurs in seconds; other people can feel like they have been gone only moments to find it has been days. Your soul flight will be completely unique to you.'

'Don't you think it would be better to wait until I'm with the shaman?' I make my last desperate plea to prolong the inevitable.

Leo briefly exchanges words with the elders. 'Yaskomo, the shaman, is aware the journey needs to commence now, as the eagle is a sign from the spirit world. You will meet him at the point of your journey when the stars align.'

I really don't get the whole 'stars align' thing that they keep mentioning so I don't bother asking and move on to more practical issues, like my rumbling stomach.

'Are we eating first?'

'No, you will not eat, it is a far more powerful and insightful experience when abstaining from food. The only thing you are to ingest is the ayahuasca mixed with the sap of the lupuna tree.' He indicates the pot hanging over the fire.

'And that is what exactly?'

This time Jeremy answers. 'Ayahuasca is a brew of pyschoactive decoctions prepared from the *Banisteriopsis caapi* vine mixed with leaves of dimethyltryptamine, or DMT.'

I just stare at him blankly. His scientific explanation is as helpful to me as Yaku explaining it in his native language.

'It was described by a Harvard ethnobotanist in the 1950s as having divinatory and healing purposes.' It sounds like this provides some credibility that otherwise wouldn't exist from Jeremy's perspective.

Leo chimes in. 'It's also known to provide spiritual revelations regarding a person's purpose on earth and give insight into being the best they can be, by accessing a higher spiritual dimension.' Leo and Jeremy seem to be teaming up to offer a balanced science-meets-spirituality explanation. How lovely!

'Are there any known side effects?'

'Vomiting and potentially diarrhoea,' Jeremy replies. Hmm, not so good. 'Medically, it is a reaction to the mild toxins released in your stomach as a result of ingesting the brew. But spiritually, it is the release of negative emotions and energy built over the span of your human life.'

'I'm impressed.' I try to squeeze Jeremy's hand wondering when he had time to do this research, although it shouldn't surprise me. This is well and truly his forte. He shakes his head apologetically, rejecting my touch.

'So you're both saying I should come through this more enlightened, understand the universe and my place in it, and maybe even a little lighter than I am now, correct?'

They both laugh.

'More or less, sweetheart, yes, that's the idea. But hopefully not too much lighter, you're perfect the way you are.' His eyes glance at Leo's, almost pleading for a promise that that is all that will happen to me.

'And I could be gone minutes or days, we just don't know?'

'That's right. But know whatever happens, Alexandra, physically we will be right by your side.'

'I'll never leave you, AB, you know that.'

'I do, yes.'

I regard each of them solemnly. Why does drinking this seem so much more serious than having a potent 'cheers' with Jeremy as we embark on one of our many wild adventures? The absinthe that I drank in Sydney, when all this began, pops into my mind. But I know, we all know, why this is different. My life and future freedom depend on the outcome of this journey.

Yaku passes me a cup of the steaming brew.

I look around, absorbing each of their faces in the light of the flames.

'Anyone else partaking?'

'Just you this time,' Leo responds. 'Our legs will remain firmly on the ground. Bon voyage, Alexandra.'

'And you won't speak to me until it's over?'

He shakes his head. My time has obviously begun.

Jeremy squeezes my hand for the last time before releasing me to the waiting spirit world, mouthing the words 'I love you' as I take my first guarded sip. No 'skol' or 'cheers' this time.

The potent potion is difficult to take at first, but with each sip I adapt to its bittersweet taste and it warms me from the inside. I can detect the slight hint of peppermint and ginger and wonder whether these have been added to the mix in an attempt to calm my stomach. There is no use asking, as no one will answer me now anyway.

I'm not sure whether I was expecting something dramatic or not, but I remain seated and relaxed around the fire as I finish the potion, just as everyone else sits relaxed, in silence for quite some time. The flames appear to lick their faces and they warm my body from the outside.

My reverie is interrupted as I hear the sudden screech of what looks to be the same eagle in the twilight sky. This time it isn't circling around the lupuna tree, it is determinedly closing in on our site. Suddenly my vision locks onto its tiny, beady eyes, and I can see clearly its white underbelly and black wings, even the striped feathers encircling its legs. I try to disengage to see if the others are concerned by the closeness of this massive bird of prey, with a wingspan seemingly as wide as a man is tall, but my gaze remains fixed and it seems to be swooping directly toward me. I fear the enormous bird is going to come crashing into me, knocking me off my seat, and my arms automatically come up to cover my face and protect me from its huge clawed feet, but instead I rise from my seat and am lifted to the great heights it can reach.

Suddenly, I am seeing this great land through the harpy eagle's eyes. I watch below as our little gathering is left behind, sitting perfectly still like tiny figurines, the flames of the fire becoming the size of a firefly as we rapidly ascend further into the sky and soar above the earth. This is an awesome experience.

As we continue, I am at one with the eagle and the earth below us looks like a mere marble, its insignificance from these heights almost overwhelming. All fear and foreboding is lost. I only feel happiness and hope. I'm surprised by the clarity of my thought processes — for some reason I expected to feel drunk from the elders' concoction.

It's as if we are in transit to somewhere else but I don't know to what or where. That is, until I abruptly disconnect from the eagle and plummet downwards. My body feels exactly like it did when I was hurled from a plane, blindfolded, with Jeremy, the same G-force penetrating every extremity. Yet this time I can see the eagle flying high above me, and the earth accelerating toward me from below. I am attached to no one, have no wings and seem to be on a one-way collision course with the ground. My heart is racing and I'm starting to panic. Surely this can't be soul flight, Leo never mentioned anything like this …

The ground comes toward me so fast I'm sure my speed is increasing by the millisecond. Gravity trips me up and I tumble into an uncontrollable spin, unable to determine up from down, this way from that. I'm gasping for oxygen and my brain feels like it could implode with the pressure of relentless rotations. Then I smash into the ground and feel as though my body has shattered into a million tiny pieces, forever lost in the atmosphere.

Oh, dear lord, am I dead?

Lake Bled

Madame Jurilique is furious. 'What do you mean we haven't received any response? We have been tracking her every move and now you tell me she has simply vanished into thin air? This is simply impossible. I explicitly stated that she was to call the number provided the second she landed in Europe.' Madeleine frowns. Her is heart pumping hard, but it should be in anticipation of Dr Alexandra Blake's arrival, rather than her frustrating absence. 'Absolutely nothing? You're sure?'

She slams down the phone, wondering what on earth could have gone wrong. Again. The instructions were perfectly clear and she knows they were delivered successfully. Madeleine believes herself to be an excellent judge of character and she knows that Dr Blake would never risk her children if she were able to save them from any harm. It was the perfect plan. That is, unless she doesn't turn up.

For the first time she concedes that she might have been wrong and her face scrunches in fury. First Josef, now this. She slams her fist onto the desk and as she does she catches a reflection of herself in the glass wall of her office.

Momentarily distracted from the task at hand she turns, horrified at what she sees. The reflection shows a more-than-middle-aged, stressed, wrinkled face that should be smooth and refined. She certainly paid enough for her last face-lift. She couldn't possibly be due for another one, surely?

She instantly whips out the hand mirror she keeps in her bottom drawer to take a closer look. My god, what she sees is appalling. Crow's feet, deeply furrowed frown lines. And her neck! It looks like a turkey neck. When did this happen? She has always prided herself on her immaculate physical state …

She ponders a moment and then considers that it must be the additional stress that those people have caused and anger is welling up inside her again when the phone rings. She quickly places her mirror back in the drawer, lest anyone comes in her office and thinks she is vain. The call is internal and she's in no mood for any more bad news after the day she has had.

'What?' she screeches into the handset.

Exasperated, she listens to one her managers explaining that another member of her team has not turned up for work after complaining yesterday about having to self-test the products prior to market release, as per Xsade's company policy. Does she personally have to deal with every detail in order for this organisation to run smoothly? Obviously, she does, as her manager continues to whinge into her ear.

'Why don't *you* test it, then?' she snaps.

She half listens to the manager's aggravating voice as Dr Blake's absence continues to play on her mind. She is incredulous to hear the manager tell her of the company policy of testing products on each person only once, lest it skew the results. Honestly, they must think she, their Managing Director, is a complete idiot. She interrupts the ramble.

'So what you are saying is that you've already tested it, correct?' Apparently so. 'Which product are you referring to specifically?'

She listens. 'The chemical peel, is that what you said?'

Madeleine is immediately more interested in this conversation given that the composition of this new peel is designed to replicate results achieved by plastic surgeons, albeit for a limited time.

This may be the first bit of good news Madeleine has had all day as the vision of her face in the mirror flashes before her eyes.

'Fine. I will lead by example and test it myself. That way there will be no arguments down the track from anyone else. I'll be down in ten minutes.'

She slams the phone down and makes the calls she needs to make. The first to alert her information technology experts to prepare for Dr Alexandra Blake's sordid life to go online, and confirming that only she, the Managing Director, personally, is to have the final approval before it goes live. And the second call is for her security team to commence the search to fetch Dr Blake and/or her children, from wherever they are hiding, immediately. At least now, she feels she is being proactive.

She was going to check on that traitor Votrubec to see how he is enjoying his paralysis, but given Blake's arrival has been deferred, she instead makes her way down to the beauty lab to remove some of the harshness that her face has been accumulating in recent times. They can all wait. And she recognises only too well that she's long overdue for a bit of 'me' time.

Madeleine settles herself into the salon-style beauty couch after having changed out of her Chanel suit into a less than classy elasticised towel that leaves her shoulders and neck bare. She can't remember the last time she lay down in the middle of a working day, and even though technically this is still work, she feels a little decadent.

Her skin is thoroughly cleansed and toned, which doesn't cause her any concern. She has a full range of cosmetics in her office to redo her make-up afterwards, and she finds herself relaxing into the rhythm of the circular motions on her face.

'Would you like both face and neck, Madame?'

'Yes.' She considers her sagging neck and knows it will need more than a peel to re-establish its youthful appearance. She also knows that in this job she needs to look as young and vibrant as possible, unlike the men who are able to age gracefully with their greying and balding heads.

The technician applies the peel with a thick brush, thoroughly painting Madeleine's face and neck. She covers Madeleine's eyes with solid pads before adjusting a large ultraviolet light over her upper body. Once it is close enough to activate the mask, the machine is secured in place.

'This will need to be on for at least twenty minutes. I will check your progress, so please, relax and enjoy.'

'Don't wait around here, go and do some other work, I'll be fine.' Madeleine's voice is muffled as she tries not to move her lips too much. 'There's no use wasting precious company time.'

The technician is about to mention that company procedures state they are to stay within the room when the machine is in operation, but remembers her manager's warnings about the boss's ferocious temper, so she places headphones over her Managing Director's ears and quickly scurries out of the small room, quietly relieved that she has been dismissed.

Madeleine is also happy to be left alone to plan her next steps. She didn't get to this position by not taking risks and she's certainly not going to stop now. A little to her surprise, her stressed body relaxes with ease, the classical music soothing her mind, and she finds herself rather indulgently wafting off into a delightful sleep.

Jeremy

Ever since Alexa arrived back from the lupuna tree, the activity in our small camp ratcheted up tenfold. The elders, usually so calm and tranquil, have been busy with their herbs and potions for the preparation of the first soul flight brew.

I have to admit, I'm not one hundred per cent convinced that the toxins in this mixture won't have side effects for Alexa. I have known her body for long enough to know how it can have a massive response to any unusual substances or chemical imbalances. As soon as Leo shared his plans with me I started researching the details of ayahuasca.

I was both surprised and reassured to find that there are dedicated retreats around the world where people can experience this phenomenon for themselves, which eased my mind a little but not completely. The last thing I wanted was for Alexa to be spending her time vomiting in the heat of the jungle. I had promised Leo that I would not give her any pharmaceutical drugs during her journey, to maintain her natural state, but the elders were willing to accept my suggestion of adding ginger and peppermint into their concoction in the hopes of settling her stomach. We'll see if it works.

I feel much happier having completed her medical back at Avalon. She is as healthy as an ox, to use a non-medical term. Her bloods are good, her cell counts excellent, BMI perfect, reflexes as they should be. At least I know she couldn't be in a better state medically to embark on this spiritual journey of Leo's. More importantly, I sense that she is now mentally up for it. Our time at Avalon seemingly calmed her nerves, though I can't say the same for mine. The least I can do is ensure she maintains this level of physical health and wellbeing until we reach the natural conclusion of this nightmare. So far, so good.

I can't take my eyes off her as she takes her first sip of the steaming brew. She is braver than any woman I know and this stems from her willingness to explore the unknown and question the known. Who knows whether this will change anything in our lives, or whether she will ingest the potion, enjoy the high and then everything will continue as it was before.

No, I shouldn't be so negative. I owe Leo more than that and I have enough confidence in both his IQ and EQ to be assured that he isn't sending us on some wild goose chase, even though at times I can't help but feel as though we're searching for the elusive golden egg.

Nevertheless, as promised, I try to focus my mind on sending positive thoughts supporting Alexa.

The elders have asked us to stay seated with her around the fire until her spirit leaves her physical form. God knows what that is meant to look like. Is she meant to fly away on her chair as we wave her goodbye, or does her body go limp and lose all muscle control? I focus intently on her physiology, as I want to memorise any changes in as much detail as I can.

It has been about ten minutes since she finished the brew and she has been making eye contact with us as if she is waiting for something major to happen. Unsurprisingly, it hasn't. Her gorgeous green eyes are shimmering as they gaze into and reflect the light of the fire. I do notice they continue to dilate the longer she stares, rather rapidly actually. I'm tempted to wave my hand in front her face to see if she still registers our presence but I've been told not to touch her or interrupt her line of sight to the fire, which apparently helps her succumb to the powers of the ayahuasca. I also don't know exactly what impact the sap of the lupuna tree will have, as that was a last-minute addition as per Yaku's request. Why? Because the tree told him so!

I think back to the discussion I had with Leo when he told me this. 'You cannot be serious, Leo. How the hell did a tree tell Yaku that it would take responsibility for guiding her soul flight?'

'It's the way things work in nature's playground, Jaq. You saw that Alexandra was connected to the lupuna tree from the moment she arrived here. We wouldn't have been able to keep her away from it even if we wanted to. What is it that you are really worried about?'

'I'm worried that I haven't done any research on this tree; I didn't even know it existed before she pointed it out. What if it's full of toxins and poisons? It could kill her for all I know.'

'I doubt that the amount they are talking about would kill her. Besides, some shamans regularly use it in their remedies and the elders haven't alerted me to any deaths.'

'Okay, but as you are well aware, Alexa is not of the Wai-Wai people and we know how sensitive she is to drugs. This could be no different. We just don't know.'

'No, you're right,' he says calmly, 'we just don't know. But you're comfortable with her having the ayahuasca?'

'I would say resigned is a better word than comfortable.' He raises his eyebrows at my pedantic nitpicking. 'Okay, yes. I am.'

'Good, let's see how this unfolds and we can make the decisions we need to make along the way.' Leo puts his hand on my shoulder. 'She is up for this, Jaq, you need to let her do what she knows she must.'

For the first time since this Amazonian journey began, I feel a bit overwhelmed by the trust I know Alexa has placed in me to get her through this, based on the faith I have in Leo. I can't deny I also have the tiniest sliver of doubt that we are going so far into the

171

unknown that I may *not* be able to help her. I share this thought with Leo.

'I hope you know how much trust I am placing in you, my friend, that this will end well.'

'Yes, I'm well aware of that, but as you also know, nothing is ever assured in this life. We can only do the best we can.' He looks steadily at me as if to assuage my concerns. 'However, I do believe what Alexandra is doing will provide some of the answers.'

I feel as though I'm swinging from a rope connected to a helicopter, hanging on for dear life and having to trust the driver to understand both the terrain and weather patterns to ensure our ultimate safety. Being this out of control, not in the driver's seat, never sits well with me, and I've been forced into feeling this way when it comes to Alexa too many times recently. It's unnerving to say the least.

The twitching of AB's fingers immediately brings me back to the present. I'd give anything to be able to shine a light in her eyes and check her responses. She looks lost in space, eyes almost fully open and unblinking. Her twitching hands could mean anything from low blood sugar levels, the beginning of a partial seizure or the result of some change in her neurological condition.

As every part of me wants to check her pulse, I feel the heavy weight of the elders' eyes pinning me to my seat. I look at Leo and his eyes beg me to let this be. Damn this silence around her. I never thought it would be harder for me, than her.

Her eyes remain wide and her gaze is locked on the fire as the twitching continues up her arms and then takes hold of her toes and lower legs. She looks as though she is experiencing some form of mild convulsion. If I weren't so well acquainted with her medical state, I'd swear she was having the beginnings of an epileptic fit. Her eyes start rolling around in their sockets as the convulsions continue to seize her body. My heart feels like it is held in a vice as I see the love of my life experiencing this, and having to hold back. Every part of me wants to help her, to ensure she is alright.

She is clearly having a horrific reaction to the toxic shit they've given her and I go to get up to retrieve my medicine bag only to find I physically can't lift myself up. What the hell is going on here? It's as if my butt has been superglued to the seat. The elders' eyes are in the same trance-like state as Alexa's were moments ago, and Leo has closed his eyes and sits calmly with his palms open and resting in his lap. Am I the only sane one here?

Still pinned to the chair, I sit helplessly watching the woman I love have a seizure that has become so severe she now topples backward out of her chair, her head and body thumping hard on the ground as I release a scream even louder than the eagle's cry we heard from the lupuna tree earlier. My god! The second she hits the ground, her body becomes limp, almost lifeless. At the same time I am freed from the chair and fling myself off almost landing directly on top of Alexa's body.

Desperate for any response I lift her arm, check her wrist for a pulse and pull open her now closed eyelids. Nothing.

'Leo!' I scream out, desperate to get his attention. 'Leo, get my bag. She's not responding.'

Everyone is still sitting contentedly around the fire as if they are locked in position. Fucking hell, this is my worst nightmare. I lean down so my face is just above her mouth to feel for any whisper of breath. Nothing. I check for any sign of a pulse — it's absent. I place my ear on her chest for any sign of her heartbeat. Fuck. I'm momentarily torn between leaving her and racing to get my bag. The others are still not responding to my pleas and remain fixedly in a trance. I'm left with no choice but to race over to our tent, fetch my medical kit and run back to tend to her.

When I return, desperately trying to open the bag on the way, the others have left the fire and surround her body.

'You'll all need to move. I need to start CPR and she may need adrenaline.' Fearing the worst, I desperately search in my kit for the drugs I need, before I start pulling up her top to begin CPR.

Takasumo, the most grizzled of the elders, carefully picks up her hand, closes his eyes as he places Alexa's wrist between his palms and says, 'No, okay now.'

'What?' I shout. I sound like a madman, as their mood remains unnaturally steady.

I grab my stethoscope to listen to her heart and, thank god, I can hear the weakest of beats. My own heart is beating so fast I feel like I've got ten times more adrenaline pumping through my body than I have waiting in the injection beside me. I pull her shirt down and check the back of her head for any damage when she fell. It seems okay, though she is still unresponsive. I continue with every check that comes to mind and though her vitals seem to be improving, her blood pressure remains slightly lower than normal. I take a few moments to calm myself as I listen to the strength of her improving heartbeat in my ears.

What the hell was all that about? I look at her body and her colour is returning: her lips are pink, her cheeks slightly flushed and she looks wonderfully at peace, nothing like the short, sharp convulsion I just witnessed moments ago. Everyone else appears calm and at ease.

'Leo, what was that? Did I miss something?'

'Sometimes, when a person ingests ayahuasca, they can have a reaction like that when the soul leaves the body. It usually lasts less than a minute before the physical body adjusts and re-establishes its normal rhythm.'

'So, you're telling me Alexa's soul has gone?' I am really attempting to sound as controlled as possible and try to keep the sarcastic edge out of my voice.

'In a way, yes. That is why we remained by the fire until she had settled, to ensure its safe arrival at its destination.'

'She was flung from the chair!'

'These chairs aren't very stable. A few movements and they can topple over, I've done it myself a couple of times,' he states with a chuckle, but my death stare makes it clear I find none of this the least bit amusing. He changes tack. 'You didn't steady it for her?'

I am really having a difficult time hearing all of this, and his question confounds me. 'I, well, I couldn't move. It was so strange.'

'Sometimes it's difficult letting go of the ones we love, and when we do, we tend to imagine the worst. She is in a safe place, Jaq. No harm will come to her and she will return more enlightened than when she left.'

His words hit me like a brick. I glance back toward Alexa, and though she's unconscious, she looks peaceful and calm, as though she is enjoying a deep restful sleep. I am forced to reconsider my version of events. It is only then that I consider the possibility of my heart and my mind being in conflict with one another.

Even as I'm thinking it through, I can feel my deep commitment to Leo and my absolute love for Alexa. I think of Leo's request for me to refrain from speaking and remain seated so she can embark on this journey, and of my fear of losing her, never wanting to let her go. I honestly couldn't bear for us to be separated again after so many years. I feel like we've been waiting an entire lifetime to reconnect to each other. A future without her in it, even temporarily, is completely unacceptable in my mind and in my heart. It's as though I was being forced to choose between keeping my promise to Leo and my love for her.

My heart knew I wanted to reach out to help her, but my brain seemed to override the impulse, making me immobile. When I come to terms with this realisation, I admonish myself for even vaguely considering the elders having some spiritual or magical hold over my body. I'm relieved I have managed to find a logical explanation for my behaviour.

Although Leo assures me that low blood pressure can be a symptom of soul flight, I'm not one hundred per cent convinced so I begin my meticulous documenting of Alexa's medical state. This at least keeps me preoccupied in the short term. While I'm detailing her vital signs, the elders talk to Leo.

'They'd like to move her, Jaq, but didn't want to interrupt until you'd finished your research.'

'Why? Where?' I suddenly feel like I'm turning into Alexa with so many questions flooding my brain.

'They want her to be closer to the lupuna tree that is protecting her. The closer her body is to her protector, the safer she'll be, just like people are when they embark on soul flight with the shaman.'

Who am I to argue? It still sounds like madness to me, but if they believe she will be safer, I won't be disagreeing.

'That's fine, Leo.' I try to temper my tone, as I'm a bit embarrassed about my previous outburst.

He nods to the elders.

We carefully pick her up and carry her light frame on a stretcher to the lupuna tree. It's dark now and we will take turns keeping vigil around her apparently soulless body. I reluctantly leave her to have something to eat and, if I can, to catch a few hours sleep. The noises of the jungle initially keep me wired until I am lulled into a deep, dreamless sleep.

Alexa

It is like nothing I have ever experienced before. A different time, a different place and it can only be described as simultaneously ethereal and visceral. I am everywhere but I'm nowhere — the sensation all too unreal. It's as if I am watching a movie but from the perspective of being both the director and the actors and even part of the set itself. I can see them and hear them, even understand them, but they cannot do the same. They are playing their roles and I'm floating about the scene, within it, yet invisible, untouchable.

My senses are on high alert, absorbing the feelings of those within each scene, but maintaining my own self. It is the strangest form of unreality imaginable and I can only surmise this must be my version of Leo's soul flight. I immerse myself in both the process and possibilities.

My vision shifts and I can suddenly focus. I see a mother putting a young girl to sleep; she looks to be

179

about five years old. The mother is lovingly stroking her forehead, gently caressing the strands of her long dark hair away from her face. She gently kisses her cheek goodnight and the girl's smile speaks volumes of the love she has for this woman. I can feel the emotions from each of them in my heart, as though I'm invisibly connected to their deepest thoughts. I remember my own mother doing the same thing when I was small, just as I do now for my own children.

The mother draws the makeshift curtain and takes a last look at the girl before closing it fully. She returns to the candle in the middle of the round table. The kitchen is rustic; we are in a time where water is fetched from the stream in a bucket, bread is homemade and clothes are scarce and valued. She walks over to the fireplace that is keeping the night chill out of the small dwelling. Lighting a taper from its burning flames, she illuminates a circle of candles and sits in the middle of the almost bare room, as if in deep meditation.

The scene suddenly flashes and changes rapidly before my eyes, as though some one has flicked through many pages of a novel to continue somewhere else.

The same woman is entering another home in which she is warmly welcomed. The family embraces her and thanks her for coming to them. I can feel their trust in her just as I feel the woman's quiet confidence in the task she has come to perform. She has a satchel slung over her shoulder that she is about to open when her young daughter comes running in. The girl looks similar to me the year I began school.

'Mama, I just want to be with you, please, can I watch?'

The mother raises her head toward the elders of the house they are in and they nod in unison.

'Of course, Caitlin, come here,' she says calmly.

There is a sick boy resting on a blanket in the corner of the room. He is older than the young girl but is slight and frail. He looks desperately unwell and as I look toward his body, the unnatural stench of his illness permeates my being. Though it is offensive and vile, I can feel the compassion they both have for the boy lessening the strange sense of his odour.

My curiosity pulls me in closer to the scene, to the sick child, just as the mother moves to him. I feel connected to her; I feel her love and commitment to healing this boy regardless of any risk to her own life from his disease. Linked by some indescribable bond, we move closer. From the sheen of his skin I can see the boy has an acute fever. He is weak and I sense that the foul smell is eating his body from the inside out. He is gravely ill.

Taking her time to feel his tortured body, the mother carefully smooths her palms over his arms and legs. Her every movement is watched intently by her daughter, Caitlin. She then places both palms on either side of his face and closes her eyes. She seems to be deep in prayer or thought and begins chanting some sort of incantation. The young girl quietly moves across the room to kneel by her mother's side, also placing her palms on the boy's skin, replicating her mother's actions.

The family remains watching from afar, the fear in their eyes recognising the tenuous hold the young boy has on life and sensing the magic in the room. Long moments pass before the mother and daughter withdraw their touch from the boy and again open their eyes as though released from a spell.

The mother returns to her satchel and removes some herbs that she places in a mortar and pestle. The woman of the family adds a few drops of hot water to the mixture and nods her approval to continue. The mother reaches for one last item, and indicates that the family should turn away, not observe the last step of this process. They do so, maintaining their silence, their grief for the boy evident in their hunched bodies.

Caitlin continues to watch her mother with an intensity and curiosity that I recognise in myself. The mother takes a small dagger out of the satchel and deftly pierces the skin of her middle finger, squeezing three drops of blood into the concoction before discreetly replacing the dagger and sucking the remaining blood from her fingertip.

'You may turn around now,' she states quietly to the family as she grinds and stirs the ingredients with the pestle. 'This must be given to the boy from a place of the heart. Only a mother's love will help heal him now; continue to watch over him in his rest.'

The mother of the boy steps away from the rest of the family and walks over to the boy. She cradles her dying son in her arms before raising the concoction to his lips. She helps him open his mouth and pours it in, little by little. The father rushes over to their side with some additional water, which the mother gives to the boy to wash the medicine down his throat. He coughs a little before they lay him gently back on the ground and return to the healers.

'Thank you, Evelyn. You are our last hope.'

She acknowledges the family before packing her satchel with her few items and holds her daughter's hand at the wooden door. 'We shall continue to pray for your son's health.'

The family stares after the pair as they leave, feeling exhausted, but for the first time they have hope in their hearts.

A few days later Caitlin is out feeding the chickens when she sees the young boy walking along the side of the road with a hefty bucket in his left hand. At full height, he is much taller than she. He has a healthy glow in his cheeks and a strong stride. He looks nothing like the fragile body barely able to move in the corner of the room. A smile lights up her face as she realises that her mother's magic has helped remove all signs of illness and infection from the boy's body.

She runs toward him and he puts the bucket on the ground to receive her hug as she wraps her small arms around him. She glances up at him, holding his gaze with her large silver-green eyes; the radiating warmth in them indicates that he shares the same joy in his heart as she does in hers. She feels secure in her mother's magic and though not expressed in words, Caitlin knows that he will protect and help others as he travels his path in life. She knows they are bonded by her mother's blood and that somehow their connection, however brief, will be meaningful in the future.

I see my own eyes reflected in Caitlin's and realise I experienced the same sense of calm serenity from Leo, when he captures my gaze, a trust that everything will work out as it is meant to. The completeness of Caitlin's connection with the boy reverberates through my entire ethereal being.

Caitlin has watched her mother work small miracles all of her young life. Evelyn has a kind heart and shows such compassion for others that the young girl wants only to follow in her footsteps. Her mother never accepts direct gifts or payments for what she does, but they also never want for life's basic necessities. It's as if the village itself has some unspoken agreement to maintain their existence; it is never discussed, it merely occurs.

Often Evelyn leaves at night for a few hours, when she thinks her daughter is sound asleep. She goes deep into the forest and partakes in rituals that are intimately aligned with the cycle of nature. She can feel when and how things need to happen, the awakenings of spring and the heat of the summer, the turning of autumn and the temporary death of nature in winter. Every season is as much a part of her body as is the earth itself.

On nights when the moon is full, she leaves the house for longer periods and comes back to the small house with her hair matted and wild, clothes torn and dirty and sleeps long into the next day.

People within the village feel her raw energy and presence when she is close to them and although they know this woman is one of the most compassionate among them, they are also a little afraid of her, of a magic they don't understand or allow themselves to fully believe in. Unless they are in need themselves, they tend to keep their distance. Their fear of the unknown both entices them closer to her and eventually turns them from her.

As Caitlin grows older, she spends as much time as she can with her mother, wanting to learn and understand the gift of her magic so she can one day make it her own. Once she commences bleeding, her mother teaches her things about her magic that she couldn't before. She explains that although they can talk to each other openly, it should never be discussed with others. Caitlin understands they have a duty to use their gift for the good of others. She also knows, but doesn't understand, why people have an inherent fear of the power of the blood gift, which is why it can only be used in the context of unconditional love. Her mother explains this is even more important with times changing so rapidly and a sense of darkness and menace descending on the world.

Evelyn asks her daughter to promise to keep the power of her blood a secret and she solemnly makes this vow. Caitlin always wondered if she too has this gift, the healing magic in her blood. Her mother slowly lowers her shift over her left shoulder and Caitlin sees the small heart-shaped mark beneath her left shoulder blade. She has seen this mark many times before when they have bathed together.

'This is the mark of the blood.'

Caitlin raises the palm of her hand to her left breast, where she has the same mark. She had not realised until now the power it represents.

Evelyn places her hand over her daughter's. 'As your breasts continue to grow, your mark will become hidden. This is a sign of the shadows that will soon darken our earth and our lives. You must keep yourself safe and out of harm's way. When the time comes, someone will come into your life who will understand you and their need to provide you with protection. You will know who to trust by looking deeply into their eyes and you will see the truth in them. Just as we do now.' The gaze between mother and daughter is intimate and close, never threatening or tyrannical. 'Trust your intuition. This will guide your journey through life. Even if I am not by your side, know that I am always with you, loving you, bound to you.'

The two women embrace each other, not knowing what the future will hold but with a strong sense of the responsibility their gift has bestowed upon them.

* * *

On the night of the next majestic full moon, Caitlin pretends to be asleep as her mother lightly kisses her cheek. Evelyn closes the timber door leaving her daughter behind and escapes quietly into the forest.

The girl waits only a few moments before following her mother along the same path, the lucent moon paving the path before her eyes.

At one point, her mother turns around, hearing the rustling leaves and smiles wisely before continuing her journey deeper into the forest. Her daughter stills then sighs with relief that her mother hasn't seen her. The ground is littered with the falling leaves of the forest providing padding for her bare feet. An owl hoots from the trees above, as if acknowledging her forbidden presence in the deep forest at nightfall.

Eventually Evelyn enters a clearing and Caitlin drops behind, hiding behind a grand elm tree. Her heart pounding fiercely within her chest, she attempts to steady her breathing and calm her nerves. She hears a rustling in the trees on the other side of the clearing where her mother has disappeared before she hears the low chanting of voices.

Worried about being discovered in case others arrive along this pathway, she quickly climbs up the tree, giving her an uninterrupted view of the clearing and the proceedings below. The chanting quiets to a whisper, as if it belongs to the forest itself, and she sees her mother emerge naked, except for a wreath of native forest flowers around her head, the last of the season.

Evelyn begins to sway and dance along with the light breeze tantalising the trees. Caitlin senses their energy and connection with her mother below as if they are becoming one. She is illuminated in the clearing and her body looks beautiful and bountiful with her arms raised above her head and her hips undulating like the branches in the wind. The daughter has never seen her mother look so vital, so vibrant.

The hidden, chanting voices become silent as their naked bodies emerge from the trees and form a circle around Evelyn, all bowing their heads toward her. After a few moments of meditating with the sounds and breath of the forest, they too begin to move like Caitlin's mother, but with slower movements as if waiting for the rhythm to enter their bodies.

The chanting begins again, much louder than before, as they raise their voices to the heavens and spread out around the clearing, each carving out their own space and energy in their movements. Evelyn moves toward a slab of rock at the edge of the field, lays down on it with her hands falling back behind her head and spreads her legs, wide open. One at a time, both men and woman approach her, bending to kiss the inner lips between her legs.

Evelyn writhes and moves in a delighted trance as each person takes their turn, touching her sex with their lips. Then they return to the clearing and recommence their alluring sounds and move in a trance-like state of sheer sensuality, each of them pleasuring their bodies until they release their ecstatic cries as if paying homage to both heaven and earth. This continues for some time as until they all eventually lay silently in the field, surrounded by nature and basking in the light of the moon.

As clouds pass over the light of the moon, they pick themselves up from the grass and silently return to the hidden canopy of the forest, never speaking a word to one another. Caitlin, wide-eyed and worried about being seen, hurriedly descends from the branches of the giant elm and hastens home.

Early the following morning, a heavy pounding on the door awakens both women from their deep sleep. Soldiers enter their home and Evelyn is physically dragged out the front of their small house. Her hair is roughly held by large calloused hands at the back of her head, her face shining in the thin light of the dawn.

'Is this she?'

A man standing off to one side nods his head, deliberately keeping his eyes away from Evelyn, who is staring directly at him. He slinks away in the shadows behind the gathering of the small crowd.

'You are pronounced witch, woman. You shall be burned at the stake.'

Caitlin's wails pierce the air as the mother is hauled away by the guardsmen. She lunges forward and grabs hold of the edge of her mother's shift and screams with every ounce of energy in her body. Her fear for her mother soaks through to her bones. She has been the focal point of her young life and it's as though the very essence of her heart is being ripped from her ribcage.

The soldiers, holding each of her mother's limbs, roughly kick Caitlin away as another guard grabs her around the waist, preventing any further progress being made. Why is her mother not fighting back? Where is her magic to stop this from happening?

This is worse than any nightmare Caitlin has experienced and she shuts her eyes and quickly reopens them just in case this is all a horrible dream. But instead she watches her mother being shoved into a wooden cage with three other petrified woman with ashen faces. Evelyn's eyes are filled with tears of sorrow and longing toward her daughter, but her physical presence remains calm, almost as though she knew this time would come.

Accepting this fate, the end of her life, she turns to her hysterical daughter and says clearly, 'Be strong, my love, for this is our destiny, so long as men fear power in women.'

Caitlin falls, crushed and abandoned, to the ground. Her screams can be heard far in the hills, as she is left with a hole in her heart as round as the moon and she understands that she will never lay eyes on her mother again.

* * *

I, too, feel as though my own heart is being crushed. My feeling for Caitlin is so strong, I can only believe our connection is based on kinship somehow. I feel both the mother's pain and the daughter's anguish and fear, like two souls being brutally ripped apart.

I want to run to her, save her, help her and love her. I reach out, but heartbreakingly I know I can't touch her. I want her to know that my love, like her mother's, will always be with her. No physical separation will

ever be great enough to keep them apart and that
one day, somehow, somewhere they will be reunited.
But I can't, I'm being pulled away from the scene as I
desperately try to cling to the sobbing girl.

Jeremy

As soon as I awaken from my slumber, I grab my kit and make my way to Alexa at the lupuna tree to relieve one of the elders, Mapu, who is keeping watch over her. From afar, she seems to be resting in exactly the same position, looking content and relaxed. That is, until I am close enough to see the sheen on her skin and feel the heat from her forehead.

'How long has she been like this?' I ask, my panic rising.

'Her okay.'

It's still dark so she can't be too warm from the heat of the sun. I grab a small camping deckchair and take out my tympanic thermometer to take her temperature. As I suspected, she has a slight fever at thirty-eight degrees Celsius, though she is lying peacefully. Actually, she looks like Sleeping Beauty, in the light of the half moon shimmering through the forest canopy and I'd give anything to be the one to awaken her from the unknown of this deep sleep. Surely she should have experienced some form of coherent consciousness by now and what in god's name could be causing her fever?

I take out my torch to examine her body for any sign of infection; something may have bitten her on our journey here. I go check her eyes for dilation but Mapu guides my hand away and rests his hands beneath his head to illustrate she is sleeping before clasping them together like bird's wings to indicate she is far away or flying.

Feeling totally hamstrung, I'd give anything to wake Leo to discuss exactly how long he believes this process should last. Agitated by Mapu's patience, I raise my water bottle to him and indicate I'd like to give some to Alexa. '*Água?*'

He shakes his head and instead picks up his own potion and hands it to me. I take a sniff and notice its sweetness, assuming there could be some honey in it. Even though I'm uncomfortable giving her things I don't fully understand, I respect that I'm in their world and while she is in this state, I have to trust that they are better qualified to ensure she gets out of it, though I swear if she remains unconscious for the next twenty-four hours I will be flying her out of here to get her the medical attention she needs.

I moisten her lips with the liquid and carefully let some drops fall into her mouth. I wet my clean handkerchief with my water bottle and gently run it over her limbs before laying it on her forehead to cool her. And then I wait because really that is all I can do.

At sunrise Leo appears and relieves Mapu. 'Do you want some rest, Jaq? I can get Yaku if you'd like.'

'No, I'll be staying right here, thanks.' If I could do thirty-hour shifts during my early career, I can certainly do them now.

'How's she been?'

'She had a slight fever a couple of hours ago but that seems to have settled though I can't explain why. She's had some fluids, but otherwise she hasn't budged.'

Just as I say the words, Alexa shoots up into a seated position and is gasping for air.

I'm so shocked I fall off my seat. 'Shit!'

We're both taken aback though Leo is more composed than I am. I move straight to her side.

'Alexa, sweetheart, are you okay? Can you hear me?'

She looks around, startled, but then seems to recognise our faces.

She nods that she can hear us before saying urgently, 'I need to go back, I need to know, I can't wait. Where is Yaku? I need more ...'

'Slow down, slow down. Where have you been?' In my peripheral vision, I notice Leo slipping away.

'A different time, place, I don't know, Jeremy, but I know it will help me understand everything. I need to go back before I lose them forever.'

I don't have a clue who she is talking about, but she looks agitated until she sees Yaku return with Leo and a cup in his hands. Only then does her face break into a smile and her hands reach out to take the cup. I feel a little panicked.

'Are you sure you want to do this, sweetheart? I'm not sure it is safe for you to have any more, you've had a fever.'

'A fever?' This seems to divert her attention from drinking.

'Yes, it's gone now but —'

She interrupts me. 'They burnt her, that's why. They burnt Evelyn, they believed she was a witch but she wasn't, she was a healer with special blood. She had magic but she was good, kind and had more compassion than any of them. I need to go back to check if her daughter is alright. They took her away.' She is speaking like a madwoman, her eyes darting around the forest as though she is looking for these unknown people.

I look anxiously toward Leo, at a loss. He kneels down beside the stretcher and cradles her face gently in his palms. Without uttering a word, he looks deeply into her eyes. It is only then that I remember I'm not meant to speak to her. She inhales before her body shudders on her exhale, as though she is releasing tension and calming down. He nods without breaking eye contact and she raises the ayahuasca to her lips and swallows its potent contents. They remain that way until she finishes and Yaku takes the cup from her hands.

Their eyes remain locked until Alexa's dilate like before and she slowly closes them as if her lids are too heavy for her to control. Leo carefully lowers her body back onto the stretcher and she is gone again, to whatever world this Amazonian concoction is taking her to.

Leo turns to me. 'Let's take a walk, you need a break.' He speaks to the elders in their native tongue and they nod their heads. I hesitate. 'It's okay, Jaq, they won't let anything happen to her. They understand where she is better than we ever will.'

His outstretched hand rests on my shoulder as he senses my reluctance. I take another look at AB, who has once again returned to her Sleeping Beauty state and I fleetingly consider if I'm helping or hindering what she is going through with my anxiety about her wellbeing. She certainly appeared more agitated being here than wherever she was, so with this in mind I agree to go with Leo to clear my head and stretch my legs, knowing that he will have some words of wisdom to share, as always.

* * *

When we return, Yaku informs us it is time to go downriver. The shaman has sent a message letting them know that his moment to receive Alexa is close and she needs to spend time with the village women to prepare for this event. With no small degree of cynicism I ask how this message was received. Which animal or tree communicated this to the elders?

Leo asks them and points in the direction of our small camp. 'Other members of the tribe, Jaq, they travelled upriver this morning and will return to the village with us.' A cheeky smile appears on his lips as though he can read my thoughts exactly.

'Oh, right,' I respond, a little embarrassed.

'You know, my scientific friend, it's not all voodoo and magic in the jungle.' He laughs at me. 'Let's get organised.'

We stretcher Alexa's body to the canoes waiting by the riverside. She isn't fully unconscious but she's not here with us with any awareness either. My heart is in a constant state of dulled anguish seeing her like this, but my head tells me to ignore the pain and focus on the greater good.

Leo told me on our walk together that his soul flight occurred over a five-day period and that the spiritual awareness reached climactic proportions when his physical body was at its weakest. Apparently, Alexa still has some way to go. Not the greatest news from my perspective, but at least he is trying to manage my expectations moving forward. As long as she continues to retain fluids, I've promised that I won't interfere with the process. I hope I don't regret it.

Floating down the river on the handmade wooden canoes is a serene experience. The Wai-Wai only use their small outboard motors if they need to go upstream, or against the tide. It's surprising how fast the tributaries feeding into the main river system actually flow.

It is a joy to experience the vitality and noise of the Amazon basin in this way — the abundance of life here is unimaginable. We pass people bathing in the river, washing both hair and dishes side by side. Men are fishing and women are weaving baskets and waving as we float past their tiny villages. Kids are playing and splashing on the river foreshore, their laughter tickling the air. Alexa would love to see all of this activity against the backdrop of the greenest, most intense rainforest in the world.

We leave the main river and head back toward one of the offshoot tributaries. Leo yells over the noise of the small motor from the canoe next to mine. 'Not far to go now, maybe an hour or so.'

I nod in acknowledgement and marvel at how they find their way around this massive and intricate river system without the aid of any technology or jungle street directory. As I look toward Alexa, I notice she is again completely unconscious and wipe a few strands of hair from her face. In doing so, I notice two small dark stains on her white shirt and my heart immediately skips a beat. What now? If I didn't know better I would say it looks like old blood.

A little alarmed, I unbutton her shirt to find that it appears to be coming from her breasts, having seeped through her bra.

'What the hell?' I mutter more to myself than anyone else. I glance around before I discreetly pull down her bra to find both of her nipples covered with dark, coagulated blood. Just as I'm attempting to stay calm and think of some diagnosis for this, I am distracted by shouts of excitement.

'Jaq, look. River dolphins, pink dolphins, just behind us, playing in our wake,' Leo calls over from one of the other canoes.

Under normal circumstances, this would be an amazing experience; under these circumstances I'm left staring perplexed at Alexa's bloodied chest. Other than friction from running, or issues with breastfeeding, I can't think of any medical condition that would cause this and even so, it would be fresh rather than this dark, coagulated blood.

'Is everything okay over there?' I hear Leo yelling again.

'I'm not sure. There's some kind of blood on Alexa's nipples,' I don't mind yelling back in English, given the others' understanding of our language is so limited.

'Really?' He sounds as shocked as I am. 'Is she still bleeding now?'

'No, not that I can tell.'

'And it's just on her nipples?'

I quickly scan the rest of her body. Other than her nipples and her inability to communicate with us, she seems perfectly fine. 'Yeah, just there.'

'Wow, that is weird. Do you think it could be some form of sexual stigmata?'

Only Leo would be quick enough to come up with a comment like that. I throw him a look from my canoe that seriously hopes he is joking.

'Just sharing a thought ...'

I shake my head in response. What the hell could cause this? Concerned but also intrigued, I reach for my kit and take a swab for testing later and seal it in a bag. This journey gets weirder by the hour.

As I sit, baffled but unable to do much at this point, one of the pink dolphins rears up right beside where I'm sitting, with its mouth open as if it is smiling at me. I'm so caught off-guard, I can't help but laugh in response to what looks like the cheekiest grin I've ever seen. It distracts me enough from my unsettled thoughts to fleetingly consider what Alexa would say about this if she were deciphering it from a psychological perspective, interpreting a dream.

Strangely enough, this thought lightens my emotional burdens and for the first time since she sipped the ayahuasca, I feel as though everything will somehow work out. As soon as I note this thought, the pod of endangered pink dolphins vanishes into the depths of the river and we don't see them again.

I swear this jungle is messing with my head.

Part Six

Change is the essence of life. Be willing
to surrender what you are for what you
could become.

Reinhold Niebuhr

Lake Bled

Her Managing Director has essentially dismissed her, so the technician decides to have a quick coffee as she hasn't had a break for hours and figures five minutes away won't do any harm. She had been about to head off when her manager called to say Madame Jurilique was on her way down. She loves her coffee steaming hot and always likes to get the kettle as it boils. This time is no different, except when she begins pouring the water into her cup she sneezes, causing her to drop the steaming kettle. Boiling water splashes over her hands and wrists scalding her skin and leaving her screaming in agony with what looks to be third-degree burns. A member of the management team finds her writhing in pain and, bypassing first aid protocols given her assessment of the seriousness of the situation, immediately summons the new head physician, whom she had had dinner with a few nights ago.

Dr Jade is carefully preparing to administer the sophisticated drugs to his predecessor. He is particularly keen to make an excellent first impression on Madame Jurilique, whom he has respected and admired from the employ of his previous company for many years. He can imagine the risk Dr Votrubec now presents to Xsade, given he knows their formulas and secrets, so Dr Jade justifies his boss's decision to incapacitate him in this way and surely this will be more comfortable than being bound and gagged, as Votrubec currently is on the other side of the room.

Not bothering to look into the harrowed eyes of the man before him, he measures the exact quantity of the injection just as his pager buzzes its emergency tone. Reluctantly, he carefully replaces the full syringe back on the tray knowing the timing and sequencing of these drugs is the key to the success of this procedure. He reads his message, quickly grabs his medical bag and exits the lab, forgetting to lock the door behind him as he runs toward the emergency.

Josef, though unable to breathe easily through his gag, exhales an enormous sigh of relief. He needs to get out of there and fast. This may be his last opportunity.

* * *

Madeleine continues to enjoy the ambience of her daytime respite to the sounds of Rachmaninoff. Dreams about the successful launch of Xsade's new drug and the appreciative crowd's standing ovation as she finishes her speech, dance around in her head and ensure her unconscious state.

* * *

The new scientist inductees continue their tour around the facility. As they enter a laboratory where a new chemical compound is being mixed and tested, Salina slips discreetly away from the main group to check the rooms down the corridors for any sign of Josef, keeping her head lowered as she passes a security camera.

She opens a fire escape and quickly moves down the stairs to the next level to continue her search. This place is much larger than she first suspected. There are a few silver-suited volunteers in one of the larger rooms and she apologises and backtracks. Hearing footsteps coming her way she increases her pace as fast as she can without attracting attention, thankful she's wearing silent trainers and opens the next doorway she can access.

As she closes the door behind her she turns around to see the bound figure of a distraught man, instantly recognising him as Dr Josef Votrubec. Relief and adrenaline flood her body as she races to his aid, swiftly undoing his bonds with a slice of her pocketknife. She cautions him to silence before flicking the light off as they hear footsteps shuffle past the door. The door handle turns and they both freeze in horror until they hear a voice declare, 'No, this can't be the room, it must be the next one.' Both breathe a collective sigh of relief as the door closes again.

'My name is Salina, I'm a friend of Dr Quinn and Dr Blake. I am here to get you out,' she whispers to him.

Josef will take all the help he can get to avoid the drugs that will render him totally immobile. 'Thank you. They will be back any moment, we need to get going now.'

Salina notices the cut on his cheek and the bruises on his wrists and forearms before throwing him a lab coat.

'Are you hurt? Will you be okay to walk?'

'Yes, I'll be fine. But neither of us will be if they catch us in here when they return. I know an emergency passage out of here. Follow me.'

Just as they are about to open the door to check if the passage is clear they hear a massive explosion above them, followed by silence, then the sound of screeches and screams.

Salina is not wasting a second. 'Go, I'll follow you.'

Josef grabs hold of her hand and they stumble along the corridor, before disappearing entirely from the view of the security cameras as they slip through a white door that will eventually link them to the same route on which he took Alexa. The building rocks from another explosion before evacuation alarms are sounded and they immediately increase their pace, their senses heightened by fear for their lives as they prepare to take flight up the spiralling stairs to higher ground.

Alexa

It takes me a while to re-establish my connection with the past world again, but I'm more confident this time, knowing a little more what to expect from such strange sensations. As I float above the land, scanning my surroundings, relief washes over my being as I eventually sense where I need to be and allow the vision to draw me in once again.

* * *

The soldiers take Caitlin to a large town to await her fate — whether she is to be declared a witch or not after her mother was burned at the stake. She never knew such a world existed outside her small village.

Alone, and with a leaden heart, she is still overwhelmed with grief when she is brought before the high priest, who is draped in incredibly ornate garments that she'd never imagined could exist. He declares that now she has been separated from evil, her hair should be shaved and she should earn her penance as a slave to god. So long as she shows no sign of witchcraft, her life will be spared, otherwise her death will be necessary to ensure her salvation.

She is taken away and locked within the walls of a monastery where she is told she will remain for the rest of her living days. Put to work as a maid for the church, she does the cleaning, washing, assists in the preparation of meals and serves the monks. She is not to speak, only to be spoken to. She is not allowed to make eye contact with anyone she serves, in case her potential for witchery curses others. Her lonely life continues without pity or love and her heart continually aches for the loss of her mother. Over time, her hair returns to its original length, although it must always be kept in a tidy braid and hidden behind linen.

One evening, in bed and exhausted yet again from the relentless daily grind of her work, visions flood her mind as she remembers the sight of her mother in the clearing, her legs spread apart as she lay on the surface of a rock, allowing people from the village to kiss her most private parts. She recalls their reverence toward her mother and tries to reconcile this with the teachings of the church she now finds herself confined within.

A tear falls from her eye in memory of the loss of her cherished mother, as it does most nights. Tonight, though, for the first time, she allows her hands to wander to her own private place between her legs. Her fingers fondle shyly into the deeper layers of her flesh and she feels her opening moisten in response to her touch. This feeling soothes her, connects her to her core, more so than anything she has experienced since being taken away. As her fingers continue to caress and play they discover a secret point of pleasure and she gasps aloud at the heady sensation.

These feelings temporarily subdue the inexhaustible pain and cruelty she has both witnessed and experienced in the recent past and for a brief moment, she allows her mind to be set free as a fragile cry escapes her lips through the door of her dormitory.

Within minutes of this occurring, a figure runs toward her, towering above her bed in the darkness and grabs hold of her hands. Caitlin screams with fright as her wrists are roughly seized, the evidence of her grave sin immediately exposed by the slippery fluid on her fingertips.

'You wretched, evil girl … after everything we have done for you.'

Her arms are stretched and bound above her head, and attached to a ring in the wall. A cloth is stuffed in her mouth and secured with a rag tied around her head to subdue her cries lest she disturbs the other servants.

She spends the rest of the night trapped and shivering, unable to sleep due to her fear of what may become of her in the morning, yet unsure of exactly what she has done wrong.

Hours later, Caitlin struggles to see what is going on when she hears the old priest talking to someone as he pauses at the doorway. 'She can no longer remain here. She is dirty in the eyes of god and her mother declared a witch. It's an intolerable situation. Any ordinary form of work is now out of the question. Her sins are an abomination.'

She strains to see who the old priest is speaking with and recognises a well-dressed man, whom she has served on numerous occasions when he has dined with the priests.

'What will become of her, Father?' The man's voice is gruff but his accent is educated. He is not young, nor old but always immaculately attired.

'We may be able to torture the demons out her, and should she repent before God she may undergo some cleansing. This has worked for some but it may take many years. My fear is that the rack will do her no good as, now that she has engaged with the devil, there will be no stopping her attempts at deceiving others in her witchery.' There is a pause and Caitlin's nerve endings remain on high alert. 'I feel the only option is the wheel. This way we'll know one way or another whether she be witch or not. God will either have mercy on her and grant her salvation at the gates of heaven or she will descend into the depths of hell where quite probably she belongs.'

At these words Caitlin screams into her gag and thrashes her body wildly, causing her nightshirt to rise up high on her thighs. She has learnt from her time here that barely anyone survives the wheel, least of all a young woman declared a witch. She knows that after a few turns of the monstrous contraption everyone drowns, particularly as it so often gets stuck and the person tied to it remains trapped under water.

'She will need to meet death and declare herself before God, just as the flames took her mother. There is nothing more we can do to help her.'

The well-dressed man steps into the tiny room and moves in closer to inspect Caitlin in greater detail, as she writhes on the bed with fear in her eyes. His hand lingers over her thighs under the guise of adjusting her nightgown to ensure her decency, while the priest remains distracted at the door adjusting his robes. She squirms beneath his touch, unable to alert the priest nor prevent the man's firm fingers pressing into the tender flesh of her inner thigh as she watches him appraising her curvaceous body and pert breasts, his eyes lusting over, rather than making contact with hers. Her muffled screams are barely audible to herself, let alone to others.

'Would you consider another fate for this sinner, Father?'

'It depends what you have in mind. She is a risk to society and herself, her urges now proven to be uncontrollable. I caught her in the very act of the forbidden myself, hence her restraints. She cannot be trusted alone, lest her fingers continue to search for the devil.'

'I see.' The man, never looking directly at her, ensures Caitlin's gag is secured before sliding his fingers along her décolletage and deliberately lingering over her breasts. The slightest of smiles quirks his lips as Caitlin's body freezes in fear, her nipples responding uncontrollably to his touch.

'She would need to be securely bound at all times, to give her any hope of salvation. Given her lineage, we already know she is unfit to be wed and to reproduce.' Reluctantly removing his hands from her body, the man continues his discussion.

'On the condition that I keep her restrained, and away from society, would you consider allowing me to resolve this quandary for you?'

The priest contemplates this offer for a moment; it would certainly save him a good deal of paperwork. The Church authorities aren't so quick to burn the condemned these days without due process being followed. He also has no mind to deal with another young, vile creature and her tireless screams, begging for forgiveness when being tortured, which of course comes far too late. The evil has already possessed their souls and the noise just gives him scorching headaches. The men exchange looks that indicate a deal sealing her fate could potentially be brokered. Caitlin, desperate to hear what the men are discussing, lies silent and still, her eyes wide with alarm.

'She would need to be permanently marked, to readily identify her as unclean to anyone who happens to cross her path.'

'That could certainly be arranged, Father, though the fewer who come in contact with her the better from my perspective,' he reflects, returning his gaze for one last salacious glance at Caitlin lying helplessly on the bed. 'Perhaps an additional offering for the restoration of the church's altar in preparation for Easter may help lift her bevy of sins.' The priest has been hoping to restore the altar for many years, but funds have needed to be allocated elsewhere and Easter has always been the most sacred of events in the church's calendar.

'That's a fine idea. I do believe we could certainly come to some suitable arrangement. God bless you for your kindness and generosity to the church. I just pray our Lord recognises your goodness at the gates of Heaven.'

The men converse with ease as a chill descends on Caitlin's body and she begins to shiver from head to toe.

'One more thing,' the priest adds as they turn to leave. 'Never look into her eyes, they will trap you in their evil. It has happened before.'

'Thank you for the advice, Father, I shall take heed.' He picks up a hessian sack from the floor and as if to prove to the priest how sincerely he takes his words, fully covers Caitlin's gagged face before leaving the room. 'I shall send my men to collect her later this morning.' They close the door behind them leaving Caitlin trembling with the fear of her unknown future instead of the fear of death.

* * *

Caitlin has no idea where she is. She arrives at her new destination in the same state she left the monastery.

The only words spoken to her during the transit involved the new rules that would govern her life. They involved addressing her new owner as 'master' at all times when being spoken to and facing the wall with her eyes closed whenever anyone enters the room.

Her hands remain bound together in front of her and it isn't until she hears the door close behind the men who fetched her from the monastery, that she dares attempt removal of the sack covering her face, along with the stuffed handkerchief in her dry mouth.

Hungry and desperately thirsty, she gasps in relief as she notices some water and bread on the bench, devouring both in seconds. What is to become of her now?

She eyes the dark room cautiously; there are no windows and she looks to be in a stone basement of some kind. There is a wooden ladder attached to the wall connecting with a horizontal door that seemingly forms part of the floor above. There is no handle and no means of escape. She huddles into the cold corner of the room in despair, wondering how her life has turned from such light with her mother to such desolate darkness in such a short space of years.

Someone enters the cell and Caitlin cowers in the corner covering her face with her hands, not knowing what to expect. She hears her new master's voice at the same time as she feels his firm hand grasp the back of her neck, lifting her to a standing position facing the wall. Before turning her around a soft black hood is placed over her head. Fear of the unknown ripples through her body as she detects the smell of molten iron wafting around her cell. Held in place by her master, she feels a rough hand grasp each ankle as she listens to the conversation unfold between the two men.

'Neither the Church nor God would ever forgive me should she escape,' her master explains. 'One as dangerous as she, the daughter of a witch no less, is intent on practising her craft.'

Caitlin feels heat in the room, then feels the heavy wrought iron being clasped around her extremities. She notices that, at the mention of the word witch, the tension with which the blacksmith is working tightens around her flesh as her new master continues chatting to him.

'Her wrists and ankles will be forever bound and chained within these walls in order for her to repent her wicked life.' His message is loud and clear as though he wants to assure the blacksmith how seriously he is taking the words of the priest. Caitlin's movements become severely restricted by the addition of heavily-weighted chains put into place by these God-fearing men. Her body remains limp and despondent as she wonders how her life turned into such a miserable existence.

Caitlin implicitly understands from overhearing her master that he appreciates his elevated position within the Church's community and will do anything to ensure this continues. He bids the blacksmith farewell and returns to her. Running his hands along the curves of her body as he attaches her bound wrists to the wall he whispers close to her ear: 'You understand that your life belongs to me now, don't you, my pet?' Petrified at his proximity she is unable to respond.

'Answer me,' he says in a low commanding voice as his fingers gently caress and stroke her neck and shoulders. Caitlin has never been this close to a man, let alone been touched by one the way he has touched her. Her mind is in a spin as his musky, sweat-filled scent permeates her senses.

She tentatively nods her head, not wanting to say the wrong thing.

'Speak, my pet, and answer me knowing who I am to you.' She can't help but scream into the cell as she feels a sharp bite as he takes her flesh between his teeth on her lower neck. Caitlin quickly tries to ascertain the meaning of his words before replying.

'Yes,' she pauses before adding, 'master.'

'Good, pet. You learn quickly.' His caressing fingers return to her available body as she remains hanging. She gasps as he unbuttons her shirt and releases her breasts one at a time. She can feel the bulge in his trousers against her but doesn't understand why it is hardening against her.

'My job is to remove your witchcraft, which have no fear I shall take seriously. Your job is to accept your fate and your new life. I own you and your body from this moment until you die. Do you understand what this means?'

She feels his breath on her back before he turns her around, her arms still bound above her head and attached to the wall. Guilt, shame, and humiliation course through her as she grapples with the pleasure she feels as he fondles her breasts. She can't reconcile any of the wild emotions rushing through her as her palms break into a sweat. She loses all concept of coherent thought as her body responds to such previously forbidden feelings. He pinches and twists her nipples, which sends a sharp, shooting sensation through her entire body that immediately tightens in her lower belly, her body involuntarily thrusting against the wall as she gasps at the painful shock of it.

'I will ask only once more. Do you understand what this means?'

Caitlin doesn't really understand what anything means: the force of the feelings shooting through her body at his proximity to her, his rough handling of her private parts, the fear pounding through her nerves. His fingers continue twisting her nipple as his teeth clamp down on the other one. The only words she needs to know from this point forward immediately escape her lips.

'Yes, master.' She screams through her hood. As soon as she utters these words his torturous twists turn into a long slow suckling of each nipple. She is deeply embarrassed by her feelings and the response of her body as something ignites in her groin and noisy groans escape her lips, echoing around the confines of the cell.

'Good pet, I'm so pleased we have reached this understanding.' He turns her around to face the wall and she feels the sharp sting as his hand comes down hard and fast on her buttocks before he promptly turns around and leaves.

Caitlin is left alone in the cell with nothing to focus on other than the confusion of her conflicted feelings. Though she fears her new master, and never knows whether she will be submitted to pleasure or pain, she also fears her loneliness when he leaves. Sometimes she wonders whether death would be any worse than living out the rest of her life in this blackened stone cell, never seeing another human soul again. Every time someone enters fear rises up within her, never knowing what to expect, but always knowing that whoever arrives, thanks to her master's guaranteed preamble, they believe she is akin to the devil incarnate.

Her master has taught her to face the corner with her eyes closed whenever she hears someone enter the room so her face can be completely covered with a hood. The one time she failed to obey this command she was whipped until she lost consciousness and food didn't arrive for some time; her only nourishment was drinking water from a bucket in the corner. Caitlin understood, from that point onwards, that every aspect of her diminished life is in his hands and she never makes the same mistake again, learning to meticulously follow his orders and instructions.

Her cries or screams don't seem to bother the people who come and go so she is never told to be quiet, though she understands her pleas fall on deaf ears. This darkness is her new reality and she begins to lose all sense of any other destiny. Day by day her body becomes his and her spirit weakens.

* * *

Caitlin no longer struggles when her wrists are clamped at an angle above her head and her ankles similarly anchored to the wall. She has no choice anyway, given the weight of her chains. Her cotton nightshirt is unbuttoned so her fully naked form is exposed underneath, her body opened in a spreadeagled position, only her face covered with the hood; as usual, she is prevented from witnessing the proceedings in the room with her own eyes.

'Today is the day you are to be marked, my pet, and I'm rather looking forward to the results. The evil in you may even enjoy it. We shall see.'

Caitlin has no idea what this means as her senses immediately shift to high alert. She inhales the bitter stench of the basement through her hood as well as the strange, astringent smell of alcohol, just seconds before she feels the sting on her wounds and cries out through the fabric with each swipe.

'Calm, my pet, there will be no whipping today. This young man is ensuring your ongoing health.' Her master's large hands cup either side of he face as her wounds continue to be tended to.

'Hold still, almost done.' Caitlin is surprised to hear kindness in the young man's voice, but no longer trusts anyone, especially male voices who talk to her when she is blind, bound, naked, and at their mercy. This man, in her mind, is no exception. She just knows that the stinging pain he administered was almost as bad as the whipping itself. She braces herself for what may come next.

She feels him hesitate with each stroke, sensing that he, like the others, has been warned about her witchery, as though he is trying to distance himself from her fate as a condemned woman.

Sensitive hands fondle her right breast, firmly massaging in circular motions. They are not her master's large, rough hands. No one has ever touched her so tenderly; Caitlin doesn't understand what she is feeling but at least it is not pain. Regardless, she has no way of preventing anything he may do to her body.

The man continues kneading her breast and though she remains on high alert for pain, she finds herself inexplicably relaxing enough to release her from her hyper-tense state, allowing her body to go limp under his touch. Caitlin is as surprised as the young man when she hears a light moan escape from her throat.

'That's enough, Lyon. She is never to experience pleasure without pain; that is God's will and it keeps her witchery at bay. Do it now.' She hears her master's command from the other side of the room.

'Yes, sir.' Lyon immediately stops massaging and pulls away from her as though she has tricked him into doing something that he shouldn't. The smell of alcohol fills her nostrils again as the cool ointment is wiped on her nipple. He pinches the tip of her nipple, lightly at first but then he twists it until she gasps in pain and her fear returns like the opening of floodgates. As if sensing her apprehension, he tightens his grip on her areola and she feels a sudden pain shooting through the sensitised skin of her protruding nipple. Caitlin's body jerks as she releases an almighty scream, sending her chains clanging against the stone wall as she attempts to catch her breath in an attempt to adjust to the shocking, burning sensation of her pierced, tender flesh.

She vaguely hears her master's voice in the background of her mind. 'Good work, continue. I'll be back.'

The man's hand then fondles and massages the left breast. This time Caitlin knows what to expect and won't allow herself to be lulled into any false sense of security as she attempts to prepare her body for the pain to come.

She waits a long time with her blinded eyes squeezed shut and her breath held, but nothing happens. Adrenaline continues to pump through her veins from the last stabbing pain, though the fear of the anticipated pain heightens the impact on her. Lyon's voice is so close and quiet against her ear she thinks she could be imagining it in her delirium.

'You have the symbol, under your left breast.'

Caitlin freezes in fear of his discovery of her secret, one she promised her mother she would never discuss. How could she possibly keep it covered in a position such as this, with someone so closely inspecting every intimate detail of her breasts and body?

He lifts her left breast; she can feel him examining it carefully, without pain. Her heart thumps in her chest so hard and fast she can hear it pounding in her ears. Anticipating death, she awaits her fate in the darkness ...

'You are a woman of the heart, not a witch.'

She immediately exhales but is not sure why as he continues to whisper in her ear, pushing part of the covering aside so his voice is less muffled. She can feel the warmth of his breath as he speaks to her.

'My mother told me this story every night before I slept. I know it word for word as she told me time and again.'

Caitlin remains still as she wonders how a bedtime story could possibly have anything to do with her.

'Once upon a time, there was a kind woman who lived in our village. She was referred to as "the woman of the heart" and could be identified by the birthmark of a heart on her left shoulder.'

Caitlin freezes in shock, unable to believe she is hearing the story of her mother from this man.

'There are only a few women with such a gift of magic and healing; they are revered by the common folk and their magic needs to be protected. Each generation is blessed by a woman of the heart, a true healer of the sick and desolate. One day, a boy so sick he was at the door of death was touched and blessed by such a woman. He returned to full health within three days, a true miracle in the village. Her daughter, also of the heart, attended the healing which made the young boy's recovery much faster. The young boy was given the gift of life, instead of having it taken from him. His mother told him, "If by chance you should ever meet a woman of the heart, and who is so marked, it is your duty to protect her from those who wish her harm." The young boy would grow into a strong man who would be clear in his destiny, understanding that his life would be dedicated to protecting the women of the heart, just as they had helped him.'

Caitlin doesn't say anything, not knowing how to react. She knows this symbol on her body should be hidden, should never be discussed, but she also remembers her mother speaking of men who would protect her when the time came. Still untrusting, and unable to look into the young man's eyes to see the truth, she remains silent.

'I know this story is no fable,' says the man, 'because I am the boy, the boy you and your mother healed when I was to die. It is my duty to protect you.'

In spite of her determination to remain unaffected, Caitlin's eyes fill with tears and her body quivers with emotion as she hears these words.

'I will need time but I will ultimately ensure your safety. That is my promise.'

Caitlin exhales with relief and hope, even though she knows she can't verify his words. But it has been so long since there was anyone who showed her compassion.

'However, to protect and help you in the future, I must follow through on your master's commands today and do this first. I am sorry.'

Another hot white pain flashes and she screams louder and harder this time. The build-up of frustration, physical pain and emotional agony finds its release from her body in one last bloodcurdling scream. She slumps in her restraints, as her body adjusts to the pain in her nipples and her heart. In doing so, she experiences the strange sensation between her legs that she felt the night the priest found her, a tingling warmth that spreads from her groin to her belly. At least she knows that she can still feel — whether it is pain or pleasure makes no difference to her. None of this makes any sense, but now she has some hope, where moments before she only had despair. She believes the warmth in her body is a sign of this hope. So she temporarily relinquishes her spirit to her captivity and accepts her fate. The quiet, kind voice, the perpetrator of her pain and her surprising warmth, is literally the only hope she has left.

* * *

Caitlin has no world outside the four walls of her prison. There is no light, for weeks no one speaks to her. In the endless darkness her mind becomes acutely aware of senses other than sight. She can't remember the last time she heard a woman's voice, saw another human being, smelled the rain or the touch of fresh air on her skin. Let alone be given the opportunity to look into someone's eyes and see the depths of their soul. She misses this connection more than anything, never knowing until it was taken away just how much it was part of her being.

Her life consists of the comings and goings of her master who saved her from execution but seems intent on dooming her to a living hell and Lyon, the man who pierced her nipples and tends to all her wounds, regularly checking to ensure they are healing.

Her master beats Caitlin using some kind of riding crop or leather strap, not so much to cause any permanent injury or concern, but enough to ensure that the traces of witchcraft that were entering her body are kept at bay, in order to fulfil his commitment to the priest and therefore the Church. He reinforces with his words and actions that as long as he continues with frequent punishments, the magic will be unable to settle in her bones, thereby aiding her potential salvation. He explains that to protect her from herself and her evil, she shall be fitted with a chastity belt to which he alone has the key.

Over time, Lyon inserts progressively heavier and larger rings, ensuring that she is clearly marked as per her master's promise to the old priest. Caitlin doesn't understand her confused feelings for Lyon, the faceless man who knows her secret, and is ashamed to admit she looks forward to him fondling and touching her nipples when he comes. She finds herself unable to hide or control her obvious arousal from him. Her master is never far away when Lyon is in her cell and the risk of them exchanging any words are too great.

One evening, just after he has replaced the nipple ring and left, her master arrives and slides his fingers between her legs, feeling for himself the warm moisture between them.

'My pet, your nipple rings arouse you, do they, now that they are fully healed?' Caitlin freezes. He lifts her leg and grips it in his hand while his fingers penetrate her inner folds. She can feel the wetness within her clearing his path as her body spontaneously heats beneath his touch.

'I asked you a question,' he says firmly as he removes his fingers and abruptly slides them into her mouth. 'But I agree, this time there is no need for you to respond when the answer is so obvious.' He covers her tongue with her own juices and she has no choice but to taste the sweet saltiness of her sex.

'Wouldn't you agree? Answer me, now, so I can hear your voice.' He deliberately leaves his fingers stuffed in her mouth.

'Yes, master.' She mumbles the muffled words and prays for mercy.

'Suck them clean, you dirty pet.'

From this point onwards Caitlin's captivity changes. Her master rewards her for her complete submission by enabling her body to receive almost unbearable pleasure. He understands every response to her body before she knows it herself. He takes his time to locate every hidden sensitive crevice and how it responds to his touch, whether it be firm or soft, fast or slow. He recognises that she is unable to control her gasps and moans

226

whether it be from pain or pleasure and relishes in the noises her body produces under the control of his touch.

Caitlin comes to understand her master appreciates routine and expects perfection. His arrival in the basement is preceded by a bell, at which sound she removes her clothes, places the hood over her head — as he is forever fearful she may look at his eyes and ignite her devilish magic — and is to bend over a sloping board he has made especially for her.

On her knees she bends her body over the raised platform, her buttocks protruding with her head lowered. She must connect her nipple rings to the attachments on the board and rest her arms by her body awaiting her master's arrival. Sometimes he pins her arms behind her back, connecting her wrists together, other times he stretches her arms out in front, locking them beyond her head. Occasionally he leaves her arms free. Every time, however, the nipple rings control her movements more effectively than any other restraint, ensuring her stillness and his ultimate control over her body. He has explained to her that this simple act, by trapping the most feminine part of her body, offers her the best hope of eliminating any potential witchcraft possessing her. The difference between maintaining this position with the precision he expects is the difference between a punishing beating and a rewarding orgasm, either way she is left utterly spent when he leaves.

'My pet, it is time to prepare you for penetration. To accommodate man and, once and for all, to force out the devil.'

Attached to the board, he massages her buttocks with lard, taking his time to ensure she is well lubricated before any penetration occurs. He slides his fingers along her crack before tracing circles around her anus. Her breath freezes on entry until her rectum adjusts to the plug being inserted, which settles within her.

'Keep breathing, my pet.' His large hand firms over her lower back.

She is always conscious not to wriggle or move. Each rise and fall of her chest has the potential to either stimulate her nipples, or cause instant shooting pain should she jerk too hard, and it takes all her concentration to ensure it's the former sensation she has to deal with.

Once the discomfort from the plug has subsided, although it remains firmly lodged within her, the sting of the belt hits her buttocks. Always ten strokes, five on each cheek, unless something is not to his liking, then it can be any number more. This pain she learns to manage. Her main concern is managing to keep her chest steady on the board with each blow, which provides a small distraction from the blow itself.

The best and worst part of this exercise, after the punishment for her sins has been delivered, are his questing fingers that have become expert at playing with and teasing her inner folds. She is deeply ashamed of the anticipation and arousal she feels when she longs for his touch and cannot understand how her body can experience such pleasure after the pain that has been inflicted. He has complete control of her orgasms that can either be small, releasing a few mild pants or cause great shuddering, uncontrollable spasms and reverberating screams of euphoria around her cell.

Strangely for one so committed to routine, there is never any regularity or rhythm as to how long he takes, so she can never control her breathing enough to manage her trapped body. She both fears and longs for the feelings of ecstasy he causes that allow her to escape momentarily from this earthly world.

Every few days Lyon appears in her cell to bathe her and tend to any wounds on her body. He brushes her long hair and scrubs and trims her nails. It is his job to ensure she is clean and acceptable to her master. He does a thorough job of looking after her and though he has never spoken again of her being a woman of the heart, she senses the kindness in his touch.

Her master, while able to elicit almost unbearable pleasure and pain over her body with his clever fingers, never penetrates her vagina and is delighted when her anus is ready to accommodate his manhood.

'My pet, congratulations on your progress. You are finally ready.' Caitlin's breathing quickens as she realises what is going to happen. She is stunned when she receives no lashes on this day. His mastery over her body ensures she reaches a shattering orgasm before she feels his penis penetrate her from behind. Her master's fastidious preparation makes her first experience of sodomy more pleasurable than Caitlin would have ever believed possible and he gifts her with multiple orgasms, leaving her absolutely exhausted.

That night she receives a banquet almost fit for a queen and she has an appetite to match the volume of food delivered into her cell. Just as he controls every aspect of her physical being, she senses her spirit completely surrender to her master, allowing herself the luxury of forgetting the world she had once known.

Her master tells her that he has sent a message of gratitude to the old priest for suggesting she be marked. He proclaims the nipple rings have provided the key to the successful submission of her witchcraft, enabling her to live a more pure life and recommends their use for other offenders under the influence of the devil. He believes that surely this triumph is a clear sign from god that he did the right thing by saving his pet's life and is grateful he did so. For reasons undisclosed to Caitlin, he now believes he can move on with his own life.

* * *

I'm drawn away from the scene and I'm left with thoughts and emotions swirling around my psyche. For the first time in my life, I have to consider that this is where my secret fantasy stems from, rather than some psychological deficiency leading to masochistic tendencies. The intense feelings of being bound, blind, punished and pleasured that have haunted me my entire life, but never made any logical sense, have just been played out in front of me. Feelings I have felt personally, that I know mirrored Caitlin's. A sexual fantasy I shared with Jeremy very briefly years ago that formed the basis of my thesis have just been replayed, relived by me.

Caitlin's fear was my fear, her shame my shame. The shame of desiring something that seems so evil and wrong, but wanting it so much because the sheer pleasure of submitting to it was undeniable. Sexually awakening my body, awakening the feelings that lay dormant for so many years, has brought me to understand that my carnal needs derive from a space and time inextricably linked to my ancestry. My feelings and desires were ignited by arousal and sexual acts that stem from centuries ago. I can't help but wonder how much more we have to learn about our psyche, how much more we have yet to tap into. After all my years of psychological study and experience, never before would I have considered this to be a potentially viable explanation for sexual preferences. Yet, I've just witnessed the very source of my tendencies, my arousal. Sexual acts that challenge my personal boundaries, yet excite me beyond belief.

I could feel the confusion in Caitlin's feelings, the turmoil of never wanting to give up on her mother and her own destiny; almost craving the physical pain of the beatings to subdue the emotional pain and anguish in her heart. All the while, her body reacted against the absolute intrusion into her secret orifices yet greedily accepted the orgasmic highs, just as I have found myself in similar situations throughout my life. Jeremy awakened me to anal pleasures in my youth, though

I desperately wanted to avoid it from fear of the unknown pain. He re-awakened my sexual being when I had believed I was past my use-by date, allowing me to explore the dark fantasies of my mind, never judging, though gently coercing, yet always right by my side. I understand intimately what Caitlin was going through, how she was desperately trying to maintain control in an environment in which she had none.

This irreconcilable fantasy of mine, that I have to admit was a major impetus in my studying psychology in the first place and was a direct influence on my thesis, appears to be a fragment from a past life. One that Jeremy recreated during our weekend together, which has led me to experience a sequence of events I would never have believed possible.

I could have sworn my own nipples were being pierced as Caitlin's were, feeling the searing pain as it happened and then the erotic aftershocks she was determined to bury and ignore. The tips of my own breasts still feel swollen, aroused and tingle with the memory. Even though my physical body is weak, my mind has never been sharper. It's as though the insights I'm receiving are being processed at higher levels in my brain.

The vision of Caitlin in her cell is no different to how the image has played around in my dreams for years, albeit in a different time or century. A shameful fantasy that has haunted me since adolescence, preyed on my mind, teased me to attempt, to understand. I was never brave enough. In all my studies, my prescribed theories,

232

never once did I consider that these raw emotions and feelings might derive from a real time and place.

I'm shocked at this discovery, but desperate to understand Caitlin's destiny and how it may link further to my own. I send myself back into the ether with these thoughts swirling around my brain.

* * *

One day, her master appears in her cell without sounding the bell, something that has never happened before.

'Turn around and face the wall.' She hears his booming voice as he enters. Caitlin has not seen her master's face since the day at the monastery. She quickly follows his instructions as she has been trained to do, lest he should immediately pull out his belt. He places the hood over her head before addressing her in an abrupt tone.

'I am to be married so you will be moving to the forest. Lyon will take you. Listen carefully to my rules, as they are not to be broken. Do you understand?'

'Yes, master.' Caitlin's voice reflects the shock she was feeling.

'You will not leave the forest.

'You will not remove your nipple rings.

'You will wear your chains and chastity belt on the night of the full moon.

'I will attend to your punishments to keep your witchcraft at bay once a week. Lyon will prepare you.

'You are forbidden to speak to anyone other than myself or Lyon.

'Should you disobey any of my rules you will be tried as a witch. Do you understand?'

'Yes, master.'

'Whom do you belong to pet?'

'You, master.'

'What part of you?'

'All of me, master.'

'Never forget it.' He slaps Caitlin's buttocks to reinforce his point and binds her wrists in front of her.

'Lyon, get in here. She's ready to go.'

* * *

Lyon takes Caitlin to a small cottage deep in the woods on her master's vast estate, where she will have no contact with society. As outlined, her master punishes and pleasures her once a week, to ensure her witchcraft never sets in. Lyon continues to take responsibility for Caitlin's ongoing wellbeing, given they are the only two people who know of her existence. He ensures she is bound and blind for her master's weekly visit and most importantly that she is hooded, fully bound and chained within the tiny house with her chastity belt firmly fixed to prevent her sinful fingers, every night of the full moon, when she is of greatest risk to herself and others.

Caitlin, having believed she would never escape either the dormitory or the basement that confined her, can't believe her good fortune at these new arrangements and is deeply grateful to Lyon for having organised it with the master. After years of death and darkness looming over her, she rejoices in the solitude of the forest. As long as she obeys the rules, she has more freedom than she has experienced since the death of her mother.

Instead of feeling violated by the ongoing constraints in her life, she counts her blessings that there is hope where there used to be none. She understands that it has taken Lyon many months to sway her master to make these arrangements, to give her a life outside the cell and reconnect her with nature and she is deeply grateful to him. Other than Lyon, she still longs to look into the eyes of another human soul and Lyon assures her that he is working toward making that a possibility.

One day Caitlin is embracing the feel of the sunshine on her deprived skin, humming as she plants a small garden near the cottage, when she hears a rustling in the bushes. She stills.

'Hello,' a voice calls, 'is anyone there? I heard you singing so I'm hoping you can hear me.'

Caitlin runs back to her cottage, fearing for her safety. Though she secretly longs for human interaction, she knows it is forbidden. Hearing heavy footsteps running toward her, she speeds up, almost making it to the cottage to close the door behind her but she trips on her long skirts and topples over, knocking her head against a rock.

As she opens her eyes, she feels the softness of her bed beneath her and turns to see a tall man standing in the tiny cottage, drinking from his flask and staring directly back into her eyes.

Her heart stops beating for a long moment as their eyes connect with one another. She can sense this man's good nature along with a restlessness and lack of control. She also knows that her nipples have instantly hardened at the sight of his tousled dark hair, mischievous green eyes and cheeky grin.

'My name is John. I brought you in here when you hit your head.'

Not wanting to break any rules lest she be punished, she remains resolutely silent.

He had been appraising this beauty singing in the forest for well on an hour. Her long dark hair is braided in parts and looks as wild as the forest in others. Her lithe limbs and curvaceous body ooze sensuality and he was immediately drawn to her, almost dangerously so. As he carried her inside he had opportunity to feel her soft warmth against his own growing erection. After he carefully laid her on the bed, he stepped away, able to absorb her beauty as she rested. He noticed the outline of the rings connected to her nipples and was initially taken aback. Who is this woman? He has been with many women and has only encountered this once on his travels, though he didn't get close enough to touch.

They maintain their steady gaze in silence, his arousal strengthening as he notices her nipples swelling beneath her blouse.

This man captivates Caitlin, it's as though he has the power to put her under a spell, not the other way around. She has never experienced such feelings and her breath quickens as he takes a step closer, as if he is being magnetically drawn to her. She watches intently as he kneels beside the bed, his eyes reflecting her own soul as if they have met before. She senses she is privy to a secret and unexpected homecoming, as the beat of their hearts regulate their breath to each other's tempo. Their longing for each other is undeniable as the atmosphere intensifies between them, their limbic systems in overdrive trying to accommodate the raw sexual energy they are experiencing but not understanding how or why this is happening. Just simply knowing their union is meant to be.

Slowly, he reaches out to her and silently she allows him to touch. She knows not whether to expect pleasure or pain from this man before her, never having felt the softness of a touch without the preceding punishment. Her feelings for him are both rapturous and confused as she finds herself increasingly unable to control the responses of her own body.

He senses her apprehension and smooths her creased brow with his thumb; without a word he soothes her concerns. Totally absorbed in the beauty of her face, he continues his exploration of her features, his thumb sensually sliding along the profile of her face, eventually circling her lips.

She inhales deeply, parting her voluptuous mouth allowing him to tease and play with her tongue. The feelings that are literally taking her breath away transfer to her groin and a cry of anticipation escapes her lips.

His hands move down to explore the curvaceous terrain of her body. He takes his time, adapting the rhythm of his touch to her breathing. He's aching to peel back the clothes covering her, but he forces himself to go slowly. Inch by inch he slides her dress up her thighs, the intensity of his gaze letting her know how hungrily he anticipates what wonders may lie beneath.

Her breath stills when his hand slides between her moistened loins. She releases a soft moan at the sensitivity of his touch.

Ignited by her sounds, he positions himself alongside her and unravels her body of all clothing. He has never felt such fierce desire for someone, and marvels at the sight before him. He kisses her lips, softly at first, before deepening the kiss as his passion rises.

She clings to him but he gently lays her back. The last thing he wants to do in this strangely sacred moment is rush his exploration, lest he neglect some of the intricacies her body has to offer his touch. He positions her arms above her head so her neck, breasts and arms are available for his lips to explore. He slows his pace even more so, inhaling every scent he can extract from her body, never wanting or needing someone more under his skin. He plays and tantalises but never penetrates.

Caitlin has never felt more alive or desired. She is so moved by these feelings, tears escape the corners of her eyes just as wetness builds between her legs.

Flashes of her beloved mother in the field flood her mind as she wonders if these feelings that she is experiencing for the first time could be what her mother felt; she remembers how beautiful and sensual she looked as she danced and the people worshipped her body. It is with these thoughts that Caitlin finds the courage to explore his body, just as he did hers. She too kisses and plays, fascinated by the responses she can elicit from his body at her touch. Never before has she been allowed to look at or explore a penis, only ever felt it blindly behind her. She is in awe of the size and hesitatingly kisses its tip. A little fluid erupts from its head and she tastes its saltiness as he smiles beneath her, encouraging her to continue.

The muscled strength and nakedness of this beautiful man intrigues her, his warmth and masculinity offering her a magical connection she never knew two people could share. Soon they are fully acquainted with one another's bodies, and having taken the time to discover an understanding of each other's most sensual and responsive areas, their intimacy reaches new heights.

For the next few hours their lovemaking is passionate and bold, raw and tender. She loves what he can do to her breasts with the rings, arousing all sorts of alluring sensations both externally and within her. Every time he pulls or nips her tips, she feels as though her groin will explode with desire and at times it does, leaving her wondering in shock how he achieves these uncontrollable eruptions within her.

He strokes her hair and her body until her erotic convulsions subside to quivers, until they can reconnect again. He wants her to feel everything her body is capable of under his touch and her own. So strong is his attraction to this exotic, curvaceous creature his erection never subsides, and he makes the most of every moment they share.

Caitlin loses her virginity to this charismatic man who encourages her to surrender her body to experience the wonders of human intimacy and ecstasy. Their lovemaking has enabled their minds and souls to connect, as though their bodies were intricately designed for each other. Rather than carefully having to manage her movements to accommodate her punishments, she craves his phallus and the feeling of completeness it creates within her.

He is more than willing to satisfy her desires, as many times as she wishes.

* * *

John tenderly kisses Caitlin's sleeping lips after he has dressed, knowing his men are awaiting his arrival further down the river. He had already been gone too long. Though he knows their meeting was mere chance and that it is impossible for them to progress beyond this brief interlude given his gypsy lifestyle, he knows he will never forget this emerald-eyed beauty with wild dark hair and exotically ringed breasts. He bids her a loving farewell.

When Caitlin wakes she wonders whether her feelings were all part of an erotic dream. She lowers her hands between her legs and feels his seed within her. She smiles a private, indulgent smile that she has been given this opportunity to experience such sheer human joy. Finally, she feels as though her destiny has changed course for the better, for she knows that this man, whoever he was, only adored her — fear was not part of his being. Caitlin never sees him again.

Over the next few weeks, she sees less and less of her master and she wonders why. Her breasts are swollen and tender and she notices a firmness in her belly. Lyon has been looking after her and she asks him.

'I'm not sure what is wrong with my body, it's changing.' He moves toward her and places his palm on her belly.

'How did this happen?'

Caitlin isn't entirely sure what he means, so remains silent.

'Caitlin, your master didn't do this, please answer me.' Concerned by the fear in his voice she turns around, unable to meet his eyes. She is unsure whether to tell him the truth but also unsure about what is wrong with her.

'Tell me, was there a man here?' he asks gently.

'Yes.'

'Did he penetrate you?'

'Yes.'

'You are with child.'

Caitlin almost collapses in wonder. How did this happen? It is a miracle, a sign from the gods, that she should procreate. She can't deny the smile on her face or the tears of joy in her eyes.

'What are we to do now?'

Feeling euphoric though sensing his despair, she bravely but tentatively steps forward and embraces him with the warmth of her body. Slowly he looks at her face and their eyes meet. She feels his warmth and compassion, knowing that her mother's blood healed this man. They are connected. He will protect her by taking whatever role he needs to play … it is his destiny.

'We must leave this village and travel far from here before your master returns from his trip and finds you like this.'

Wasting no time, Lyon organises what they need for their imminent departure. He removes Caitlin's nipple rings for the last time, symbolically releasing her from her captivity, and closes the door behind them on their past. Together, they move far away. Caitlin delivers healthy twin girls, and Lyon raises them as his own daughters. Both are blessed with the sign of the heart on their skin, signalling their healing blood. He spends the rest of his life protecting and providing for his cherished wife and her daughters knowing they alone provide the lineage to their sacred bloodline. Caitlin is tentative at first about trialling the healing power of her blood, but her confidence grows as her daughters age. Their life continues comfortably, as man and wife, knowing that their bond to each other goes far beyond such ceremony, and reaches into the very core of their souls.

* * *

As I float away from Caitlin's life I see fragments of the twins' lives and their children, their children's children and so on like cards flipping quickly through a pack. It provides me with a sense of their healing blood being diluted, its magic fading over time, and ends with my own grandmother smiling warmly and knowingly. She encourages me to continue on my journey with her outstretched hands and if my eyes could shed tears they would be reflecting the love in my heart for her, as she died many years ago. In desperate hope, I reach out to touch her and her image floats away into the ether.

As this occurs, I feel my ethereal presence being pushed into a vortex. Everything around me is tinged in dark red before the vision clears and I see Jeremy and Leo watching me during the experiment as I swirl toward them in the whirlpool of life. As I pass through this turbulence, and the images of the men, my heart pumps loudly around me. I feel like I am the life force of the healing blood itself and everything stills other than my beating heart and the energy sending blood coursing through my veins, until I am forcefully pulled through its energy to the other side and return to my earthly state.

Gasping for air with my eyes wide open, I find myself staring into the eyes of my ancestral companions — one my lover and the other my guardian. We three, whose destinies have finally collided after centuries of missed opportunities, have ignited the enigma of my blood. I now have the knowledge that Leo more than likely has had for quite some time: that we played an incredibly important part in each other's past lives, that in essence, all of this is meant to be.

I wonder whether they are part of each other's lives because of me, or whether they too have their own unique connection to each other. I consider the fleeting arrival and departure of John in Caitlin's life and their physical allure connecting them as if their limbic systems were communicating in a way which gave them no choice but to awaken each other sexually — the exact same way I feel toward Jeremy. Never being able to deny him anything he asked. He awakened me sexually just as John did Caitlin, and I thank god that we were granted another opportunity to be together after our lives separated us from each other the first time. I have so many questions flooding my brain as I consider the events of my recent life since reconnecting with Jeremy. I wonder about Leo's experience of soul flight, his reading of my thesis and the results from Jeremy's experiments.

Although I understand that there is something unique in my blood under certain scenarios, I know I don't have a heart-shaped birthmark on my body and, to the best of my knowledge, neither do my mother or sister. So although I know the ancestry of the blood relates to me, I don't have the sign, nor do I understand how it came about in the first instance. As always, I seem to have more questions than answers but nevertheless, I am learning that despite my frustrations everything gets revealed as and when it needs to be, and not beforehand.

I can't believe I was concerned about experiencing soul flight when it has already revealed so much. I relish the sounds of the Amazon, being at one with nature and barely hovering above my physical form. I am aware of being moved, but have no control of my limbs so merely accept what happens. I feel no pain, no discomfort. I just have the awesome ability to fly wherever the wind in the sky takes me. I wonder what more I can possibly learn from this insightful and magical journey.

Lake Bled

The national police have sent a map through to Martin's phone detailing what they believe is an entrance into Xsade's facility beneath Lake Bled. He meets up with Luke, and the members of the task squad, at the entrance of a massive storm water drain on the outskirts of town through which they hope they can make their way into the illegal complex. Martin is pleased they have come prepared; fully armed and with equipment that may be required should they need to make their way in by force. The elite group debrief and agree on a plan of action for when they gain access to the facility. They switch on their flashlights and cautiously enter the cavernous tunnel.

Xsade's security system has recorded a breach in their facility, and the Head of Security is glad he's on duty, filling in for one of the team. This provides him with a hands-on opportunity to run through their new procedures. The alarm is sounding in their offices and security cameras that continually scan the perimeter are now confirming infrared images of humans penetrating secured access points. The security chief immediately presses the lockdown button for the security gates. Unfortunately, nothing occurs and he wonders whether there has been a malfunction.

Now that the figures are in clearer view on CCTV, he sees they are heavily armed. Fearing they are entering the facility to steal patented formulas, he begins procedures to protect the facility by instigating a series of explosions. This new equipment was recently installed under the explicit instructions of Madame Jurilique to protect Xsade's intellectual property. It has been designed to alert all employees to evacuate the premises and fully protect and secure their confidential assets. He can't believe his luck in being on duty when it needs to be utilised. He presses the detonate button. And pauses. Nothing happens. He presses it again, twice for good measure. This time the system activates both the alarm and the explosions to deter the intruders. That should stop them in their tracks. He has a chuckle as he considers the old girl Jurilique wasn't so daft in spending shareholder funds on this new system after all. He settles back into his chair to watch the action on his multitude of screens. He shouldn't need to be evacuated if all goes to plan.

* * *

Martin and the team have made steady progress into the depths of the tunnel. But suddenly, about two hundred metres in, they feel the ground beneath their feet quake before they hear the rumble of the accompanying explosion.

'What the hell was that?' Martin yells.

Unsure whether to move further into the tunnel or run, they pause a few moments to assess the situation. Another loud boom thunders in their eardrums as they cover their ears with their hands.

Martin's concern for Salina and Josef reaches fever pitch, knowing that in all probability they are inside the facility. His unwavering commitment to Leo propels him forward faster and deeper into the tunnel with Luke following just behind him. They reach a locked steel gate and yell to the police that they need their equipment.

Just as they catch up and ignite their blowtorch to cut through the bars, they hear muffled screams coming from beyond the gates. After a few minutes they can see people pouring out of the darkness in the tunnel, some wearing silver suits, some in lab coats and others in plain clothes. They are covering their faces, protecting themselves as they run forward toward the security grid blocking their passage.

'Quickly, people are trapped, they need to get out of here.' Martin's usually controlled voice is laced with an undercurrent of fear, particularly as he notices smoke escaping from the depths of the tunnel behind the crowd. The police commander is urgently shouting instructions to his men. The crowd has reached the gate and is screaming for release, terror evident in their eyes as their screams grow louder. As one bar of the security gate is cut open, bare hands grab hold of it and loosen it further, bending it backwards and forwards.

The police shout at people to stand back as they go to start on the next one when someone from the depths of the crowd pushes through yelling that he has the code. After much shuffling of bodies, he finally makes his way through and with trembling hands enters a code into the keypad on the side of the tunnel wall. The gate swings open and the crowd cheers before surging forward, stumbling over each other and almost crushing some people, everyone desperately seeking the freedom of fresh air and the sky above.

Martin and Luke, stunned to see some children in the crush, help them and some women to their feet and set them on their way.

'I'm going in,' Martin yells. 'I need to find Salina and Josef.'

'It's not safe,' warns the commander. 'You heard the explosions. It could have been anything in a lab like this.'

'Do you have chemical masks?'

He nods and gestures to one of his men to get them out.

Martin turns to Luke. 'You need to leave the tunnel, it's unstable. Check the surrounds of the lake, they might be there.'

Luke hesitates.

'I want you out of here, now. Go.'

'Okay. I'll see you out there.'

'Run, make sure the others are alright.' Martin breathes a sigh of relief as he sees Luke turn around and run back out toward safety. He lost one of his men once and has never forgiven himself.

The commander hands him a mask which he fits over his head and covers his hands in gloves, ensuring none of his skin is exposed to whatever may have exploded in there. Another smaller explosion rocks the ground and more people come trickling out as Martin, followed by the commander and a small group of his men, make their way inside Xsade.

People within the facility scurry around like rats on a sinking ship, searching for any path to safety they can find as the evacuation signals deafen their ears. The scene is utter chaos, but thankfully there isn't too much smoke just yet. The police assist as many people as possible, pointing in the direction of the storm water tunnel until they are the only ones left in the immediate area.

Martin yanks a fire extinguisher from its bracket on the wall when a flicker of flame catches his eye from a doorway down the corridor. He bolts toward it, praying to god that Salina and Josef are not trapped inside, and enters. He closes the door to the lab to contain the fire, hoping like hell that the labs here have been made as fireproof as possible and breathes a sigh of relief as he notices the ceiling sprinklers are working.

He sees a pair of legs in the adjacent room lying on a lounger, emerging from beneath a massive machine covering the top half of the body. He indicates this to the commander before using the weight of the extinguisher to bash through the glass of the locked door.

He has no idea whether this person is dead, unconscious or sleeping, but they obviously haven't heard any alarms or felt the explosions. Both men try lifting the equipment off, but it appears to be secured in place.

They realise it is a woman trapped under the equipment, so the commander grabs hold of one of the legs and shakes it — both legs jerk in response. The next thing they hear is a bloodcurdling scream. The woman's legs and arms are flailing on either side of the machine covering her upper body. They see the ultraviolet light inside the equipment as the woman's screaming continues.

'My face, my face! It's burning! Help, get it off me.'

Still unable to budge the weight of the equipment, Martin searches for the power source, eventually flicking the switch and yanking out the cord to cut off the supply. The woman sounds in unbearable pain with her limbs thrashing about in every direction.

As Martin rushes back, he trips over a Louis Vuitton handbag and dislodges his mask. It is only then that the putrid smell of burning flesh penetrates his nostrils so intensely it causes him to dry retch on the floor beside her. The commander is still having no luck when they hear and feel yet another explosion further down the corridor of the facility.

As Martin pulls himself together in one last attempt to free this trapped, burning woman, two people covered in blood and smoke appear at the door.

'Salina, Josef. My god, are you alright?' By the looks of them both they have been through a lot.

'We are okay, Martin,' Salina replies. 'What are you doing here? What's going on?'

'She's trapped, we can't get the machine to release. It's computer encoded or something and won't budge.'

Josef immediately drops beneath the machine. 'The equipment locks down when the system has been corrupted in some way. There is a manual override located underneath that will release it.' They hear a loud click as the machine finally comes away and reveals a ugly mess of mottled, bloody flesh beneath it.

Salina immediately turns her head to vomit in the corner as Josef covers his nose the best he can with his shirt and assesses the damage.

'Pass me that water,' he yells to the commander who is standing next to a water jug and some glasses. Josef carefully rinses water over the raw, burning flesh, fearing for her life rather than her looks, which he knows will never be saved.

Another explosion rocks each of them off balance.

'We need to get out of here, now, this place is about to go,' the commander yells.

'You go, I need a couple more minutes or she'll die,' Josef answers as he remains focussed on the task at hand.

'You two go. I'll carry her when Josef's finished. We'll be right behind you.' Martin isn't budging without knowing both Salina and Josef are safe.

They all exchange tentative and worried looks between them before the commander and Salina make their way toward the tunnel.

Josef frantically prepares some cold, wet compresses and applies them to her face before carefully wrapping a bandage from the first aid kit around her entire head and neck. It is only at this point he recognises the ostentatious diamond ring on the hand of this victim as Jurilique's. He immediately stills.

'What's wrong?' Martin asks, concerned that yet another explosion has rocked the floor and they are still here.

'Nothing.' Josef's medical training and desire to save lives easily overrides any other thoughts he might have about his disturbed and corrupt ex-boss. He wouldn't wish the pain of these burns upon anyone, even a woman like Madeleine. Josef registers the desperation in her terrified eyes before he covers her face completely in an attempt to save the burned flesh.

'Okay, that's the best I can do right now.'

Martin goes to hoist her up over his shoulder but Josef grabs his arm to stop him.

'No, we must try and keep her face as still as possible, otherwise blood will rush to her head.'

The two men carry her out, face up, as fast as they can. Fire and explosions chase them out of the facility and into the storm water tunnel.

Part Seven

The earth does not belong to man: man
  belongs to the earth.
All things are connected like the blood,
  which unites one family.
Man does not weave the web of life; he is
  merely a strand in it.
Whatever he does to the web, he does to
  himself.

Chief Seattle, Letter to all, 1854

Alexa

I am slipping into varying states of consciousness with ease though it is increasingly beyond my control. Sometimes I am fully cognisant of what is happening around me, other times I merely slip into another world and time. I am vaguely aware that my body doesn't want for much but my soul is vital and hungry to show me more so eagerly takes me away. I can hear sounds around me but still no one speaks to me so I'm never distracted from my immersion in the spirit world.

It is during one of these returns to consciousness that I become aware that I'm surrounded by the women of the tribe. There are no men in this hut, just women chanting around my resting body. I don't have the energy to lift my head from my lying position so I merely turn it from side to side. My eyes widen as I focus on what is happening around me. The women are in simple traditional clothing, which barely covers their bodies, and one of them is wearing an elaborate decorated headdress made from feathers and beads.

We are in a small, enclosed thatched hut and the air I breathe is thick and hazy. It stems from some smoking rocks and plants in the corner, presumably a form of incense.

No words are spoken. I don't feel the need and know they won't be returned anyway. I'm comfortable with this and not speaking seems to preserve what little energy I have. I abstractly wonder about my children, knowing they haven't been in my presence for however long this journey has taken in its timeless dimension. I perceive reassuringly they are safe and that, in their minds my absence has not been too great. This knowledge provides me with a sense of wellbeing for them.

I make eye contact with the woman in the headdress as she comes toward me to lift my head in her arms. Still chanting, she brings some liquid to my lips and tips it carefully into my mouth, before lowering my head back onto the stretcher. My eyes close as their chanting increases in volume and I recede into the eye of the eagle flying high over the lush lands of the Amazon.

I come to again with awareness of small, light strokes being painted on my body. I can't move, my body is too weak. It is as though I only exist in this body through my eyes, though I can still feel every sensation. I'm disconnected but aware.

My insights to date have been profound, though my inability to move my physical form means I haven't been able to record anything in my journal. This world and the past world shift and blur with ease. I can't remember when I last saw Jeremy or Leo, as time is no longer a measure that I comprehend. I'm assuming they are close but I understand that this preparation I am going through with the tribal women attending to me is somehow strictly women's business.

I notice I am naked. My body is being decorated with fine lines of dark paint, no doubt extracted from some plant or flower. I can only gather I am being prepared for some from of ritual or sacred event. I can't imagine what but given everything I have seen and experienced — if that is the right word — on my soul flight so far, I know I needn't prepare, just accept whatever happens. Perhaps my time has come to finally meet the shaman.

I am perfectly still as the chanting woman continue their activities around me, my body content with being a canvas for the women's artwork. Considering the minute detail with which they are applying their strokes, this is not a project that will be completed any time soon.

Once again my head is lifted and I feel the warm, herbal liquid entering my mouth and moments later I am flying again.

* * *

The battered ship lands on the shores of Ireland from the freezing waters of the North Atlantic Ocean. Some men are weary, some dead but most eager to ravage this newly-discovered land. Batons in hands and helmets on heads, the men scour the countryside in search of civilisation, food, shelter and wealth of any kind to extend their empire. These huge Nordic men, covered in animal skins, are silenced by their leader as they notice the shimmering flames of fire atop the hillside. Their robust bodies stride steadily closer to the scene and bear witness; unusually for them, they still as they watch, mesmerised by the vision before their eyes.

Under the light of the moon, at a time when twilight never converges into full darkness, lie six women and six men. They are positioned on each of the twelve rocks in a circular formation, removing what simple garments they have from their bodies. As they become naked a woman covered only by her long black hair and a wreath of golden flowers around her head rises from the centre of the circle as though from flames and kisses their genitals as if igniting their passion. She moves clockwise around the twelve, as though she is giving them permission to feel, touch and explore each other in their most sensual parts. She returns to the centre of their circle and begins to chant and dance; different tempos and rhythms appear to signal a change in connection to each person. The men move in one direction, the women the other, back and forth as their frenetic exploring continues, the sexual moaning heightening within the entire group. The lady with the wreath, in their centre, continues writhing and dancing and moving, her chanting reaching ecstatic levels as she takes on an almost goddess-like form and the small crowd gathers in closely around her. As this occurs, I sense my spirit being drawn directly into her body and we become one. I am her.

The pure sexuality of this ritual is pounding through my veins and I notice its energy has subdued the violent intentions of the Nordic men as they watch us. Their heightened arousal temporarily suspends their need to plunder and despoil. The twelve bodies surround me, worshipping me as their high priestess and I eagerly open myself up to them, granting them access as I spread my arms and legs wide and throw my head back. Each concentrates on a different part of my body: my neck and ears, each of my breasts, my thighs, my belly and my sex. I reach new heights for them, my people, toward the glory of our goddess. The only part of me left untouched is my mouth, which continues to release an almost unearthly yet soulful sound. I am secured by strong hands, my legs spread wide as my body is offered high to the stars above. Tongues and fingers fondle my sacred openings with reverence, as my body quivers in the pleasure they elicit, and a soulful song, going beyond ecstasy, pierces the night and reaches the heavens. The bodies wrap themselves around me until my heavenly sounds subside, gently lowering me back to earth glistening, quivering, idolising me. Only when I am completely still and close my eyes, do the others partake further in their sensual activities. Each man and woman partner off and complete the act that ensures the birth of the next generation.

The chief of the Vikings notices most of his men are now pleasuring themselves around him given what they have just witnessed. He forms his lips to emit a low-sounding growl to attract only their attention. Some in the peak of the act attempt to swallow the sounds of their own release. They move toward the local people as a uniformed and disciplined group to do what they do best — conquer. As the leader nears the dark-haired goddess, she remains perfectly still on the ground as if in a trance, palms placed over her heart.

The Viking chief sends his men back to the ship with their human bounty, others are sent to continue their hunt for food. The giant white warrior towers above the serene woman, taking her in, absorbing her beauty, recalling her sounds. He lowers his body over hers, kissing her hard, slamming his tongue into her mouth, as if trying to touch those soulful notes. He takes hold of her breasts, twisting them with his calloused hands. She lies still beneath him. He removes the cloth covering his throbbing phallus, which reveals the virility of his manhood. He positions himself over her body, but just as he moves to enter her, her large eyes flash open like a bolt of lightning, temporarily blinding him with their shimmering emerald gaze.

Never one to be taken against my will, my body rises slowly and confidently from the earth and guides the Viking to his knees, so we are equal in height. My unblinking eyes meet his, overpowering his strength with my magic. I position my moist, naked form above him, my long hair barely covering my breasts and I lower my glistening thighs around his majestic girth, knowing I will be able to take him deep within my loins. I, the high priestess, throw my head back, baring my throat, releasing him from the captivating trance of my gaze, and take wild control of his pleasure until he is completely under my sexual spell. He holds me in a vice-like grip with his arms as if his soul depends on the essence of my beating heart. Our lust for one another grows until we are both consumed by mutual passion for one another, losing all sense of consciousness, until he explodes volcanically into me, releasing his Viking seed into my belly as though we are creating the earth itself. His low guttural cries of 'Freya' merge with my heavenly voice as we two become one.

Sated under the evening stars, this is the first act of kindness and warmth the Viking has ever experienced in his life. The first willing touch of a woman. As I see his tears, I see Jeremy's smoky green eyes reflecting back and recognise the explosive beginning of our united souls, establishing a most sacred and blessed path for centuries to come. Anam Cara.

As high priestess I kiss the tears as they begin to slide down his face replacing aggression with love. We remain connected in the lush green field, kissing and caressing, soothing and adoring until he finally becomes flaccid enough to withdraw from my body. In the light of the breaking dawn, he strokes a small heart-shaped birthmark positioned just above the nipple of my left breast and tenderly kisses it, gently this time, just as I did for him.

The union of our two souls, Jeremy's and mine, forever bound in the magic and power of these origins that sparked the essence of the healing blood.

It is only at this realisation that I am released from the body of the high priestess and return to my ethereal state.

I see that the Viking never returns to his ship and he never kills again. The priestess and the Viking travel the northern lands — she offering rituals to the gods and goddesses in return for health and fertility, he teaching men to embrace, not fear, the sexuality of women. Their union is one of love, lust, and desire, never tiring of each other sexually, only craving and exploring the carnal nature of their beings.

Time travels into the future and they have twelve children, symbolically representing the conquest that brought them together. Three of their daughters have heart-shaped birthmarks somewhere on their bodies, on their left sides: one on her foot, one on her shoulder and another on the cheek of her bottom. They have their mother's gift of soul singing and healing, displaying greater compassion and spiritual awareness than the other children. Their mother teaches them fully of her magic and their craft is passed down many generations. The heart-shaped birthmark fades over the generations, becoming instead a mark of legend and abstract magic as opposed to reality ... But then again, all legends seem to be founded in some form of truth when you tap into their source.

* * *

I now understand that none of these events have occurred by chance; they all lead to this watershed in my life. I have been given the privilege and gift of witnessing my ancestors' lives, the fragments of my soul. I know I have the power and courage to put the past behind me and venture, unafraid, into the future with the man my soul has been searching for centuries to find. With the circle complete, I intrinsically know that integration will be possible when the stars align, just as Leo said to me.

* * *

When I next open my eyes to this earthly world, I am sitting up and my hands are being held by a man I have never seen before. We are seated cross-legged and I am mesmerised by him. His headdress is more elaborate than anything I have seen on my journey so far and is decorated with many feathers of the most colourful birds in this immense jungle.

I can feel the energy running between our palms as though it is literally pulsing through our bodies and regulating each beat of our hearts. I don't see anything else around me, so absorbed am I in his presence.

Once our eyes lock, I hear the first pounding beat of a tribal drum; it is slow at first as though it's attempting to attune itself to the rhythm of our bodies. I remain locked to this man both physically and mentally.

We temporarily lift up out of our bodies and fly together but not too high, just enough for me to absorb the scene below us, illuminated only by the fire burning and the fullness of the moon. My heart fills with warmth when I notice from above that Jeremy and Leo are sitting beside me and the shaman. Their eyes are closed.

As we float above everyone I notice the women who have been tending to me are chanting and dancing around the fire with their men, to the increasing beat of the drum. They remain calm, as though preparing themselves for what is to come.

I take a moment to have a good look at my body, one that I would not have recognised as myself just months ago. It's as if I have been transformed in every possible way. My hair, now longer than it has been for years, has tiny braids weaved through it, with feathers and beads interlaced between the parts that remain wild and free. My body is lithely toned from little food, and trekking through the jungle. My skin has a healthy glow beneath the intricate designs swirling around my limbs, shoulders, back and belly.

Many strands of beads of varying sizes are hung around my neck, some reaching almost to my belly. I have an intricately-woven skirt sitting around my hips, barely covering my private parts. My breasts are bare other than the necklaces — each areola has been painted with reddened dye and the tips of my nipples black, as though they represent all-seeing eyes.

The woman I'm inspecting looks wild and exotic. Under different circumstances I would have denied it could ever have been me, but I know she is the culmination of the many visions I have witnessed via my soul flight. She is completely serene, like a goddess awaiting some form of reincarnation. No sooner has that thought flickered through my mind, than I am abruptly reunited with my body with a virtual thud.

My hands have been released by this man with the powerful magic sitting before me. This time I sense everything around me and can look into the eyes of the men who have orchestrated this journey. Jeremy, though looking tired and a little overwhelmed by what surrounds him, is full of love and appreciation, and ultimately awe at being involved in this event.

As I turn toward Leo, I recognise him fully as my soul's protector, the man who has been there for me in many lives, looking after me and my bloodline when it was most at risk. I now understand why my discoveries on this journey regarding my past were so important to him, to us.

The drumbeat suddenly stops as does the chanting and dancing. The four of us are seated in the middle of a ring of people, by the fire. Nobody speaks; it is as if even the jungle surrounding our clearing has suddenly stilled and awaits what will happen next.

A moulded clay cup half filled with a steaming brew is presented to the shaman by the same woman who tended to my body and spirit before I awoke here. I can't remember the last time I had solid food but also feel no need for it whatsoever. The shaman inhales its aroma deeply and chants something as he raises his eyes to the heavens above. He is wearing a pouch over his own embroidered skirt and he digs into it, retrieving a handful of powder. He sprinkles it into the cup and it hisses and smokes when it hits the liquid.

He takes the first sip and bows his head for a moment. He then passes it to Leo, who passes it directly on to me. Both Leo's and Jeremy's eyes are firmly fixed on me as I pause to inhale the scent of the concoction. It smells quite bitter, like the others, and in this light it's difficult to determine its colour.

Aware that this is what I am here for, the climactic point of my jungle journey, I take a decent sip of the concoction, swallowing its heat quickly in case I'm put off by its odour. I too, bow my head, though not in respect; it just makes it easier to encourage my system to retain the brew and accept its taste, as its potency and power are having an immediate impact on my mind. I steady myself before handing the cup to Jeremy who, continuing our clockwise motion, hands it directly back to the shaman. He ingests another mouthful, then as it makes its way back to me, this time around Leo accepts a mouthful.

I remember Leo mentioning at some stage that the primary purpose of our meeting was for the shaman and I to fly together and that he would determine via my spirit if anyone else needed to accompany us. If this were necessary, any additional people would play a secondary role in the experience, so I can only assume this is why Leo is partaking on the second round. As does Jeremy when I pass the cup to him. There is an almost bittersweet aftertaste this time as I adjust to its flavour. Its heat warms my bones from the inside out.

This circular process of sipping continues until the last mouthful is swallowed by the shaman. When the cup is returned to the woman in the headdress, he indicates for me to hold both of his hands and we again reconnect by looking deeply into one another's eyes.

The drums and chanting recommence in the firelight around us and with a nod of the shaman's head Jeremy and Leo place each of their hands above and below ours. I feel the energy from their palms begin pulsing through my body, as though the beating drum is trying to synchronise with our beating hearts.

After a few moments of being lost in the shaman's gaze, the ground shifts violently, as though I'm looking through the lens of a camera being swung rapidly from side to side, yet I can still feel my body remaining firmly anchored to the ground. The sensation is quite different to the experiences I had on the journey to this sacred place.

Suddenly the shaking changes and there is some great pull, yanking my heart and mind away from my physical being. The force is strong, gripping and relentless, until finally I detach and start spinning. We all start spinning round and round, faster and faster, until our bodies are a liquid blur surrounded by a circle of light created by the flames of the fires. We become one entity as this dizzying feeling continues. I feel like I need to grasp their hands more firmly lest I fall out of this speeding ring and go smashing into a rock.

Faster and faster we go, I can no longer see their faces or eyes, just the outline of the ring of gold encircling our diminishing forms. When the spinning reaches the point of speed where I think I will be physically ill, it suddenly stops and I'm immediately plunged into a darkness so black, I can't see the hand in front of my face.

The sound of my thumping heart almost consumes me. The silence and darkness are absolute, though rather than sitting as I was when I accepted the shaman's brew, I am standing still as if I am on the cusp of some great unknown. Even though I feel my heartbeat continuing to pound within my body a sense of calm and resolve infiltrates my nervous system. I feel sure that all will be well and I will embrace my next steps rather than fear them.

I temper my breathing with this new confidence as my eyes and body adjust to the mysterious darkness. For all I know I could be in the core of the earth or the outer realms of the universe. A small flicker of light appears amidst the black. I can't be sure whether it is tiny and in front of me or large and faraway. I have absolutely no spatial awareness or any sense of depth or breadth. After a few moments it increases in size and looks as if it is indeed moving toward me. What began as a firefly now looks like flame, but just as I begin to feel its heat on my body it splits into two, one remaining directly in front of me and one behind me.

The light reveals a shadowy outline of two female bodies holding glowing lanterns on top of bamboo shafts. One of the women has nipples painted in the same way as mine, the other has two golden rings through hers, making them pert and erect. Seeing them sends a rush of blood to my own. Their breasts are barely covered by the beads hanging around their necks. They too wear short embroidered skirts, similar to mine, but less elaborate. Our headdresses are all different so I assume they must depict some meaning I have no knowledge of.

No words are spoken. The women wrap a cord around my waist in the same way it is wrapped around theirs and connect us in a line. The woman in front of me starts walking and I follow. Even though there is enough light to show us the immediate path of my steps, I have no sense of what the blackness surrounding us holds. No sense of the sky above, or the depths below, or whether we are inside or outside. Nothing is too warm or too cold, other than the flames guiding our steps. We move solemnly and silently forward, one step at a time.

In the distance I hear the deep beat of a large-barrelled drum; it sounds like the heartbeat of the earth itself and my footsteps readily adapt to its pounding rhythm, deepening my trance. We make our way further along the meandering path until we turn a sharp corner and stop. Each of the women takes one of my hands to ensure I don't take a further step without their lead.

The drum stops. I'm suddenly blinded by a vision of gold before me, and everything halts in this moment.

My heart, my fears, my hopes, my world, my being.
Transfixed.
No breath.
No senses.
Just enveloped in gold.

The beat of the drum kick-starts my heart and my body becomes submissive to its slow, deep call. My vision clears and I see that we are in a giant cave, larger than I have been in before. We are positioned at the mouth of the cave, high above the women who prepared me for this event, who are seated on the ground in a large, though not fully-formed circle. In a semicircle behind them are massive drums being pounded by the men of the tribe, their sound penetrating the cave and ricocheting through our bodies, connecting our minds and our spirits.

We continue our threaded journey along the outskirts of the cave until we join everyone in the depths below.

I am disconnected from my companions and delivered to the centre of the circle. We are now standing and I am surrounded by twelve women who, like me, are in a deep state of trance, not necessarily of this world. I am the thirteenth woman, standing alone in the middle, but knowing I am surrounded by compassion and unconditional love. I allow every pore of my being to soak up these feelings as the throbbing beats of the massive drums take control of our bodies and we move to their rhythm, while some of the women join in chanting with their melodic voices providing depth and harmony to this spiritual awakening. Our bodies cease to exist as separate entities and we are joined as one. I completely lose myself in the majesty of this moment, my unconscious taking over my mental state.

Once again, I can see everything from two perspectives: from my own eyes, and the entire scene from above. I am being lifted high into the air by the women, as if I am being offered to the gods. They take me to an alcove, on a higher level of the cave, that looks like an ancient altar and lay my limp body within the circular frame that awaits there. I have no fear as my wrists and ankles are stretched and bound to this circle — I only feel acceptance and love. Once secure, it is pulled into an upright position and my body is held up, bound and spread-eagled, as the women form a circle around me. It's as if I always knew this would happen, that it was meant to happen, and that all will be well. I know, without a doubt, that this event is the culmination of my ancestral lives and my earthly experiences since reconnecting with Jeremy. Right here, right now.

I look up toward the only natural light in the cave to see an opening, revealing the heavens above. Before my eyes is Venus, the brightest planet in the sky. I am in awe of its celestial beauty and I feel like my body has been opened so far and wide as an offering in order to receive her universal gifts. Her light awakens my sensuality and desire and rather than feel restricted by my restraints, I feel bold and empowered by them, knowing they anchor me to the earth, ensuring I'm grounded by gravity, lest I should fly away to be with her forever. I can feel my vital essence simultaneously homing in on my past and future, seeking reconciliation in the here and now, so old wounds can be healed to enable the richness of my future.

I move my hips to the continued beat of the multitude of tribal drums and summon the men who have played such significant roles in my many lives. As my eyes look skywards, searching through the cave's opening, my peripheral vision catches the licking flames of the fire beneath as Leo emerges from the depths of the darkness.

He positions himself behind my body, sliding his smooth hands along the curves of my body and joining in my seductive dance. I cannot see his face; as he is my past, our eyes will never meet in this moment. I allow my body to feel the sensations my protector is creating, knowing there is nothing to fear, no sin to repent, that he is in his rightful place in my life. His fingers explore me as if he is preparing to say goodbye to my body, but never my soul.

Jeremy appears from the circle of women, as though they have blessed his sacred passage to be before me at this precious moment. Our eyes lock and we become lost in our combined emerald gaze. I understand that this is the man the universe has been waiting for me to connect with fully, deeply, for centuries, since our original union when the blood magic began.

The sensations cascading over me are otherworldly as these two men surround my body, one before me, one behind me. I remain as open to them as I do to Venus above, willing them to adore my body, wishing for our ultimate union more than anything else in the world. Knowing there is no jealousy or remorse in their feelings, knowing they understand the importance of the roles they both play.

Leo to unlock me from my past and Jeremy to provide the key to my future.

As the tribal drums increase in beat and tempo, my bound body becomes increasingly fevered by their explorations, and impatient for our connection to be complete. As a dark crescent creeps across Venus, Leo's phallus teases my back passage and smooths against the split in my cheeks. His hands wrap around my breasts, kneading their bountiful flesh as Jeremy steadies my swaying hips and longingly and lovingly kisses me, deep into my mouth, seducing me in preparation for what is to come below.

Their concentrated focus on my body is sending my mind spinning out to the stars above. I revel in their worship of my body, desperately wishing I could touch them in return and embrace their masculine forms, but I also understand that is the future, not the present. So I remain open and restrained between them, for them to explore and access at their whim, kissing and stroking and suckling. Their movements become languid and slow against my skin, tantalising my plumped erogenous zones with considered strokes from fingers and tongues, carrying me right to the edge of the precipice and leaving me there. Oh, such tortuous bliss.

My vulva pulses in response to the sensations they are creating, my wetness calling to them to become more intimate with my openings, to become one with me. These men in my life continue creating heavenly ecstasy as my need for them to fill me completely builds unbearably. I throw my head back and cry out with pleasure, relinquishing all control to lust and desire and surrendering completely to the pleasures of my physical body. I can't speak but for my helpless moans, I am too far gone.

My beads and skirt are removed; touch is entirely intimate, skin on skin. Every nerve ending in my body feels like it has been teased to life, awakened to the pleasure of what is and what is to come. I only ever feel the sweaty warmth of Leo's body behind me, never meeting his eyes. His hardened phallus slides with ease over my curves and within my cracks, his arms and hands roam freely around my waist and breasts and legs. I find it difficult to hold the weight of my body as I fall under the orgasmic spell of Jeremy's playful fingers dancing within the folds of my engorged labia.

Leo stretches my cheeks wide and finds his place, slowly and sensitively embedding himself in my back passage as I release gasps of heady pleasure. Once positioned, his hands wrap around my breasts, kneading and massaging as Jeremy spreads my moist thighs and fills me where he knows he belongs.

I have never been so wholly taken. My body quivers in desire as I wantonly accept them inside me, rejoicing in the fullness.

I have wanted this since I dreamt of it many years ago, always wondering what it might be like, never knowing if I was strong enough or brave enough to endure it physically. And finally I am gifted with this exquisite pleasure, impaled to the very core of my sexual existence. A pressure so intense, so intricately balanced that if it were the slightest bit greater it would descend into pain. A pleasure so absolute, it defies all my expectations. I had no concept of how complete this would make me feel, physically, psychologically and spiritually.

Surrounded, enfolded by their masculinity, my body accepts their pumping rhythm until they find perfect unison in their thrusts. With my arms and legs anchored high and wide and their arms stretched out horizontally holding onto our circular frame, our three bodies are connected in a way that redefines da Vinci's famous drawing, Vitruvian Man, becoming a new symbol of this perfection. Our synergy blends the spirit of the divine feminine with the virile masculine as their seeds simultaneously erupt into the core and essence of me.

I balance on the cusp of heavenly ecstasy. Jeremy and I are still gazing into each other's eyes at the wonder and awe we have for each other. At knowing we could never have been together without Leo or his soul's guardianship of my gift. We have waited more than centuries for this ultimate connection, our communion of relationships, to finish together what we've always been destined to do and be. This is so much more than sex, or lovemaking, or even the gift of marriage. What we are experiencing together at this very moment in time is beyond religion and borders infinity.

Our pasts meeting our present, to enable our future.

We three are one. Always have been. Always will be.

Embraced in love, entwined in touch, we roll, we spin, we caress, until time becomes an irrelevant measure in our existence.

Never have I experienced a more sacred moment than this explosion of sexual communion we have been blessed to share as the stars align before us. As the dark shape covering Venus is lifted and she returns, my ecstasy reaches celestial heights and our combined energies are consecrated. I am as complete as I will ever be, every moment of my life and ancestry has delivered me here as I lift out of my body and ascend to the heavens above.

It is if Venus is communicating directly with me, flooding me with her gifts of love and fertility. My heart now beats for her, in her honour, as I bask in her glory. I could stay here forever as my mind's eye sees the universe from her perspective.

A place and time before man tainted religion by his greed and need for power and control, where sexuality was rejoiced in, and the female form revered for our ability to recreate and reproduce on earth. Where nature and rebirth is celebrated and woven into the very fabric of humankind.

I overflow with images of goddesses and high priestesses who were worshipped for their fertility and creation by civilisations, so maintaining the balance and source of universal order by nurturing both Mother Earth and the children she bore.

Beauty and nature and sex and love and intimacy. Will this universal connectedness ever be given permission to reconnect? It seems our egos have allowed our minds to take centre stage for too long, allowing science to replace spirituality in dictating our new path as the progression of our species continues. Our behaviour, our health, our wellbeing influenced by this new regime, but disconnected somehow. Man-made drugs that ensure our longevity and lessen our pain, designed to make us happier and healthier, yet we wonder still why we are so discontent.

I feel unexpected gratitude for my bravery in embarking on this journey, for being willing and open to exploring the undiscovered, and engage once again in creativity, imagination and play. It has kept my soul vital and strong within my consciousness. I understand that the time has arrived, that enough is enough. Now more than ever before, we long for the reconciliation of our sensuality and our soul. For the earth to heal it needs nurturing, it needs loving. Change is upon us and it requires the ultimate communion between science, sexuality and spirituality, the need for a higher state of consciousness.

As Venus relinquishes me, I am left surrounded with a warmth and love that is as absolute as it is complete.

Her brightness recedes as the full moon obscures some of her brilliance, our act of sexual intimacy remains illuminated and our purpose becomes immaculately clear. We three exist to foster this integration.

The purpose of everything I have been through these past months crystallises. My meeting with Jeremy, the conditions of my time with him forcing me to leave the shell of my old self. I reflect on my deliberations in accepting Jeremy's proposal and how at the time I likened it to being Eve accepting the forbidden apple. My redundant values were based in origins I never fully investigated, I merely wafted along with society's tide. A code that delineated right from wrong, black from white, in a world that was clearly never meant to be either. But when I finally embraced my sexuality and let my old conventions and assumptions fall away, I was again challenged by science and threatened by fear, which only served to strengthen my resolve and clarify my thoughts about who I am and what I stand for.

And now this. I have been so honoured to be able to take this journey into a spiritual universe beyond the realms of plausibility in my mind, so that instead of questions, I now have answers. Knowledge of what lies beyond our human limitations, the knowledge of unconditional universal love and connectedness that each of us have a choice to embrace and make a significant and meaningful part of our lives.

As these realisations settle, Venus beckons me to join her one last time before she disappears into the skies once more. My lovers disconnect from my body behind me as I follow her, intrigued. I feel my essence spiralling toward her in some sort of vortex, as though I'm being magnetically pulled from the core of my bellybutton toward her secret world. The spinning stops and I find myself in a cave that could only be described as womblike. It feels soft and cushioned and completely serene, in shades of pink and rose and fiery orange. I hear the subdued thud of Mother Earth's heart continually beating, soothing our souls.

I am not here in any physical form, but I understand that I belong here, have always belonged here. This is where I come from and this is where I will ultimately return — though I also know that in the deepest level of my soul, I have never truly left.

My thoughts, my feelings and my love are overflowing through my spirit, wave after wonderful wave, infinity replenishing itself, over and over again. The feeling is so pure and so strong I know it stems from the source of life itself. It is part of me, it is all of me, it contains me. I am it. I am the mother of unconditional love, nurturer of the earth. I am both the heart and the womb, embracing and embraced by the divine feminine.

From around the circular walls of the womblike cavern, I can feel the presence of others, at one with me yet slightly separated. We should be united, but we are not ready yet. I am meeting the oldest and deepest souls of my sisterhood, welcoming me into their sacred union. They share my love and I their wisdom, each soul having their own unique gifts and talents. They have been waiting for a long time for my arrival so that our circular connection can be complete.

My soul is replenished, refreshed and invigorated from my connection with my sisterhood; I feel the core of my belly being pulled again in the opposite direction, away from the infinite comfort of the secret womb. I become the tears I shed in both joy and the knowledge that I don't know when I'll return to this heavenly and sacred place. Until the stars align again.

The light of Venus diminishes as the bright moon temporarily blinds me to her presence. It as at this point that I return to my physical being and darkness descends on both the heavens above and devours my conscious state.

Part Eight

Risk — more others think is safe
Care — more than others think is wise
Dream — more than others think is practical
Expect — more than others think is possible

Cadet Maxim

Alexa

I open my eyes to blinding lights and an excruciating pain in my head, as if an axe has sliced it in half. I close them immediately with the hope that the pain will subside but have no luck.

I try to move my arms to feel what is wrong with my head, but find that I can't move them from my side. My stomach churns and I feel my body violently and involuntarily heave itself forward and project vomit into the air around me.

God, I feel awful. Unable to ascertain what has happened to me nor what is happening around me, I collapse backwards in a hot sweat when the retching subsides. The faint sound of subdued voices swirling around me become distant and deadened, as blackness takes me far, far away.

* * *

I hear the intermittent beeping of a machine before any other cognition occurs. I'm laying down flat and feel a dull pain in the side of my head. I pause for a moment before I'm brave enough to open my eyes. I don't know where I may find myself physically, mentally or spiritually or even what century I may be in as my consciousness returns slowly but surely.

When I do, the brightness is overwhelming and I have a flash of memory of opening my eyes at Avalon after having been blind and in darkness with Jeremy all those months ago. Where on earth am I now? I can't be in yet another version of Avalon, can I? My head hurts even thinking and my body feels weak. I notice a drip in my hand and groan inwardly, wondering if Jeremy has gone completely over the top again in his doctor role. Where am I? Where are my children? Why am I alone?

Unconsciousness steals me away again.

* * *

Next time I wake, I find my hand being held and Jeremy sitting by my bedside. I turn to look toward him, and the journal he's been reading falls to the floor as he jumps up from his seat.

'Alexa, sweetheart. Don't try to turn your head, just keep still.' Instead, he moves so he is in my line of sight. He is smiling at me, but I don't miss the deep concern etched in his face and eyes. I smile back and notice how dry my lips are. I must look a sight.

'Hi,' is all I can manage in a raspy voice.

'Well, good morning, Dr Blake. It's great to have you back.'

Where have I been, I want to ask, but instead say, 'Where am I?'

'In Boston, Massachusetts.'

'Oh, right.' I really do jet around these days. My simplistic, home-and-work lifestyle seems like a distant dream these days. He notices my confusion.

'You were in the Neurological Intensive Care Unit at the Brigham and Women's Hospital. We brought you here as soon as we realised that you had a depressed fracture of your temporal bone and might have ruptured your meningeal artery.'

He has a tendency to bombard me with medical jargon at the best of times, let alone when my head feels like this.

'Will I be okay?'

'Yes, sweetheart.' His smile exudes confidence and the back of his hand tenderly strokes my cheek. I feel myself relax from the tension I didn't know I was holding. 'It looks like you will make a full recovery and there will be no permanent damage, just some mild headaches for the next month or so. You're been under excellent care in here. This hospital is affiliated with Harvard and I do much of my work with the depression centre here. We were very worried for the first forty-eight hours, given your vomiting, but since then your recovery has been excellent.'

Oh no, not more lost hours of my life.

'How long have I been here?'

'Just less than a week. We didn't want to take any risks when it comes to your brain, GG.'

I look at him, puzzled, and his brow creases immediately.

'Oh, I see, you're testing my cognitive abilities. Don't stress, J, I know I'll always be your gorgeous girl.'

His relief at my words is palpable and we both smile as he squeezes my hand.

'I don't remember very much,' I say.

'You've been on strong painkillers and mild sedatives to give your body time to heal, so you've more than likely been wafting in and out of consciousness. Sometimes the drugs can even cause hallucinations or at least some pretty vivid dreams.'

Trying to decipher what was real or not is too hard for my brain.

'Where are Elizabeth and Jordan?'

'They're here too. They've been in and out, mostly in the afternoons. They understand you've needed your rest but they'll no doubt be thrilled to speak to you.'

'So they're back from the Amazon? Is everyone okay?' I try to sit up and he gently rests his hand against my shoulder to keep me still while he presses the button for my electronic bed to raise me up.

'Everyone is absolutely fine. No wild animal attacks, no infectious diseases. It sounds like the kids had a ball, as did Robert and Adam. They've been making a slide show of all their photos and it sounds like they'll be penpals with Marcu for years to come.'

'Oh, that's great. What a relief they're well.' I rest my head back on the pillow. 'So what happened to me? Or more like, why does something always happen to me? It seems that every episode in my life lately ends with me needing a drip.'

Jeremy notices my hand twitching as he holds it. 'Don't worry. We'll get rid of the drip as soon as we can, as soon as you've eaten. Would you like some water?'

I nod. I can tell he wants to accommodate my every need, making me feel cherished and loved from the inside out.

'You don't feel nauseous, do you?' He sounds like he's reprimanding himself for not asking earlier and I want him to stay in Jeremy mode, rather than revert to doctor mode on me.

'No, I feel good. Tell me, what happened?'

'What's the last thing you remember?'

'Jeremy!' I raise my voice and it comes out as a husky screech. I'm not playing that game with him. Besides, there are so many distinct, weird and wonderful memories going through my head that I'll need a while to process them before they will be in any reasonable order for discussion. Just the thought of it right now makes my head hurt.

'Okay, okay. You need to stay calm. Do you remember the shaman?'

I nod.

'We were all sitting with him and everything went a little weird. Leo and I have had a brief conversation, but we have slightly different versions of what occurred, so we thought we'd wait until you were feeling better to piece it together. It seems as though some things were real and some things just happened in our own minds. Either way, we were standing up and suddenly your body started convulsing like it did the first time you had the ayahuasca —'

'What do you mean, convulsing?'

'You don't remember?'

I shake my head.

'Each time you drank the most potent blend, you experienced varying degrees of convulsions. It scared the living daylights out of me at first but then I became more used to it, knowing in less than a minute you'd be in a "calm and otherworldly" state — by the way, those are Leo's words, not mine.'

He pauses and kisses my hand before continuing.

'Anyway, this last time, the time with the shaman, you had no convulsions at the beginning but later, after you ended up standing, it was as though some invisible force took over your body and you were spinning, with your head thrown back, moving around the clearing we were in. We didn't know whether to stop you or let you go and you kept going faster and faster until you fell over, smashing your head on a rock.'

I raise my free hand to the bandage on the left side of my head, just behind my ear.

'We were suddenly released from the trance-like state we were in and as soon as we saw you were injured, we organised to make our way back to Miami at once. But when you started vomiting in the plane, I wanted you under the care of my colleagues in this hospital, immediately.'

I see the depth of his emotion, the fear for my life, flash past his eyes as he recounts his story. I squeeze his hand as it rests in mine.

'Well, it seems like it was a good decision, and if you say I'm going to be fine, I know I will be.'

He returns to the present and to me, and kisses my cheek. 'Yes, sweetheart, you will be fine and it's excellent having you back. Do you need anything for your pain?'

'I'm not sure. My head is still aching but it's not too bad.' He presses the call button for the nurse.

'You'll need to take it easy for a while. You had to have a small blood transfusion shortly after you arrived here.'

'Really?' This is more of a shock. Even Jeremy looks a little unsettled.

'Your blood wasn't coagulating as well as we'd hoped so the surgeon thought it best after cleaning your wound and well ...' He hesitates.

'What is it, J?'

'Well, AB, there was blood on your nipples during your soul flight and I couldn't understand what was causing it. It appeared to be old blood rather than fresh, it's really quite baffling ...' He scratches the side of his head as though he is still attempting to come up with an acceptable scientific theory.

Caitlin's face appears in my mind. 'Wow, that's amazing. I really must have been connected to her.'

He looks back toward me, into my eyes. 'Connected?'

'There is so much to tell you. Let's just say, during my soul flight, this girl Caitlin, well, it was me too, I suppose, in a strange way —' I realise this is going to much more difficult to explain now that I'm back in the 'real', present world '— had both her nipples pierced so I imagine that's why mine ended up that way. I was connected to her, Jeremy, as though part of me was actually her. I felt what she was going through.'

He looks at me thoughtfully. 'You know, sweetheart, before the trip to the Amazon, I would have said you were stark raving mad, or at least a little mentally incapacitated from the blow to your head, but since experiencing everything we have, even I have to admit there are some things science and medicine can't explain. And I have the blood sample to prove it.'

I look at him. 'From my nipples?' I say, astonished.

He nods. 'Although it is the same AB blood grouping, it's definitely not your blood, although there are distinct DNA attributes that are similar. It's utterly perplexing.'

I can't help but grin. 'That's because it's Caitlin's.'

So much is coming back to me with these words and thoughts, so many realisations I didn't have before my Amazonian experience. I close my eyes, momentarily recalling the insights I received from the universe, the reason I'm here, with Jeremy, the reason Leo was in my past and will be in my future and what we can all achieve together. I hear Jeremy in the background telling me I need to rest as much as possible if I'm to be with everyone for Christmas.

I'm snapped back to reality so fast I can't believe it hasn't dawned on me before now. The memory of the situation I left behind me rises up and shakes through my entire body like a blanket of dread.

'What's wrong, Alexa, you've just gone deathly white.' Jeremy scans the monitor as a nurse arrives in the room.

'Jurilique? Am I a condemned woman?' My limbs are trembling as I picture those photos and headlines and imagine the worst of what my children may think of me now. No wonder they're not here with me, they may not ever want to see me again after what I've done …

'I think she's going into shock again.' The nurse rushes to my side adding something to my drip and pages another doctor.

Jeremy, tell me. I cry the words though they only form in my brain as paralysing fear spreads through me. He holds both my hands and stares deeply into my eyes as warmth envelops my body.

'There's nothing to worry about. Just rest now, sweetheart, close your eyes. All will be well, I promise you.'

I attempt to stay focussed as long as I can, but the room recedes along with Jeremy's loving green eyes, taking me away yet again to a place of nothingness.

* * *

I wake up looking out through the elevated bay window toward a spectacular winter wonderland and need to pinch myself to prove I'm not dreaming — again.

I have always wanted to experience a white Christmas and never had the opportunity and here I am, in Whistler, British Columbia. Everyone has gathered at Leo's ski chalet and although I'll miss my family and the seafood feast followed by a surf at the beach which comprises a hot summer Christmas back in Australia, I know I will make the most of every minute experiencing this magic time of the year with the kids in this special part of the world. That is, if they ever come in from snowboarding — they are obsessed by this new sport, and by the sounds of things Jeremy and Robert are taking every opportunity to take them out as often as they'd like.

I still seem to need quite a bit of rest so my nights are long and days are intermittent. Jeremy tells me this is a good sign and part of the healing process, as long as my headaches are kept at bay, which they seem to be. We only arrived a few days ago and I was so exhausted from the trip, I haven't even managed to step outside Leo's magnificent lodge and explore the terrain. I haven't even bothered raising the prospect of skiing as I can just imagine the response. Though I have to admit with everything that has happened, I wouldn't have the energy to even walk in ski boots, let alone carry the skis at the moment. I'm pretty content drinking hot chocolates and snoozing by the fire.

Apparently, Leo and Jeremy have spent quite a few Christmases together here with their families. This history makes the time here even more significant for me, knowing I am an embedded part of their lives now. I stretch my arms and take a moment to reflect on everything that has happened these last couple of weeks.

I was filled with joy and relief to find out from Martin that Josef and Salina were safely evacuated from the Xsade facility in Lake Bled. Apparently the new security system had severely malfunctioned causing a series of explosions much more powerful than anticipated and somehow triggered secondary explosions that caught fire and all but annihilated the entire facility. Thankfully, Salina had managed to locate Josef and they escaped at precisely the right time but not before he attempted to save Madame Jurilique who was trapped beneath a machine. Even after all she had done to him, his compassion managed to shine through. Instead of leaving her to die, he did what he could to save her chemically burned face.

Martin and Josef managed to haul her out of there with emergency crews taking her straight to hospital. Apparently the chemical burns were so severe she is totally unrecognisable and I have to admit I wouldn't wish that upon my worst enemy — which I suppose she is. The whole situation is just awful. Jeremy mentioned last night that the most recent update on her condition was that she has contracted *staphylococcus aureus*, or golden staph infection, during one of her facial operations and it isn't reacting to any antibiotics. The prognosis is that she may not survive through Christmas.

Josef was reunited with his wife and it makes my heart swell just thinking about them. He has been offered a senior position by a highly reputable German-based pharmaceutical company that Jeremy does much of his research work with. They are known to have strong ethics and a much more balanced approach to people, planet and profit, which is great news. I'm told he is weighing up between this proposal and working with Médecins Sans Frontières in Third World countries with his wife for a couple of years, taking some time out of the corporate insanity he has been in and will make his decision early in the new year.

Xsade as a corporate entity has gone into liquidation, given the funds required to rebuild another facility and the level of debt the company held. Some members of the Board are facing criminal charges, as there were five deaths as a result of the explosion in the facility, which is just horrific. Louis and Frederic were included in this tally, as well as members of the Xsade security team who realised too late the system had failed. I can't help but reflect on the demise of Madame Jurilique and how just one bad apple in a position of power can be so insidious and dangerous to the lives of others. The risk to myself and my children of her ever attempting to access or analyse our blood has completely evaporated, along with the photos and headlines that thankfully never made it on to the internet.

This news makes it worth cracking a magnum of champagne open, yet since my accident I really don't feel like drinking at all. I feel ill at the thought of it — probably because of my head. Perhaps I'll feel like a sip on Christmas Day.

A light knock on the door to this incredible old-world master suite disrupts my reverie and I puff out the pillows behind my back so I'm sitting up. 'Come on in.'

Leo opens the door carrying a tray with two drinks, some cookies and a newspaper.

'Well, good afternoon,' he says.

'Oh, no. It can't be, not again?'

'Only just. I said I'd look after you. Jeremy's taken the kids to do some last-minute Christmas shopping.'

'Thanks, Leo. You don't have to, I'm more than capable of looking after myself, you know.'

He looks at me with raised eyebrows and a knowing smile. He looks as gorgeous as ever in his polo jumper and casual trousers.

'You know the role I am destined to play in your life, Alexandra.'

I blush in response. We haven't had a chance to have much of a discussion since Avalon, what with hospitals, my constant sleeping and people coming and going. And there we have it. With this simple statement, I know he knows everything I know, and knowing Leo, probably so much more.

'There's no use fighting it is there?'

He simply shakes his head with no attempt to hide his grin.

'But I can say thank you, from the bottom of my heart, for everything, can't I?'

'Always.' He puts the tray down and hands me a cup of the steaming hot chocolate I think I'm becoming addicted to.

'While I have you alone, can I ask you some questions?' I raise my lowered eyelids to meet his gaze. I know I'll be connected to the wisdom of his eyes, and his soul, for eternity.

'Of course, Alexandra, anything.'

'There are a few things I don't understand and I know that if you don't have the answers, probably no one will.' He nods and waits patiently for me to continue. There is never any rush with Leo, he gives everyone the time and space to proceed at their own pace. I love this about him, and so much more. 'You are connected to the young doctor, aren't you, the person who saved Caitlin and ended up marrying her and looking after her twin girls?'

'The same man who was saved by the women of the heart, yes.'

'And you knew she was a woman of the heart because of the mark on her body.'

'That's right.'

'I know my body well and I know I don't have any sign or mark to indicate that my blood is any different. So I have been trying to work out why me? And why my blood? Every scene I experienced on my soul flight depicted the heart-shaped birthmark, somewhere on their bodies, but I have nothing, no mark whatsoever, yet my blood is connected.'

Leo places his cup down and takes mine from me, leaving them both on the bedside table. He takes both my hands, turning them palm up and remains silent, looking at me as though I should understand what he is trying to illustrate. My face speaks volumes about my confusion. Leo smiles.

'Do you remember when the elder checked your palms at Avalon and declared you were ready to embark on your soul flight?'

'Yes. I do.' I distinctly remember him looking at my hands and arms, turning them this way and that.

'He knew you were ready for two reasons. Firstly he was feeling your energy, ensuring that you were open to what you would experience in the jungle. Secondly, he was confirming you had the sign to form some of the missing pieces of the jigsaw we have been attempting to put together.'

'Leo, are you deliberately trying to be cryptic or is my inability to understand what you're saying due to my head injury? Because I'm lost.'

'Your palms, Alexandra, have the sign of the heart.'

I stare blankly at both palms as if something invisible will miraculously appear, as I know there are no birthmarks on them. Leo places his hands on either side of mine and pushes them together so they are joined. I watch intently as they come together and can't believe my eyes when I see that, once joined, the lines on my palms form a perfect heart shape, covering most of my hands. My shock is reflected in the wisdom of Leo's eyes.

'My dear Alexandra, you do indeed have the mark. You've had it since birth. Your head and heart lines, when combined, make a perfect heart shape, which is highly significant. Chiromancy, or palm reading, has been practised for over 5000 years, though these days we think of it as just a party trick, ignoring the ancient knowledge. Your left hand is controlled by the right brain, and is known to form part of the spiritual or personal development, some say the yin or feminine side, of the personality. Your right hand,' he raises my hand as he continues, 'is controlled by the left brain, the yang, masculine and more logical side. Your destiny reflects the coming together of these components.'

Yet again, I find myself mesmerised by Leo's calm and knowledgeable voice, a little overawed by what he is explaining about my palms.

'Caitlin's mark became hidden as she developed from child to woman at the same time as history attempted to eradicate the existence of the divine feminine. Your mark,' he rejoins my palms together, 'reflects awareness and integration. Your heart mark is only recognisable when the two parts come together. When right meets left, yin meets yang, masculinity meets femininity, observation meets intuition, science meets spirituality. However you want to look at it.'

He pauses as I continue to stare at my hands, astonished by what I can now see on my body. That which has always been there and I have never recognised until this moment. Needless to say, it's a weird sensation.

'I can't, just can't quite believe it … this is what he saw, what you saw? But you never told me …'

'Would it have made any difference had I told you then? Would it have had the same meaning for you as being told now?'

I shake my head, forcing myself to acknowledge the truth in his words and instead of keeping my thoughts to myself, I happily share them with him — my owl, my wise counsellor, my protector.

'No, it would have meant nothing more than a strange coincidence of palmistry had you told me before. Had I not seen Evelyn and Caitlin and how their blood had been marked in women through the centuries, it would have had no meaning. Had I not been given the insights of Venus and a sense of what true spirituality means I'd not be having, let alone understanding, this conversation we're having right now.'

'And what do you make of all this, Alexandra, what are your insights?'

'I know that Jeremy's and my souls have been waiting to reconnect meaningfully for centuries, since the Viking and the priestess triggered the sexual awakening of their healing blood. I know that we now have that opportunity, which had passed us by so many times during our past lives. I know that you will always be here to protect my bloodline whether it be at risk or to reunite old souls.' I look into his luminous, azure eyes and understand we share a love and a bond like nothing I have experienced before, a higher dimension, pure, unconditional love, not born out of lust and desire or anything merely physical. 'I also know that Jeremy accepts that in you, that for all the times he wasn't there for whatever reason he had the confidence of knowing that you would be.'

My insights flood my mind as Leo continues to stare deeply into my eyes and I glance between his eyes and my palms as my words unfold between us. 'I know that my role is one of integration. To form a bridge between science and medicine and the healing powers of spirituality. To work with both of you to help this happen in our lifetimes.'

I feel lighter than I have in ages having this conversation with Leo. Being around him makes me believe anything is possible and I can honestly say I have barely felt like this since being with Jeremy — each time I found blissful happiness it was snatched away. Once travelling to London and again in Orlando. Both times the Witch had come between us and both times Leo had been there to ensure we re-established our path and connection to one another.

'What about you, Leo, what are your insights about what has happened?'

'Well, it's a long story I suppose, but I think my version is that you and Jaq were always drawn to each other as if you had some universal magnetic connection. Dr Quinn would say that it has everything to do with your limbic systems, and no doubt he will continue his research into the system of nerve endings around the cortex to one day explain scientifically exactly how that works,' he says with a smile. 'Whatever it was, that connection was disrupted by any number of events in various lives. The most significant moments in this life were the suicide of his brother, which served to bring him and me together, and your decision to procreate, sending you on separate paths. The sequence of events that led to my brother and your husband being together and you being 'AB', the ultimate love of Jaq's life, was far too coincidental for me not to follow up on personally. It was as if I was being offered an incredible opportunity and my intuition was to follow every last detail of it.' He pauses, giving me a moment to reflect on his words, as our eyes reconnect.

'The experiment you underwent as part of your weekend with Jeremy awakened so many memories for me, it was as though I was reliving some form of the past I couldn't understand. The way you were positioned, your responses, it was like I knew what your body would do before you did. I have never experienced anything like it, and I knew there had to be more to it than merely witnessing an intensely sexual act. Your thesis explored the same issues I had been struggling with for years but from a different perspective. The similarities were too perplexing for my logical brain so I turned to the shaman and then everything became clear. You were as significant to me as Jeremy is to you. All three of us were and are entwined in one another's lives. If you are at risk, every part of me needs to ensure your safety, your bloodline. It's my destiny and becomes all I can focus on.'

We remain silent for a few moments, considering the bizarre sequence of events that have led us to this moment.

Eventually I sigh. 'There's still so much to consider but you're right, I understand completely. Even though the whole bloodline thing still has me baffled, but hopefully it will settle over time.'

He squeezes my palms together but doesn't release them, as though he can sense there is something else I need to ask and is silently giving me the time to do so, something I haven't felt entirely comfortable discussing with Jeremy, or never felt the time was right. I don't really know how to put this in words, but decide that after everything we have been through, nothing should be too embarrassing, so, unusually for me, I launch straight in. 'There is obviously a lot more to discuss, but there has been one thing in particular that I've been wondering about.'

'Of course.' He encourages me to continue.

'Well, when we were with the shaman and we were in a trance-like state before my accident, I suppose it was, well, I had what felt like this intensely sexual encounter. The three of us, we were togeth—'

The door flies open and Jeremy bounds on in to join us. 'Well, here you are. Still in bed, my sleeping beauty?'

I'm not sure whether I'm relieved or annoyed that we are interrupted. I know that Leo would accept that the time just wasn't right to complete this conversation and would let it go. I'm not quite as Zen as him yet but something deep inside me agrees that it serves no purpose to verbalise what happened when I was bound within the circle at this moment in time, at least.

Jeremy crawls onto the king-size bed and gives me a kiss on the lips, not in the least disturbed by the fact that Leo's still holding my palms. Leo kisses each side of my 'heart' and winks at me before releasing my hands.

Now, don't get me wrong, there was definitely a time in my life that I would have thought this was completely unbelievable. But given what I have been through with my husband, my children, my lover and now my protector, who am I to call anything weird? In actual fact, being with these two amazing men makes me feel more complete than I have in my entire life. How surreal is that?

As these thoughts flutter through my mind, the men are exchanging unspoken words that I can't even pretend to understand. They have the look of cheeky teenage boys. I try to let them have their moment but their grins are infectious.

'How did you go?' Leo asks Jeremy.

'Great, but I don't want to wait, it seems perfect now, while we are together like this.'

Again with the significant looks and silence. Leo nods in agreement.

'Would you like me to leave so you two can talk in private?' I ask. 'I feel like I'm in the middle of something.'

'Never a truer word spoken, sweetheart.'

'But absolutely no reason to leave, you are right where you should be.' I raise my eyebrows confounded by Leo's words. 'Right in between us,' he explains.

Jeremy pulls out a box from the bag he brought in with him and hands it to Leo. 'You can do the honours, my friend. Your idea, my execution.'

I have no idea what they are up to.

'We wanted to give you a combined Christmas present, Alexandra. One that reflects who you are and what you mean to both of us.' He hands me the beautifully-wrapped box. 'And this is what we came up with.'

Deeply embarrassed that they are giving me a gift and I have nothing for them. 'Oh, no, please, I haven't —' I start to apologise and they simultaneously place their index fingers over my lips to silence my words and we burst out laughing together. 'God, what hope do I have now?'

'None whatsoever.' Jeremy grins. 'So no apologies. You being here and with us is enough gift for us, so please, just open it.'

I carefully unwrap the packaging and take out the most beautiful necklace of intricately woven black leather rope with three large circles connected to it: one white gold, one yellow gold and one rose gold. It's stunning. There is a word engraved on each circle.

Past. Present. Future.

Tears immediately well up in my eyes as I'm overcome with emotion. Jeremy and Leo nod to each other, knowing they have hit the heartfelt nerve they were hoping to and they give me a moment to compose myself.

I have now been blessed with two pieces of precious jewellery that reflect every part of me. My bracelet and my necklace. They symbolise our commitment to each other throughout the ages in different ways. I have no need or desire to have a ring on my finger — I feel complete as I am.

'It's more than perfect, thank you.' I give each of them a meaningful hug.

Jeremy is eager to put it around my neck. As I bend forward I look into Leo's eyes, knowing that whatever I experienced during my trance, whether it was physically real or more spiritual, they too experienced something of a similar kind. Our interrupted conversation is no longer important or relevant; this necklace wholly symbolises our interconnected lives.

With it around my neck, I notice its weight and I love the feel of it against my skin. I pick the rose gold circle up, running my finger along the engraving. I flip it over when I feel another letter on the reverse side, an 'S'. I check the others and they too are marked with this letter.

'Three 'S's?' I look toward Jeremy, then Leo. Their grins explode into full blown smiles as they wait for me to guess.

'Science?' Jeremy nods.

'Spirituality?' Leo nods.

I shake my head, realising that they understand more than they have been admitting about my trance with the shaman and the aligning of the stars, and ultimately our entwined destinies.

'Sexuality?' I say tentatively but knowing the answer.

'Your words, sweetheart, not ours.' They burst out laughing before informing me I need to get dressed and join them in the living room downstairs. They leave together, arm in arm, like brothers and best friends, discussing the wonders of an integrated world.

As I get up from the bed I glance toward the newspaper Leo brought in with the hot chocolate. It has been folded open on a particular page and I notice it's dated from a couple of weeks ago.

People situated near the equator had the privilege of experiencing a rare celestial show as Venus was eclipsed by the crescent Moon. The phenomenon was best witnessed in northern Brazil when the Moon came between Venus and the Earth in the twilight sky. Such on event only occurs every few centuries and astronomers believe that last night's alignment was the most prominent on record.

I inhale deeply as I absorb the words in print — absolutely unbelievable! And so the stars align.

I promise myself I will never say never, ever again.

* * *

Feeling better than I have in weeks and after making myself more presentable, I emerge from the bedroom.

With my hair blow-dried and wearing black pants, a low-cut red blouse showing off my beautiful new necklace and a cashmere shawl draped over my shoulders I begin to descend the staircase to the living room below.

As my eyes sweep around the room, I pause as I recognise each face in the group of people waiting below. How many more shocks can they give me? I pause on the staircase, overcome with love for my cherished family and loved ones who are staring up toward me. Jeremy appears by my side and guides me down the rest of the stairs to join this merry gathering.

Leo has flown in my parents, and brother and sister's family, so my nieces and nephews are here. No wonder I hadn't seen much of Elizabeth and Jordan since we arrived … they will have been in seventh heaven. I hug each and every one of them as though I haven't seen them in decades. After all I've been through, it feels that way.

Jeremy's parents are here as well and I literally haven't seen them in decades. They hug me knowing I'm finally returning to be part of their family again, as I once was. I meet Leo and Adam's parents, who are as gracious and generous as their sons. Seeing them beam with pride at Adam and Robert reinforces that everything that has happened to our lives in recent times, as difficult as the journey was in parts, was well and truly meant to be.

As the path clears I can't believe that Josef is here, too, and I rush to hug him, so grateful he is alive. He introduces me to his wife, Nikita, who is a gorgeous female version of her husband and I thank him for saving my life. As I utter the words Martin appears with a woman who can only be Salina by his side and my eyebrows raise in delighted surprise. Martin secures his grip around Salina's waist, confirming the answer to my silent question. I hug them in congratulations and deep thanks for what they have been through for us.

So many wonderful people and I am just so thrilled we are unexpectedly spending Christmas together. As my fingers play absently with my necklace I go to find Leo and thank him again for everything he has done for us and for giving everyone the opportunity to come together like this. There are some things money can't buy, but I have to admit that at times like this, it does have its benefits.

Our Christmas Eve dinner is like nothing I have ever experienced before. My family, my friends, my old life and my new integrated life, all together for an enormous banquet dinner. One that I didn't have to lift a finger for. No list to prepare, no shopping, no cooking, no cleaning. Completely unheard of in my previous life so it feels very weird.

I talk, I eat, I laugh, I cry. I have never felt more love or received so much love. My heart is full and overflowing, my life never more complete. I now have no fear, only sincere hope for the future.

I tuck in my children and wish them sweet dreams, knowing there is no use in trying to temper their excitement. Christmas Eve is such a magical night for them. How lovely it is, only having to say goodnight to everyone gathered here, rather than goodbye, since we have the next week together.

As Jeremy and I eventually retire to our suite, I can't believe how happy and exhausted I feel and voice this to him as he kisses me goodnight. I swear I'm asleep before my head hits the pillow.

* * *

I wake up early on Christmas morning and take a moment to watch Jeremy sleeping next to me. I smooth his dark hair away from his eyes and just admire his beauty, thanking my lucky stars that he is mine and we are finally together. His eyes open and he catches me staring, a beautiful grin escaping his lips.

It puts me instantly in the mood. He is more gentle with me than he has ever been, stroking my body sensually, worshipping me as though I'm some exotic mystical goddess and I reciprocate. Our love is intense and sincere and beautiful, two souls connecting who are meant to be. What a way to wake up in the morning.

'That's better than anything that could come from under a Christmas tree.'

'Likewise, sweetheart.'

We lay down side by side facing each other, in awe of each other.

'That's good, because I'm afraid I don't have a real present for you, J.'

He looks at me with a wicked grin.

'What?'

'Actually, you do.'

'No, honestly I don't.' Oh dear, he is obviously excited that I might have something. 'I feel awful I haven't arranged anything. I should have asked Leo or the kids, my mind just hasn't been …'

He leans over the edge of the bed and picks up something underneath and hands it to me. I shake my head. 'No way. I'm not opening anything else until I have something to give you.'

'You can't deny a gift today of all days and I promise you, this one is as much for me as it is for you, maybe even more so.'

I look at him doubtfully and shake my head. 'No, it's not right. I'll open it later, when we're even.'

'AB, I am serious, I really want you to open it now.'

I continue shaking my head.

'How can you be this bloody stubborn on Christmas Day? It's wrong on so many levels.' He straddles my body so I'm trapped beneath him. 'Fine, I won't let you out of this bed until you open it.'

'Are you seriously going to resort to physical strength every time I refuse to do something you want me to?'

'Whatever it takes, sweetheart,' he says mischievously. Then his mood shifts. 'No, seriously, I really want you to open this, it means the world to me, and then some.' He shifts his body so I'm freed and we're next to each other again. He props his head up with one arm. 'Please, open it for me, for us.' The depth of his words have the uncanny ability of disarming me.

'Oh, okay then, please don't look so forlorn.'

I eye the box suspiciously, given that it looks exactly like a smaller version of the one the necklace came in, and take off the ribbon.

Jeremy's expression immediately changes to a nervous excitement that is rather infectious, but there's a serious undertone and I wonder what on earth he could be up to this time. The box is light and nothing rattles inside. As I open its lid, I find a small square piece of white glossy paper inside.

'What's this?'

'Turn it over.' I swear he is holding his breath as I pick it up and turn it over, realising it is a photo of some sort.

My heart stops, my body stills.

As does his, I'm sure.

Oh. My. God.

'Are you serious?'

He nods.

'It can't be, can it? When? How?'

'It can be and it is, sweetheart. Are you happy?' He nervously awaits my response.

'Twins?'

'Our twins!'

Epilogue

It is so lovely to be back home for a few weeks, away from the cold in Boston, and thankfully Jeremy understood how important it is to me that the twins will have Australian roots. So much has happened in the last year, not least of which is that my blood no longer displays any unique allele. There is no scientific reason for it, other than perhaps the transfusion I was given in hospital, but I am grateful that my AB blood is now as normal as any other person's. Jeremy organised for the storage of the twins' umbilical cord blood, containing stem cells, in an undisclosed facility. I know in my heart these cells will carry the healing powers of the next generation now that it no longer registers in my blood. We promised each other we wouldn't conduct any further research on this until the time comes, giving ourselves time to simply focus on loving them and embracing their development without distractions.

Jeremy's team has continued working on a radical new way for people living with depression to improve their lives based on the results of my 'experiment' with him — which now seems like an eternity ago — and they've made successful progress to date. The German company they partner with is about to launch a pilot program, involving a new drug to be used in conjunction with behavioural adult play theories (that I've been thrilled to be involved in developing). Only time will tell but I have never seen him as engaged and excited about life as he has been this last year and it truly warms my heart. My love for him deepens by the day.

In the next few years, Jeremy and I will work with Leo on opening his Avalon properties as centres of excellence in relation to the integration of science, sexuality and spirituality, which is exceptionally exciting and engaging work for the three of us, and is after all, the reason we exist in this world. The proceeds from the retreats will be used to fund Leo's philanthropic projects on behalf of those in less advantageous circumstances.

Elizabeth and Jordan have been so excited about this day and look pristine in their new clothes, staring adoringly at their new baby brother and sister. We are gathered together at Peppermint Bay, surrounded by the sparkling waters of the Derwent River, for the twins' naming day, having sailed down the coast from Hobart.

Jeremy holds our gorgeous baby girl, Caitlin Eve, and I have the serene Leroy Josef in my arms. Jeremy's smile hasn't disappeared from his face since their safe arrival in the world. Leo, the twins' godfather, whom we haven't seen for more than a month, has just flown in via helicopter with an exotic-looking woman. She appears to be of Native American lineage and is simply stunning. He places himself beside me with my sister, the twins' godmother, next to Jeremy, as the ceremony begins and we recognise that our twins are a miraculous extension of our souls — destiny's children.

* * *

I sidle up to Leo at lunch, who is in great spirits and was very honoured to be asked to be the twins' godfather — as if it could have been anyone else. I'm keen to learn who this new woman, Mahria, is in his life.

'It's so great to see you with someone. How did you meet?'

'Let's just say our paths crossed when they were meant to.' At least I'm now used to his philosophical yet cryptic approach to life.

'And is the connection strong?' I respond as I glance toward Mahria and then into his sparkling eyes again. As I do, I am immediately taken back to the memories of my trance in Brazil ... thirteen women in the circle. And then I'm overwhelmed by the unconditional love I experienced in the womb-like environment, where I was part of something greater, some connection not yet made, and then it dawns on me as I return to the here and now.

317

'How many Avalon properties are you planning, Leo?'

'Thirteen,' he says with a knowing smile.

Oh, my goodness. Reality strikes.

'I'm not the only one, am I?' The words barely escape as a whisper.

'Let's just say, Alexandra, that's another story entirely.'

Acknowledgements

To HarperCollins Australia, you have all been absolutely incredible, reaching new heights in efficiency and support. Special thanks to Anna, Shona, Rochelle, Melanie, Kate, Graeme and Stephanie: three published books in seven months. Who would have thought?

To Harper Collins UK — Amy Winchester, Kate Bradley and Sarah Ritherdon. Thank you so much for your wonderful support and promotion of the Avalon Trilogy.

To Selwa Anthony, my agent, for igniting this unforeseeable dream into reality and steering me through it.

To my wonderful family and friends, who have supported me while my head has been in another world for the past six months (at least). You mean everything to me.

To my husband — wow!

To my children — even though you are really proud that mummy is now an Author, you can't read these books until you are at least 18!

To all of my readers — particularly those who have sent messages thanking me for my books and encouraging me to continue writing. You have enabled a fantastic, fun and amazingly unexpected path in my life. Thank you!

To Tassie — none of this would have happened without you.

Indigo Bloome is married with two children. She has lived and worked in Australia and the United Kingdom, with a successful career in the finance industry. Indigo recently traded city life for a move to Tasmania, which provided her with an opportunity to explore her previously undiscovered creative side. Her love of reading, deciphering dreams, stimulating conversation and the intrigue of the human mind led her to writing the first novel in the Avalon series, *Destined to Play*.

BOOKS BY INDIGO BLOOME

DESTINED TO FLY
An Avalon Novel
Available in Paperback and eBook

The exciting finale to the Avalon trilogy of erotic romance that is sure to appeal to anyone who was seduced by *Fifty Shades of Grey* and is looking for something more.

DESTINED TO FEEL
An Avalon Novel
Available in Paperback and eBook

Life was going well for psychologist Alexandra Blake. Her career has taken off and she has been exploring her darkest sexual fantasies with her lover Jeremy Quinn. But her bliss is rudely interrupted when she is abducted in London, caught up in a dangerous struggle between unscrupulous men.

DESTINED TO PLAY
An Avalon Novel
Available in Paperback and eBook

Alexandra Blake, leaves her comfortable suburban existence to give a series of lectures, where she meets up with Dr. Jeremy Quinn, the man who opens her eyes and body to the world in ways she never thought possible. After a few glasses of champagne in his luxurious hotel penthouse, he presents her with an extraordinary proposition. She soon finds herself seduced into a level of surrender—and danger—she could never have imagined.